THE SAVAGE PEAK

THE MORGALLA CHRONICLES

THE
SAVAGE
PEAK

JON DAVID

bhc
press™

Livonia, Michigan

Editor: Rebecca Rue
Proofreader: Hannah Ryder

THE SAVAGE PEAK

Copyright © 2020 Jon David

Published by BHC Press

Library of Congress Control Number: 2019954361

ISBN: 978-1-64397-074-5 (Hardcover)
ISBN: 978-1-64397-108-7 (Softcover)
ISBN: 978-1-64397-109-4 (Ebook)

For information, write:
BHC Press
885 Penniman #5505
Plymouth, MI 48170

Visit the publisher:
www.bhcpress.com

Dedicated to my parents,
whose love and support mean everything.

THE SAVAGE PEAK

PROLOGUE

THE NAMING

THE DEMONS towered over her so high, she thought they might be statues. At first, she did not realize they were alive. Her lilac eyes peered up at them from beneath her hood as her tiny hands gripped the plush animal. She and the stuffed beast were almost the same size. The new power she was discovering told her things about other demons, so she did not have to ask—not everything—but certainly enough to read their emotions clearly. The four who surrounded her appeared nervous, but determined, to do their duty. Today their duty was her protection.

They wore uniforms of black leather and armor trimmed with gold symbols. Though the demons were the same species, they all appeared different. She couldn't see their faces; she thought they were very tall, but in reality, she was simply very short. Four of the greatest skilled sentenels stood ready.

The girl held the elephant tightly as she watched with concern. Though she felt secure that no harm would come to her from these four, she was unsure why she'd been brought there.

Two more figures entered the chamber, one dressed in extravagant robes decorated with gold. His hair was long and curly, as was his white beard...probably due to his advanced age. On top of his head, four horns showed through thick hair. His pink eyes peered down at the child before him, and she seemed unable to return his gaze. She focused on the marble floor, afraid to lock eyes with the strange beings before her.

"Master Udo," the servant said, "this is the child—"

"But of course, fool."

"Y-yes, Master," the servant stammered.

Lord Udo studied the child, his fingertips steepled together in front of his chest.

"So you are the one, hmm?" He pondered and smiled. "Do you speak, child?"

The girl remained quiet, for she had nothing to say.

"Look upon me, young one," Udo commanded. She could not explain why, but she felt an urge to gaze at him, regardless of her level of fear. "Do you know your father?"

She shook her head. Udo stepped closer, and the girl wished with all her heart to be away from him, far away from here.

"He is a powerful being. The most powerful...next to the Dark One. You are most fortunate to have his blood flowing through you. You will grow to be powerful and take a rightful place at your father's side. But until then, your life is in danger."

The chamber door opened again. A figure entered, dressed in black, her features concealed. Surely it was a woman by the way she strolled in with such confidence and delicacy. The small girl felt a pair of eyes on her, but she couldn't see who was peering down. The person seemed happy to see her.

"Hello, little one," the figure said in a soft voice.

The child returned a small smile.

Once she lifted her hood, the woman's scarlet features were obvious. Her skin revealed pale red scales, smooth to the touch and white horns that stretched high behind her head. Black lips, full and vibrant, glittered in the light. Her hair was the most beautiful the girl had ever seen, flowing long and white. Flickers of silver shone upon her radiant locks. Her strange, yellow eyes made the small girl nervous, but she gasped when wings emerged from under the woman's cloak.

"You are very lovely indeed," the woman said. "Do not be afraid, young one. I shall not harm you."

The words helped, and the young girl believed her sincerity and even felt happy.

"Can you fly?" the girl asked.

With teeth gleaming white, she said, "Why yes, I can. My grandmother was a dragon. Do you know what a dragon is?"

The girl shook her head from side to side.

"My name is Delilah, and that is just one of many things I will teach you."

The little girl sensed something from the woman, but she couldn't quite figure out what. It wasn't sight, smell, or sound but an instinct beneath the surface. A warm feeling emanated from the red-skinned woman. The more the child studied her, the stronger it became. An odd warmth built a bridge between the two, and they both smiled at the same time.

"You feel it, don't you?" Delilah asked. The child nodded. "It is the greatest of all gifts bestowed upon our people. All living beings, anyone with a beating heart and soul, project what we feel to the world. Demons are the only ones who can feel it. In some cases, they even use it. This I will teach you too."

Delilah extended her hand, and with some added patience, the girl finally reached out and took it.

Lord Udo spoke, but the woman didn't look at him. Her gaze was on the young, orange-skinned girl.

"Mistress Delilah, do you swear in the name of the Dark One to watch over this girl? To protect her? To teach her our ways and give her the power she will need in the coming years?"

"Yes," she said, smiling and exposing glistening white fangs beneath her black lips. "A name. She needs a name."

"Indeed."

"Something grand," Delilah added. "Something that...means something."

"Um...yes," Udo replied. "I have given much thought to this and have decided upon a name to honor our Lord Zorach and the Dark One as well."

Delilah's gaze never left the young girl. She rolled her eyes at Udo's grandstanding, which made the little girl giggle slightly.

"I have searched through the ancient texts in languages as old as the child's father, and I have found a name that..." Lord Udo rambled on, to the annoyance of Delilah and the confusion of the little girl.

Delilah knelt down, close enough so only she would hear.

"He can talk a bit too much, can't he?" Delilah whispered and winked.

The strange woman with the crimson skin made a couple of funny faces that caused the girl to burst out in laughter.

"You know, I never thought about having children," the woman went on, "but seeing you, and the potential you have, the potential that I shall see you fulfill—"

"Morgalla," Udo bellowed.

"Hmm?" Delilah replied, checking over her shoulder at him.

"The child's name. From this day forth...may all know you as... Morgalla."

During Udo's vain rambling, neither of them had heard the meaning of the girl's name, something from a long-dead language. But to Delilah, it did not matter. She smiled at the young one again. She stood, and the girl inched close, almost hugging the woman's leg. Delilah wrapped her cloak around to envelop the child. It was a simple cloth and yet to the child, it was stronger than any armor. Delilah swelled with pride.

"Morgalla."

ONE

SECRET MISSION

HELL HAS a library, and it's run by the Master of Knowledge. The stacks of books were taller than the child. But then again, most things were. The book she carried was very big and heavy. She didn't even know the subject matter, nor did she care, but its size would fit her needs. She had arranged books into four walls; in the middle of them, she had set the largest book down to sit upon. Within her small fortress of knowledge, Morgalla would fill her mind with lessons her mistress had commanded.

The ceiling of this chamber was huge with multiple levels. Shelves appeared to go on forever atop iron catwalks. Dusty books were scattered about on the floors and shelved in what appeared to be no order. No signs of life existed except for one small figure...a child of nine.

Virtually all demons, by the time they were twelve years old, had already executed their first lesser being, but Delilah had kept Morgalla sheltered among the stacks of Hell's library. Delilah had fallen asleep high upon one of the shelves. The sound of the large book plopping down on the catwalk had awakened her. All six limbs stretched the fatigue from her body, and she rose. She flapped red dragon wings a few times to return the circulation and then leapt off the shelf. Delilah glided down to where she had left her apprentice, finding her within the four walls.

"Constructed your own little castle, I see," Delilah noted.

"Uh-huh." Her voice had a tone of aggravation, slipping closer to annoyance.

Delilah ignored the child's mood. "Finish the lesson?"

"Yes, Mistress."

"Let me take a look."

The girl held up a few sheets of parchment; upon the first was her name written many times. Delilah took the sheets in her claws and flipped through them to see many other words spelled out. Morgalla kept her eyes focused on the book in front of her. Delilah, as she studied the child's writing, couldn't help but notice that the utensil her pupil had been using was digging deeper and deeper into the paper. She found some doodles on the final page curious; it was a drawing of a woman with red skin and wings, a sword in her hand.

"You're improving, child. Excellent."

"That purple boy made fun of me the other day."

"Oh? What did he do?"

"He told me all about how great his family is and how I'm nothing."

"Striking him might be fulfilling for sure," the dragon-demon said, "but it could cause friction between his family and yours. They are powerful. Do not forget."

"I won't. I just…hate him…"

"Yes, I know," Delilah assured. "Look at me, child."

Morgalla obeyed, meeting the gaze of her mistress's eyes. Delilah's clawed hands rested upon the wall of books in front of her.

"He is to never touch you," Delilah stated with conviction. "If he does…you are to tell me. Understand?"

"Are you going to kill him?" Morgalla asked with a hint of concern.

"Oh no. I'll just cut off his hand. Don't worry, it will grow back. That will be warning enough."

Morgalla giggled as Delilah smirked and winked. The woman then crawled down to the floor and made her way through the castle entrance. Master sat next to student for a moment of silence.

"Morgalla, I mean it. He is not to touch you."

"I understand, Mistress."

"Do you think the Master of Knowledge will be angry with your little...redecorating?" Delilah asked, referring to the castle.

"These books were unshelved."

"Librarians love their books. To them, they are the bricks that make up their kingdom."

"I'm making the library look nicer," the girl proclaimed.

Delilah's laugh filled the room all the way to the high ceiling, so it sounded like an ancient cavern. She then peered over at the open book Morgalla had been studying. There were pages of pictures with beaches, the sun shining upon the sand and crystal-clear water.

"Where did you find this?" Delilah asked.

"It's pretty."

"I guess. But all that sun? I'm sure it's nice and hot but...too bright."

Delilah's head suddenly snapped, and her eyes averted to another part of the chamber. She must have sensed the presence of others quietly entering the room because she stood and focused on the wall of books, then down from the catwalk to the entrance far below.

"I think it would be nice to have a house on the beach. What does the ocean smell like?"

"Shh..." Delilah commanded.

Peering down to the main hall, Delilah saw a group of demons had entered and seemed to be as stealthy as possible. They were dressed in black, their features hidden from view, but Delilah could, with ease, feel their souls. Unfortunately, their intent was not clear to her.

"There are others here," she whispered to her young apprentice.

"Who?"

"They're from the family of the purple boy."

"Eww."

"Yes," Delilah agreed and extended her hand. "We should go."

"Can I bring the book with me?"

"I...I guess. I doubt the Master would notice a book like that missing."

Delilah took the girl in her arms and leapt off the catwalk and glided down through the darkness. By the time the two of them reached the light of the main hall, the group of demons spotted them. Before they could react, Delilah had already swooped to the main gate and flew out, the child in her arms.

The Master of Knowledge had been returning, walking up the cobblestone path leading to his kingdom. He was an older demon, one who imposed his will upon the youth of Hell. Instead of joining the many wars fought upon many worlds, he kept his nose in books. Since he had grown in power, demons as young as Delilah dared not cross him directly. She flew past him in a blur, the air swooshing as her wings flapped.

He shouted. "You'd better not have taken any of my books!"

Morgalla held on with both arms and legs as Delilah's powerful limbs kept her apprentice close to her. The book was pressed between their bodies, a new treasure the child wasn't going to lose. Delilah flew towards Zorach's castle but would land in a courtyard some walking distance away. She set Morgalla down and looked around the area as if searching for something.

"Velleau," Delilah called out.

"Over here."

Both ladies watched a demon step forward from the shadows of stone. He was dressed to show off his wealth and power, dripping with gold from expensive robes.

"Did you get it?" Delilah asked.

"Yes, of course. You know I had to pull some favors for this."

"No gratitude for saving your life? And here I thought you came from one of the more honorable families."

"Do you always exploit those in your debt?"

"It's not for me," Delilah said. "It's for her."

"Zorach lets her walk around? Rather dangerous, don't you think?"

Velleau nodded to the girl, who returned a shy wave. Morgalla never left Delilah's side, staying close and holding onto her cloak.

"But you got it, right?" Delilah asked.

"Yes, yes. I got it."

The blue blood held out a small drawstring bag and handed it to Delilah. She knelt and opened it, pouring the contents onto the ground. A single item fell out. The medallion had seemingly unimpressive features. Both Delilah and Velleau were careful not to touch the trinket with their bare hands.

"Come," Delilah said to her ward. "Hold out your hand."

Morgalla was confused but did as she was told. Delilah took hold of her, making sure the girl's hand was directly above the medallion. Velleau stood a few feet away, picking something from between his teeth with his pinky claw.

"Now close your eyes."

Again, the child did as she was instructed though her pulse quickened. With the speed of a bullet and the precision of a surgeon, Delilah removed a small blade and made a razor-thin cut on the child's palm. Morgalla opened her eyes and let out a slight cry of pain. Delilah held her wrist, making sure a drop of blood fell on the trinket at her feet. Morgalla frowned at her palm, realizing the cut had already healed itself. *Demonic powers.* Delilah took the decoration by its tiny chain and lifted it from the ground.

"Excellent," Delilah said. "Here, take it. It's yours."

Morgalla held out the gift.

"For me?"

Her teacher smiled and nodded. Morgalla was shocked to watch the metal in her hand turn into a blade as long as she was tall. The sudden weight change surprised her, and she dropped the weapon.

"Easy there," Delilah said. "Not to worry, you'll get used to it. Soon it will feel as if you're carrying no weight at all."

With both hands, the young girl held the sword up. Morgalla could see her reflection in the gleaming metal. She lost strength in her shoulders, fell to her knees and set the blade on her lap, still marveling at the craftsmanship.

Her nose filled with the smell of leather as she held the gray-colored grip. The blade was dull on one end but razor-sharp on the other, much different from the small swords she had practiced with. The blade was narrow at the guard and grew wide as her eyes trailed up the gleaming, silver-like metal; again, different from the black blades Delilah made her practice with. The blade was wide near the end but came down to a sharp tip. The weapon had a knuckle guard that came out and curved like an "S" down to the head. At the head, there was a small hook just inches where her pinky finger would be. As the child held it, the metal wasn't cold.

It was a work of art meant to kill.

"There are few things in this life you can trust, Morgalla."

Morgalla stared up at her mistress with a smile. Delilah did not return it but studied the weapon instead.

"I trust you," the child replied.

"Others cannot be trusted. But this…is a weapon in your hands, under your control. You are its mistress. That you can trust."

"I…I don't know."

"First, though. I will teach you how to use this." Delilah pointed to her forehead. "That is your most important weapon. I will not always be there for you," Delilah said as she stood. "Do not look to another to save you. Do not ask a male to be your hero. This sword will be your hero."

Morgalla gazed again up to her mentor and then back to the gift in her hands. It took only a moment to decide a name for her new friend.

Hero.

Velleau watched the child with curiosity as she strolled into the courtyard, mesmerized by the weapon in her hand. He couldn't help but notice that the sword might even be even taller than its owner.

"How old is she? Five?" he asked.

"Nine."

He was surprised. "Really? She's so small."

"Don't let Zorach hear you say that."

"Hell forbid. But I was curious why you chose to get her a blade so large. My first weapon was more…"

"Yes, yes, I know—" Delilah interrupted. "More your size. Mine was the same way. But I have orders from Zorach, and I don't know when we'll be back."

"Back?"

"We're being ordered off-world."

The two of them turned towards the child who was swinging… or at least trying to swing…the sword around. When she raised it above her head, she lost her footing and fell backward.

"She seems weak for one her age. Nine years old, really?"

"Yes, really. I know why we're being ordered to leave. Isn't it obvious?"

"A little," Velleau said with a smirk.

"She'll grow into it. The sword, I mean."

"When will you be back?"

Delilah shrugged. "That, I couldn't tell you. But we won't return until I think she is ready."

"I have a feeling it will take years."

Delilah checked around the area, from the dark mountains decorating the horizon, to the black trees surrounding them in the valley. She walked to an area of some red flowers that bloomed in the garden and knelt to smell one before whispering a single word to herself. "Years."

TWO

THE LONG GOOD-BYE

MORGALLA WOULD soon forget all about the look, feel, and even the smell of Hell. Her dreams were sometimes filled with a sky on fire and the roars of warriors, but she'd wake every morning to the peaceful forest. The women, much like the peaceful monks they lived with, had all they needed up in the trees. Even if Morgalla didn't have Delilah to fly her from branch to branch, the young girl could walk among the bridges built that connected the trees. Delilah occasionally took her down to the ground…but not for long… due to the predators in the area. The rivers and streams of Jadewood were filled with life. During many months of searching from world to world, Delilah had found sanctuary on the planet Usteron. Among the forest of Jadewood, she and Morgalla made their home among the monks of the Xanxur. The trees, which grew taller than a hundred feet high, provided a quiet and safe atmosphere for Delilah to educate the child.

Meeko fish soon became a delicacy that Morgalla and Delilah enjoyed on a regular basis. Delilah often grumbled as she ate them because they were not red meat. Morgalla liked to watch the fish swim and was always depressed when it came time to feast. Delilah explained that they were prey and never to be pitied. What Morgalla adored most about Meeko fish was that they changed colors. She never understood how or why, but it was amazing to see them shift from red to gold to blue and back again. Her own powers were just emerging, and everyone around her sometimes to change color, much like the Meeko fish. Morgalla was mesmerized.

"When you face an enemy, you should never show mercy. Morgalla? Morgalla, are you listening to me?"

"Huh? What?" she said, snapping out of her trance. She was sitting on a fallen log and gazing into the stream.

"Are the fish more interesting than me or what I'm explaining?"

"Oh, I'm sorry, Delilah. I thank you for bringing me." Morgalla's voice was filled with gratitude as she peered back at the stream. "It's just...do we have to study today?"

"Every day is a lesson, young one," Delilah said, extending her clawed hand and helping her young apprentice to her feet. "I'm trying to teach you something important. Now, in life, as with all scenarios, you must strike first if you are to gain the advantage."

"Yes," Morgalla said. She trailed behind, her eyes still concentrating on the stream as they walked along the riverbed. Every now and then, her hand moved to her temple, giving it a scratch.

"This is true with all creatures, whether they be animal, demon, or...lesser beings."

Their black cloaks flowed in the spring breeze. The two figures—one with red scale-like skin and the other a light orange—both stuck out among the green and brown of the forest. Delilah had entered the stream with water coming up to her knees. She held her sword steady, ready to strike at her prey in the water.

"Will I be able to breathe fire like you someday?" the child asked.

"No."

"Aw, how come?"

"I can breathe fire because my grandmother was a dragon."

"Do I have a grandmother?"

The child's question made Delilah pause and look down at her. Morgalla sat on the fallen log, her violet eyes inquisitive.

"It only makes sense that you do have a grandmother. But who that might be, I do not know."

"What about a mother? A father?"

Delilah pondered a moment. "I'm sorry, child. I do not know who your parents are."

"But...I have them, right?"

Their eyes locked on each other. Morgalla's shined like polished glass.

"Surely you must have parents, child. But again, I do not know their identities."

Morgalla hung her head.

"Chin up," Delilah commanded. The child complied. "What is important is the *here and now*." Morgalla scratched at her temple again, and this time her tutor noticed. "What's wrong with your head? Come, let me see."

Morgalla stepped back, but just for a moment, knowing that Delilah expected to be obeyed, and meant it. Delilah removed the young demon's hood and pushed away her long hair to reveal a small bump on her temple.

"Horns. You're growing horns."

"But I don't want them," Morgalla said with serious disappointment. She scratched at the two bumps on either side of her head again.

"Nonsense," Delilah replied, standing straight. "They will be a thing of beauty. I can show you how to polish them. Oh, and you'll be able to wear jewelry on special occasions too."

She brought attention to her own pair of white horns. They were small and subtle, but she'd always found them to be a sign of power. Delilah turned and continued to ramble a bit, giddy like a schoolgirl, about doing her nails and all the fun she and Morgalla were going to have. Morgalla, on the other hand, pulled the hood back up and gave the bumps another scratch as she ran to keep up with her mentor.

They walked on a fallen log across the river, where Morgalla caught the attention of the Meeko fish again. She stopped and gawked at two who turned a bright pink when they swam up to each other.

"Hey," Delilah yelled. Morgalla's trance was broken again when she noticed her tutor approaching…"What is it with these damn fish, anyway?"

"Well, they just seem so happy, I guess."

Delilah scoffed, and her upper lip raised in a sneer.

This is going to be tougher than I thought.

She sat on the log next to her student, searching for the words to convince her otherwise. Morgalla was still quite young, and Delilah could manipulate the child's soul to follow her own, but years ago she'd decided she wasn't going to do that.

Surely there must be some way to convince her.

"Morgalla, they have nothing."

"They have each other and the river."

"Until we come along with a craving for fish."

"But until then—"

"Stop it." Delilah interrupted Morgalla's thought by kicking the water. The Meeko fish changed to bright red and swam away in a flash.

All Morgalla could do was watch as they disappeared out of sight. She frowned. Delilah knew she had been hard on Morgalla, but she couldn't worry about it. She was doing the girl a favor. Delilah's face lit up when she noticed a large trout swimming their way. Silent and still, she let her prey swim closer. With lightning speed, her blade plunged into the water, and it emerged with supper impaled on the tip.

"Ah ha," Delilah cheered. To her, the catch was a small victory, but a victory nevertheless.

The wilderness would be home for them for a long time. Morgalla grew in size and strength and was fully grown by the time she was twelve, still no more than five feet tall. Delilah became concerned. Away from civilization, demon or not, the child needed to learn all Delilah had to teach. The first lesson was survival. Finding water, hunting, gathering, and learning how to make fire was necessary.

As Morgalla struggled with two rocks to make a spark, she finally gave up, dropping them both. "But you can make fire. Why do I have to learn this too?"

"And what if I'm not there, child?" Delilah noted.

After more trial and error, Morgalla finally became disgusted and gave up completely. Delilah, having a rumbling stomach, started the fire with her breath.

The Xanxur clan, with bright blue flesh, were also difficult to miss much like the two strangers from Hell who moved in. The two demons kept their distance from the others even though the child often enjoyed watching them meditate from afar.

"Their souls are peaceful," Morgalla noted.

Delilah was quick to correct her. "It makes they're weak."

"But why?"

"This environment, child, is soft and easy. They would not survive among their own people outside of this forest."

"But we need not fear them. Isn't that a good thing?"

"Perhaps, but their weakness…I somehow feel infected by it."

Delilah gave a sneer as she watched them. Morgalla was confused with many things Delilah said. As time went on, neither of their attitudes towards the Xanxur changed.

Deep within the forest, the monks chanted their morning prayers. Often the monks' attention was diverted by the sound of metal clanging and echoing from the trees high above. They knew it was the demon woman training her young apprentice. At least the two women kept to themselves and one could barely hear the metal, anyway. The monks didn't know why the pair had chosen their forest, but as long as they were peaceful and shed no blood, they could stay.

Morgalla was too curious one morning after the chanting. De-lilah had taken a nap in the trees, so the young demon girl took the opportunity and made her way to souls below. She was unable to be stealthy because of her coloring. Morgalla snuck nearer as quietly as she could, aware of the souls around her. She spotted an adult kneel-ing on a wooden floor in the late morning mist. Two young ones, a boy and a girl, accompanied him. If she had to guess, they were not much older than her. What were they doing? She had to know.

The elder responded to a creak of wood by glancing over his shoulder. All three pairs of eyes scanned the area until they saw the young demon girl's pale violet eyes looking at them. Having been caught, she hid behind a large leaf. The elder appeared curious too. His focus jumped between the two young ones and then back to Morgalla. He motioned for her to approach.

Through the peace of his soul and the lack of fear, Morgalla knew she was not in danger, but she snuck up on him slowly, never-theless. He reached out with a piece of white chalk and a large slab of wood, dark and flat. Morgalla noticed the two young ones held similar items. She accepted them, sniffing and even tasting the chalk.

"Bleh."

The young ones snickered.

As it went with many mornings after her sparring with one teacher, she would creep down to another one. The elder looked at the work the two blue students were doing, approving of what he saw. Morgalla struggled to figure out problems that she was given with numbers. She scratched her head, sometimes counted on her fingers. She wrote down an answer and showed it to the elder.

He looked and frowned, shaking his head. Morgalla returned the frown. She checked her work and rubbed all the chalk off the board with her sleeve. She thought about the problem again, grunt-ing out of frustration. One of the other students said something quietly to another, and they both snickered. Morgalla shot a glare of anger at them.

"Shh..." the teacher said and cast a watchful eye at the two youths.

Morgalla pondered the situation some more and scribbled down something on the board. She showed it again to the teacher who studied it and nodded in approval. Morgalla smiled.

It was then they all heard a thump on the wooden platform where they were sitting. They noticed Delilah standing there, her golden eyes blazing at her young apprentice.

"So, *this* is where you've been going after breakfast, young one?"

Morgalla smiled, showing her hard work on the board to her mistress.

Delilah frowned but managed to raise an eyebrow. "Well, I suppose brains is a useful weapon."

Time passed, and each day Delilah moved faster, pushing her student. That particular morning, Morgalla decided to block the coming attack and was thrust back, landing hard on the wooden practice platform.

Delilah scowled. "Best to parry or even dodge an attack like that, until you are strong enough to block it."

"Now you tell me." Morgalla groaned, her tailbone aching.

"Up."

"Gimme a minute."

"Your opponent will not give you a minute."

Delilah thrust forward, and Morgalla screamed, ducking out of the way. "Are you trying to kill me?"

"Your enemy will, that's for sure."

They sparred more, and finally, Delilah disarmed her. Hero, the sword, was tossed over the edge. Morgalla stood motionless, frozen and not knowing what to do next.

"What are you waiting for?" Delilah asked.

"What? I have no weapon."

"*You* are a weapon. Continue the fight!"

Delilah attacked again, although it was clear she wasn't fighting at full strength. Morgalla dodged. But without a weapon, her feet and hands would have to do.

"You're holding back," Delilah shouted and continued the attack.

Finally, Morgalla swept her legs, knocking her teacher on her back.

"Ha," the teacher called. "Good."

She was on her feet in an instant, and they continued to fight. Morgalla leapt down to a large branch. Among the foliage, she clearly spotted her medallion hanging from a twig. She jumped down, and with the medal in her hand, it changed back into her sword. The change happened just in time since Delilah had cut the branch she was on, and her student was in a freefall.

Morgalla was able to land on the next wooden platform, nearly crashing on one of the monks who'd ran away, fearing for his life. Delilah was quick on her heels and disarmed her student again. With a simple sweep of the leg, Morgalla lost her footing and landed hard on the wood. She curled into a ball, nursing the bump on the back of her head.

With the pain came anger. The young demon stared up at her mistress who had neither a smile nor a frown on her face.

"There is no shame in falling, child."

Morgalla breathed the anger out of her heaving body, but Delilah still sensed the rage within her.

"There is shame, however, in remaining on the ground. Get up."

Morgalla heard the words and felt the influence her teacher had on her soul. Despite the pain in her back and head, she got up. The sharp ache that stung through her body was soon gone, but her ego was still bruised. Morgalla picked up her sword again, and the lesson continued.

Delilah wasn't all business every minute of every day. Between lessons from her and the monks, the forest was Morgalla's playground. Delilah often took her for flights through the trees and across the plains of Usteron. There were, however, places they would not venture. Delilah forbade it.

"The rest of the Usta's domain is beyond that border," Delilah noted.

"The rest?"

"Xanxur live in this forest, away from others of their species. Out there, the war is raging."

"What war?"

"Do not burden yourself with such questions, child. The remainder of the cosmos will open to you when you are old enough."

AS MORGALLA got older, horns grew from behind her ears, and soon she asked for a place of her own to live and sleep. Thankfully, there was another hut not far from Delilah's. After patching the holes in the roof, it became livable. With parchment and charcoal, Morgalla posted drawings all over the walls. After her decorating had been done, it became a home.

Her hut was tiny, barely enough room for one person, but her heart swelled with pride at her accomplishment, knowing it was hers. On this particular occasion, while admiring her work, she turned and saw Delilah standing in the doorway.

"Don't tell me you're going to say this is a waste of my time," Morgalla said, referring to her drawings.

Delilah's golden eyes examined the room. "Not entirely as long as your studies come first."

Morgalla rolled her eyes when her mentor turned her back.

"I saw that, child."

MORE TIME passed, and things became routine for the two of them. Morgalla grew into her teens and it came with a touch of rebellion, much to Delilah's annoyance. Then came the day that Morgalla's life changed forever. One morning when Morgalla rose in her hammock, the branches creaked as she rolled out of bed and landed on the wooden floor. The dreams were not violent but certainly intense, enough to make her break out in a sweat. She walked to the curtain that served as a door and opened it, the early light bathed her. The morning song indicated the wildlife had been awake for a while. She felt the chill and moisture of the morning as she stepped out to her porch. Morgalla checked the perch where Delilah usually slept but didn't see her. *Not like her to be an early riser*. Morgalla dressed in her day clothes and set out to find breakfast...and Delilah.

As Morgalla walked the wooden bridges that spanned from tree to tree throughout the entire forest, she found a low-hanging branch and snatched a few guavas. The bright yellow fruit was her favorite, and she could have it for breakfast every day for the rest of her life.

The Xanxur were awake as usual, and going through their morning prayers and rituals. Morgalla meandered along the wooden paths and bridges, coming across a group of them who had knelt to greet the morning sun. Morgalla always found their peaceful ways intriguing, but she never got too close to them. Although the monks allowed her and Delilah to stay among them, she sensed the tiny sliver of mistrust for demonkind. She marveled at them, their tattooed blue skin bathed in the morning sunlight contrasting with their white clothes. Morgalla, with orange skin and dark clothing, snuck past as quietly as she could and looked for Delilah elsewhere.

Morgalla stood on a large branch and peered out at the community of the Xanxur. She took another bite of her guava and focused on the massive forest. She heard the chanting filling the trees with a pleasant sound as the morning sun rose higher. Morgalla finally guessed where Delilah might be. Her soul was inside the chapel. She made her way down to the structure. The wood had elegant carvings all over it. Sneaking in through the darkened hallways, she heard voices at the end of the corridor. She concentrated and clearly heard Delilah and the High Priest.

"...and we have allowed you and your student to live here, so long as it was in peace," the High Priest said.

"To which, I am trying to show gratitude. Your people..."

As Delilah spoke, a controlled anger was obvious in her voice. Morgalla sensed the rage building in her teacher's soul. She guessed the High Priest was also using his training to keep his own temper under control.

"They will not ask questions. They will come and slaughter you and her."

"I didn't know your people could be so violent," Delilah said.

"They can be...when they have been provoked in such a way. This war has gone on for a century!"

Morgalla strained to hear and realized if she got too close, Delilah would know she was listening. She probably already did. Morgalla turned when spotting someone entering from the opposite end of the hallway. Stepping into the darkness, she knew who it was even before he entered into the light. When close enough, Morgalla put her palms together in front of her chest and bowed. The man returned the gesture. Lorn was one of the high priests whose height even rivaled Delilah's. He stood out from the younger Xanxur due to streaks of grey at his temples, something Morgalla found curious.

"What's going on?" Morgalla asked.

"I don't know if I should be the one to tell you. You and your teacher have been allowed to live here in peace. But now..."

The sense of urgency echoed with his soul, Delilah's too as she came out of the chamber in a huff. Seeing her apprentice, she commanded her to follow.

Morgalla had to work to keep pace with her mistress as they walked along the bridges between the trees.

"What's going on?" Morgalla asked, catching her breath.

"Damn monks and their vow of non-violence," Delilah replied.

"Delilah."

The dragon hybrid spun around, annoyance plainly showing on her face and bleeding from her soul. "What's wrong, child, is that we must leave."

"But why?"

Delilah continued swearing under her breath. She finally stopped and sat on a large branch, overlooking the valley. Her eyes squinted to the horizon.

"Did you get breakfast?" Delilah asked.

Morgalla picked another guava fruit and handed it to her.

"No meat?"

"Oh, sorry I didn't have time to hunt and kill something for you, Your Highness."

Delilah glared. "Watch your tone, child. I'm in no mood."

"Well, you're not telling me anything. Why do we have to move from the commune?"

"We must leave the planet. It is no longer safe for us."

Morgalla appeared shocked. "Why?"

"The monks of the Xanxur allowed us to stay because we live in peace. That, and we helped keep them safe from predators." Delilah scoffed. "Pacifists. But the rest of their species is driving demonkind away from their world. If they find us, they will kill us."

Morgalla was stunned. "But we never did anything to them. There has to be a way we can…"

"I have already had this discussion with the High Priest. Even if they wanted to protect us, they cannot, nor would they."

"But where will we go?"

"Our options are limited. A few other worlds are safe for us, and those that are safe might as well be Hell itself."

A sense of dread came over Morgalla, and she stared up at the sky. She hopped off the branch and paced.

"You knew this day would come," Delilah said. "We were not meant to live here our whole lives. Why are you scared?"

It was obvious that Morgalla was afraid, and she didn't try to hide it.

"You've told me stories of growing up and living there."

"And you were sheltered," Delilah interrupted. "You were not cast out to fend for yourself like some of us."

"I just think…"

"And I have taught you to never show fear. The others will latch onto it and prey upon it."

"But why go to Hell? Why not another demon world?"

"It would be the same, except for the fact that my master…your master as well, would be strongest there."

Morgalla couldn't stop staring out to the valley. A beautiful, red bird flew by. Morgalla couldn't take her eyes off it as it flew towards the horizon. Delilah approached and gently touched Morgalla's shoulders.

"I blame myself, child. Keeping you in such a place as this, I fear you've grown soft."

"I don't want to go," Morgalla said.

"We have no choice. The Usta are on a rampage, and they will slaughter anyone with demon blood."

Morgalla brushed Delilah's hands away. "Well, maybe we shouldn't have invaded their home."

The words cut Delilah's soul but not enough to dissuade her. It wasn't what Morgalla said but the defiance that annoyed her teacher.

"How many times must I tell you?" Delilah snapped.

"Don't give me the lesser species speech again."

"It is our destiny, Morgalla. Show me one species superior to ours. It is our duty to bring order to the cosmos."

"I don't know. The Xanxur seem to have order and peace."

"One religious sect among a population of millions. Can those millions claim the same?"

"There should be another place like this, a sanctuary of some sort."

Delilah snapped again, "We're not going to one of those weak worlds."

"It wouldn't be so bad."

"And be among those weak species relying on their *tek-nology*? We're stronger than Baladonians or humans."

The anger rose in Morgalla's heart. "Then why are we chased from world to world? How safe are we anywhere anymore?"

Delilah noticed some of the monks were looking their way. She seemed to know what was in their hearts. As calm and controlled as they were of their emotions, Delilah felt the slightest stir in their souls.

"Calm yourself," Delilah commanded with a soft voice. "Gather your things."

What *things* Morgalla had could fit in a small bag. Most of it was only a change of clothes.

High atop the trees, they could see for miles. Morgalla kept herself occupied by throwing a knife to a crude wooden target that Delilah had made for practice. Staring off to the horizon, Delilah sensed the souls from the armies. The demons were in full retreat to the portal and the strength of the Usta was driving them out.

With each toss of her knife, Morgalla struck the center every time with a thump. Delilah fumed, her rage boiling over as she sat on a branch.

Delilah commanded, "Come, we must be off."

"Wait, there's something I need."

"Make it quick."

The sense of urgency in Delilah's voice was obvious as she kept her eyes on the horizon. Morgalla darted around the thick branches, running here and there, her eye scanning. Usually, guavas were easy to find, but now she needed one, and they weren't anywhere to be seen. She finally spotted a bit of yellow out of the corner of her eye and checked under a large leaf and found a group of six guavas all clustered at the end of a branch. Morgalla quickly gathered the goodies into her bag. She picked the last one and held it in her hand for a brief moment and sighed.

Morgalla felt the eyes of a friend focused on her. She turned and saw the priest, Lorn, standing at the edge of the wooden path. She approached and frowned at the melancholy expression on his face.

"Why are you sad?" she asked. "I'm the one who has to leave."

"That is why I am sad. You seemed happy here."

"Almost. I mean it's a wonderful place but at the same time…"

"You felt like an outsider."

Morgalla hung her head. "I was reminded every day."

"But not by words. It was only by our souls that you knew of our…discomfort. You must realize it was your teacher's words that convinced us for you to stay all those years ago. Because she promised the two of you would live here in peace."

Morgalla smirked. "I believe I sensed your mood at the time, all of you. You were borderline scared."

"We never had demons live here."

"Then why did they let us?"

"Well, there was a debate. But Delilah made a convincing argument that you needed a home, safe and away from Hell."

"It's no longer become safe."

"I'm sorry, Morgalla. But the rest of…"

Lorn glanced away, unable to finish his sentence. Morgalla had a feeling what the words might be.

"My kind," she said.

"Yes. War is coming to an end, finally. As peaceful and open as we try to be to others, we are imperfect beings. You have the gift of insight into the hearts of others, something all demons possess. But you…"

His eyes stared at her with wonder, as if he had discovered something very precious.

"What is it?" she asked.

"You are not like other demons. You don't use your gifts for evil. Where others mold and corrupt the souls of the innocent or force them against their will, I am grateful you have not followed their path. I'm afraid…"

Morgalla sensed the presence of her mistress. She turned to a faraway branch and saw that Delilah was watching. She motioned for her student to approach.

"I guess that means it's time to leave," Morgalla said with a somber tone.

She took a few steps but had to give the forest one final look. She then gazed high up into Lorn's eyes, which gawked back in concern. He held up his hand, and Morgalla matched it. As their palms touched, she saw the sharp contrast of her orange hand enveloped in his blue one.

"Keep your friends close, Morgalla. And never lose hope."

Her expression revealed her concern and loss for words at that moment. "I…I'll miss you."

She joined Delilah on the branch.

Delilah sneered and spread her wings. "I despise long goodbyes."

"It's just unfair."

"Life is seldom fair, child."

Morgalla fought the urge to turn and give the forest one more glance. The clawed hand brushed her shoulder, and she braced herself. With a leap, gravity took over, and Delilah whisked her apprentice off to the portal that glowed red far off in the distance.

THREE

THE BURNING SKY

IT WAS the place she had seen in her dreams a hundred times. The mountains were painted black, the landscape infected with dark trees and weeds, and the sky engulfed in flames. There was no sun or beacon of light, but the inferno above provided the only illumination.

"Amazing isn't it, young one?"

Morgalla marveled at the figure who stood next to her. Her mistress, Delilah, was delighted at the sight before her as if being greeted by a long-lost friend. Delilah inhaled the air and coughed. It smelled like something strange burning. She smiled.

"How I missed that."

"Really?" Morgalla asked.

"I suppose you still have to get used to it. Do you remember the sweetness of the air?"

"No. And *sweet* isn't the word I would use."

"Want to fly down?" Delilah asked.

"No, walking is fine."

Delilah led her student down the cliff where they found a wide, stone path.

"Now remember, you can sense what they are feeling, but so can they with you." Delilah's comments made Morgalla's soul shift, something she easily sensed. "See? That kind of emotion could get you killed if you're not careful."

"What emotion?"

"Fear."

"I'm not afraid."

"Yes, you are. There's nothing to be afraid of, child. We will be surrounded by allies, and you will have me there with you."

The words brought Morgalla little comfort, but her mood changed slightly.

Morgalla found it strange, seeing the demon hybrid acting like a happy child. Morgalla struggled to keep up as they ran down the mountain path. They came to a clearing. At the end of the path was a gate. On either side of it were two bronze statues of some sort of creature. The figures had been placed on top of pedestals so high that even Delilah, with her great height, had to leap to touch them. The right statue's nose had been worn down to the polished bronze while the rest of the metal had turned black. Delilah kissed her hand and leapt to touch the nose.

She called to Morgalla, "Come on."

Her young apprentice was still apprehensive, so Delilah grabbed her hand and pulled her into the town. As they entered the gates to the city, Delilah stopped. She took a deep breath. Morgalla sensed a shift in her soul.

"What is it?" Morgalla asked.

"You gotta put on a brave face around people like this. If you think about something you hate or get angry, they won't be able to sense what you're really feeling."

"What's the point of that?"

Delilah stared at her, the tip of her claw was touching Morgalla's chest. "Important lesson about dealing with demons: Don't ever let them know your true feelings. They will use that knowledge against you."

"You never did."

"That's different. Now think of something you hate."

"That's easy," Morgalla said with a huff.

This place.

Delilah's giddy child disappeared. She was all business now. Morgalla's soul was a cadre of negative emotions. Delilah said nothing as her pace was now more of a cocky swagger. With her long legs, she was able to cover long distances in a short time. Morgalla had to almost sprint to keep up.

The buildings were mostly red and black brick. Morgalla saw businesses of various kinds, most of them related to fulfilling the needs of demons: butchers, bakers, tailors. They entered the main village square near a large statue of some sort of beast, the same species that was at the main gate, but this one had wings. Demons seemed to be everywhere, congregating around the local buildings.

"Stay close and don't make eye contact."

The town square wasn't what Morgalla was expecting at all. Demons of all kinds came and went about their business. Some talked and laughed, some walked and stared at others as if they were trying to pick a fight. Morgalla noticed that some demons had horns, others didn't. She even spotted one that had more than two eyes. One had four legs. Another had four arms. Many spoke in dialects Morgalla didn't recognize, but she swore she heard English from the lips of some.

One thing was common among all—they were all armed.

Delilah turned around as if she was searching for any familiar faces. She soon became disappointed.

"What is it?" Morgalla asked.

"It's nothing. Come over here."

They found seats in the center of the square. Morgalla hopped up on a stone ledge, her feet not touching the ground. Delilah crossed her arms.

Two young demons…young males were walking by. They were watching Delilah, specifically the symbol on her cloak as they bowed their heads to her. She returned the gesture.

She leaned over to whisper to Morgalla. "Think they might be trying to curry favor?"

"With?"

"Well, they're looking for a master to serve. Those two don't even belong to a crew." Morgalla still seemed confused. "Look around. If you're not the direct servant of a master, you had better belong to a tribe of some sort."

It was then Morgalla noticed the different colors and patterns some demons were wearing and how they had flocked in groups.

Delilah nodded to a few. "Those over there, they wear the leather skins of crocs and snakes. They're the Swamp Posse." She then nodded to another group who was wearing furs. "Those are the Black Ashes over there. They hunt off-world."

"How can you tell?"

"They didn't get those furs here. There are no animals with fur in Hell."

"Did you belong to a…gang when you were young?"

"Yes. The Sapphire Sisters."

"Where are they?"

The question was met with a shift in Delilah's attitude as her mind was flooded with memories of her youth. "I'm the last one. They no longer exist." Morgalla frowned, but Delilah continued noting various groups they saw. "Those demons over there belong to the Crimson Death Crew."

"Let me guess, they collect for the needy and homeless?"

Delilah ignored the comment, only referring to another group who was walking by, their clothes torn and disheveled. "Obviously the Dracontooth Tribe. They herd and breed dracon."

"Dracon, those animals you were telling me about once?"

"Not just any animal, the animal of Hell. They are not to be played with. Even their young could snap off a limb. We're lucky they grow back."

As Morgalla checked out the demons, she found it hard to believe that these were her own people. They seemed so much bigger than her, even the women and some of the children. She also took note that she was the only one with orange skin and violet eyes.

They continued on, strolling through the area while Delilah noted what had changed and what had stayed the same since she'd last been there. They moved past a group of tall, large demons, all of them carrying hammers of various sizes.

Delilah knelt down and whispered to Morgalla, "The Hell Hammers."

"Why doesn't a demon just serve a lord of some sort?"

"You can't just sign up. One must prove their worth. By joining a clan or tribe, one can do just that. Sometimes the lords can contract out a group for some sort of mission or task."

A disturbing thought came to Morgalla as she suddenly imagined herself as a member of one of the groups she had just seen… carrying a massive hammer or wearing red-scaled leather. "And will I have to join one of them?"

"I'd prefer not."

Delilah stopped, and Morgalla nearly ran into her. She spread her wings out slightly, her hands on her hips as she smiled at the people around, but her eyes were squinted. Morgalla surveyed the demons near her and took one step forward.

"De-Li-lah."

Morgalla watched as Delilah reached for the man's outstretched arms. His voice was deep with some sort of thick accent Morgalla did not recognize even though it was strangely comforting. Their clawed hands clasped together, and they laughed. Perhaps she'd heard the language when she was a child and merely forgot. Delilah and the demon exchanged more pleasantries until finally, he turned to Morgalla while asking Delilah a question.

"Mi cheela Morgalla," Delilah said.

Morgalla didn't know what to do. She gave a small wave to him. "Um…hi."

The demon threw his head back and bellowed a loud laugh that could probably be heard throughout the courtyard. Morgalla couldn't help but notice Delilah's embarrassment.

Delilah said something in the foreign language to the demon, and the laughter subsided. But one thing that shocked Morgalla was a comment made by the demon that caused Delilah to backhand him across his face. She shouted something to him. He wasn't offended because a smirk remained on his face as he touched her shoulder. They seemed to part as friends, and Delilah and Morgalla continued on their way.

"What was that all about?"

"He said something that annoyed me."

"Who was he, anyway?"

"That was Mordus. We grew up together."

In the distance, beyond the town, stood a massive castle. The closer they got, the more detail Morgalla could see in the intricate carvings of black and red stone. Most of the sculptures near the structure and the surrounding walls and courtyard were skulls and snakes. If it wasn't so foreboding, Morgalla might actually have called it beautiful.

"I'm starving," Delilah said.

Morgalla didn't argue. She was hungry too. As soon as they entered the castle, their sensitive noses were struck with the wonderful smell of roasting meat. Besides fish, animal flesh was a rarity for Morgalla. Most of the time she ate local vegetation, primarily fruit.

As they entered the main dining hall, the scent was stronger than ever, and the sight before them made Morgalla's jaw drop. Long tables made of thick wood were covered with food from all sorts of roasted beasts. The hall was filled with the sounds of revelry, loud voices, and laughter. There was also the sounds of crunching and crewing as hungry demons of all kinds were feasting like it was their last. Morgalla couldn't see an empty seat.

Delilah reached for a drumstick and tore it from a cooked carcass. Her fangs sank into the flesh, and she feasted. Next, she grabbed a flagon of ale and took a long drink. Her spirit was lifted immediately. Wearing a fanged smile, she beckoned Morgalla to join in.

Though all the hearts were overflowing with joy for the meal, Morgalla was still uncomfortable as she slowly stepped into the massive hall. Delilah cut a rib from a baked animal and tossed it to her. Morgalla took a bite and had to admit it was good. Her spirit too, was lifted.

Delilah offered Morgalla a flagon of her own. After a slight sniff of the drink, she returned a look of disgust. The smell made her nose burn and her stomach churn. Other demons laughed, and Morgalla thought Delilah chuckled but seemed more embarrassed than anything.

One laughing demon called out in broken English, "She's turning green."

Another suggested, "Do not worry, little one. The children are drinking a juice made from berries. Perhaps that is more to your liking."

One more round of laughter filled the enormous hall. Morgalla answered with a fake chuckle.

When she and Delilah had arrived when the feast was in full swing. They were lucky to get any food or drink at all. What Morgalla found most ironic was the juice made from berries was actually quite good.

After the evening meal, a small group of demons had gathered. The hall was mostly clear except for some of the lesser beings cleaning up. Delilah was old friends with many of them as the hall bellowed with demonic dialog and laughter. Only one was silent and still: Delilah's apprentice.

Though many spoke in a dialog foreign to her, it was not only clear from their laughter, but their combined moods that a good time was being had. To Morgalla, the comfort was was like wrapping herself in a blanket. She stayed quiet and still, though.

Kodek, a demon with a rather dominant personality, finally took over the conversation. He spoke in broken English but Morgalla was at least grateful that she could understand him. The others were silent, each on the edge of their seat.

"Hundreds of them charged forth!" He shouted, his voice carrying through the high ceiling. "Try as they might, all of them fell to my blade. Finally, when they had exhausted all of the pawns, their leader had no choice but to face me. At last, a worthy opponent!"

Morgalla took a sip of her juice. Same with everyone else she was staring at the enigmatic demon, but where the others were entranced, she was still trying to find out why the story was interesting.

"Our weapons clashed as the fire raged around us..."

"Wait, there was a fire?" Morgalla asked, interrupting.

Kodek looked annoyed. Morgalla swallowed hard. "Sorry."

"Flames raged around us. Our weapons clashed. He injured me, I injured him. Through our wounds we continued to fight. Though he was strong, it was I who was triumphant!"

Demons applauded. Morgalla didn't at first but then she saw that others noticed. She joined in the clapping.

"To celebrate, I showed my opponent the greatest of honors: I tore his heart from his corpse and feasted upon it."

"EW!" All eyes were on the young, orange-skinned demon. Her lilac eyes grew wide from the sudden attention. "What? I'm the only one who's grossed out by that?"

Delilah took a deep breath and looked at the alpha. "Kodek, please continue."

Forgetting what happened, the demon continued with his story. "His blood was sweet..."

Morgalla started to turn green and her hand went to her mouth. "You can't be serious." Seeing the eyes upon her again, she held up her hands. "If I'm the only one, I'll shut up."

Later, as the "party" broke up, Morgalla sulked in a corner of the great hall. Delilah walked up, her hands on her hips. The burning gaze spoke volumes.

"Ew?"

"Oh, come on. The guy took a bite out of another guy's heart and somehow *I'm* the weird one."

"You are only drawing attention to yourself. You make yourself look weak."

The young demon looked frustrated but her attention was drawn to one of the beings who walked around serving the demons. They were all male, and their clothing was clean but simple. Each of them walked with a slight hunch. It was clear to Morgalla what they were. To her trained eye, they didn't appear to be demons. Their skin was a pale red, almost pink, and very smooth. They had dark eyes and wore the same symbol as the one Delilah wore on her cloak.

A demon shouted at one of the servants in his native tongue, kicking him over, much to the amusement of others. Morgalla rose to see the creature fall. He struggled but got up and bowed to the demon who'd kicked him. The injured one limped away, a look of pain on his face.

"What is it?" Delilah asked. Her student did not reply, but the shock on her face spoke volumes. Delilah briefly glanced over her shoulder before taking a bite from a piece of fruit. "Do not trouble yourself. It is just a prill."

"A what?"

"Slightly more useful than a human, but still far beneath us. Never forget that."

"The mark on their heads…"

"A reminder of whom they belong to."

"But…it looks strange."

"It is a scar. Remember when I told you of those? That mark will never heal. It will be with them for the rest of their lives. All scars are a symbol indicating how weak a being is." Delilah paused a moment, noting that Morgalla was still standing and staring at the prill as he hobbled away. "Sit down. You're drawing attention to yourself."

Morgalla, with great reluctance, finally sat. "They are not demon?"

"No. If a prill makes it to the rank of soldier, he should consider himself honored."

The prill limped past, and Morgalla couldn't take her eyes off him.

"Don't do that," Delilah whispered.

"Do what?"

Delilah leaned in so others would not hear. "Feel sympathy. That emotion will get you in trouble here. The prill should be thankful they are at least useful enough to carry a weapon and fight in battle. I see we have a lot of work to do with regard to your attitude."

Morgalla's next question came with a sting. "What does my attitude have to do with it?"

"Everything. Be thankful we had a refuge, a place to retreat, and that we both have full bellies."

Morgalla said nothing but continued nibbling on her food even though she didn't have much of an appetite.

FOUR

NO SAFE PLACE

WHAT PASSED for night came, and they found a camp to sleep.

Morgalla stared into the firelight. The climate was actually quite pleasant, not too hot or too cold. There was no actual night, Morgalla noticed, because the fire in the sky only dimmed slightly. Two red lizards roasted on the fire. Delilah mentioned what they were, but Morgalla had forgotten. At least dinner smelled nice. Delilah reached into her leather drawstring bag and took out a brush. She knelt behind her student and proceeded to draw the brush through her thick, orange hair.

"Look, if it makes you feel better, we can sleep in a tree, okay?" Delilah asked.

"That's what I had planned. Look at it this way: Since you said that not many demons can fly like you, we would have a tactical advantage being up high, would we not?"

"Now you sound paranoid."

Morgalla stood. "Hey, you brought us here. It's not a safe place."

Delilah was annoyed but kept her composure. "When I was young, we slept all the time outdoors."

"But, did something happen?"

"Few and far between. If we play our cards right, we could end up sleeping in Zorach's castle. Imagine it, living in luxury."

"I don't know if I could ever sleep in the same place with all that bloodlust around. And the…"

Morgalla paused, but Delilah wanted her to finish.

"And the…what?"

"Slaves? Lesser beings? Do all demons think like this?"

"Why shouldn't we? Morgalla, we are the superior species of Hell. Wound us and we heal in moments, whereas it will take weeks for them."

"That doesn't…necessarily mean…"

"Yes, it does." Delilah spoke with conviction. "Show me another species that does that. I'll have you know that some of them actually like serving a demon mistress."

Morgalla uttered a sound of frustration. She climbed the tree to find a suitable limb to sleep on.

"You forgot your dinner," Delilah called.

She held up the roasted lizard on the stick. Morgalla took it and disappeared.

The next morning Morgalla rose to a strange screeching in the distance. It was loud enough to shake her and make her hand clench her knife. She looked over at the hammock and saw Delilah meditating on a large rock. A snake was slithering up its way through the rocky terrain. Just as it was about to snap at Delilah, a knife came from on high and impaled the beast.

"Got you breakfast."

One of Delilah's eyes opened and watched Morgalla climb down from the tree. "I saw it coming."

"Yeah, I'm sure."

Delilah stared at the dead beast. "Mmm, taupe viper. I haven't had that in ages."

She smiled at Morgalla.

"Yeah, I'm sure it's yummy."

After their meal, Delilah led them towards Zorach's castle. She nodded to some demons in passing. One even shook her hand. After the encounter, she leaned in and whispered to Morgalla, "I'd introduce you, but I forgot his name." Delilah had noticed that Morgalla smirked. "That's the first time you've smiled since we got here."

"Don't get used to it."

Delilah laughed. "Oh no, Hell forbid you to actually find humor in something."

Morgalla frowned and Delilah felt the needles in her back from her student's stare. They climbed a steep cliff. Halfway up, Morgalla chimed in her opinion.

"Why not just fly us up there?"

Delilah stopped and looked down at her. "You want everything done the easy way."

"Look who's talking? You have two extra limbs. Also if you fall, you don't have to worry."

Indeed the climb was a bit easier for Delilah since she could use her wings to help. Morgalla was also jealous that Delilah was never afraid of heights. Morgalla hated them.

They reached a summit and made it to a flat piece of rock, a demon-made cliff that overlooked the castle far below. Morgalla looked around at the intricate stone and hieroglyphs and found herself admiring the artistry. Delilah stood at the edge, overlooking the valley…hands on her hips and taking a deep breath.

"I remember the first time I flew up here." She pointed to one of the castle towers. "I soared from that tower there when I was about twelve. Drove my master crazy with all the flying I did."

Morgalla joined her, creeping inch by inch to the edge. She didn't enjoy looking down into the valley and was surprised they'd climbed up that high. Delilah's eyes were closed. The hot wind blew through her hair and joy sprang from her soul. Morgalla was starting to understand what this place meant to her and left Delilah alone for a moment while removing her cloak and taking a seat on a large rock. She removed her leather pouch and took a drink of water.

Delilah took off her cloak as well and hung it over a rock. She unsheathed her sword and started a warm-up, and Morgalla did the same. Both women sparred with each other into the late morning, each of them showing skills honed from years of practice and, in Delilah's case, experience.

Morgalla, as always, defended herself to the best of her ability, but every now and then Delilah would try to use an unorthodox attack method. Morgalla's improvisation served her well, but sometimes Delilah could catch her off-guard with a strike at the back of her hand. Sometimes the dragon-hybrid would use her wing as a weapon.

Just when Morgalla thought Delilah would make one attack, she did something completely different. Delilah swung with lightning speed but stopped the blade just inches from her student's neck. Morgalla's lips clenched into a frown.

"You're still making the same mistakes."

Morgalla huffed, much to Delilah's obvious annoyance.

"Again," the teacher commanded.

They continued to spar, and Morgalla sensed the annoyance building within her teacher's soul. Finally, Delilah, with one powerful shove, drove the pupil to the ground.

"Would you stop being so defensive?" Delilah yelled. She backed up and motioned for her student to approach. "Come on. Attack me."

Morgalla rose and turned her back for a moment, clenching her lip. She took a deep breath and prepared herself for another attack. She held up her sword, ready to defend herself.

"I said *attack*."

"It's not my style."

"It's precisely that way of thinking that will draw predators to you. Now, attack me."

The young demon's soul fumed with rage. She couldn't take it anymore as she sprang forward. Their blades connected, and they clashed with each other. A smile came to Delilah's face. Her ivory fangs gleamed. Morgalla lunged, and her mentor took advantage of the lack of concentration. Delilah dodged, and Morgalla found herself tripping and landing hard on the ground.

Delilah spoke softly. "You are angry."

"You're damn right I am," Morgalla yelled, nursing a bruised ego and aching knees and elbows.

"Your enemy will take advantage of that," Delilah noted. Her student remained on the ground for a moment, breathing the rage from her burning lungs.

After their sparring, Morgalla sat on a large rock that overlooked the valley far below. She frowned when she noted a hole in her britches at the knee. Delilah took a drink from a leather pouch and then handed it to her. She snatched it. A frown still decorated her face.

"Don't be like that. It's that attitude that might get you killed one day."

Though she was motionless, in her heart Morgalla was rolling her eyes.

"And," Delilah continued, "if you are not careful, your insolence will also get you killed."

"What did I do now?"

"Remember, child, that everyone here can tell what is in your heart. You must not only control those rolling eyes of yours but whatever is going on deep down as well."

Morgalla said nothing, only looking out to the valley.

"Oh, you don't like that?" Delilah snapped.

"No. I don't like that. What I think and feel is suddenly a bad thing?"

"In a word...yes. Cast a defiant eye at the wrong demon, and he'll cut you down. Or, best case scenario, cut out your tongue. That is what I'm trying to protect you from." Delilah took another deep breath and locked the rage within her chest. "I blame myself, child, but we had no choice. I would have loved to have kept you here or among our own kind in the world, but Usteron was the only safe place for you and me at the time."

"But you hated it there."

"Oh, indeed I did."

"The forest was beautiful," Morgalla said. "The monks...their souls were so peaceful. I didn't have to pretend to be something I'm not. Sometimes, when they were meditating, it felt like I was wrapping myself in a blanket."

Delilah scoffed. "Those monks made you soft."

"I learned a lot from them," Morgalla snapped.

"They taught you weakness."

Morgalla's hand went up in a flash. Hero had appeared in her clenched fist. The blade stopped an inch from Delilah's neck which did not flinch in the slightest. A small smile appeared.

"Well done."

A shriek carried on the hot wind, and both women looked off into the distance where they thought it was coming from. Another screech called out, and soon many had joined in a horrifying chorus. They sounded far away, but they were also getting louder by the moment.

"What is that?" Morgalla asked with a slight stammer in her voice.

A single whispered word escaped Delilah's lips. "Dracon."

Winged beasts, a swarm of them, flew overhead. Delilah ducked. Morgalla dropped to the ground. A deafening sound of shrieks and flapping wings made the young demon cover her ears. Delilah, too, found it annoying, but she held her position. Their wings made a vortex that nearly knocked the dragon hybrid off her feet.

The swarm passed. Both women looked over the edge of the cliff and saw the dracon fly down around the castle, swarming about it like a tornado. Delilah and Morgalla saw far below from the castle courtyard and noticed a large group of demons and soldiers had gathered. From the castle, a figure emerged. At first, it looked as if the structure was bleeding. A vile black substance flowed around through the courtyard.

Though they were at a great distance away, Morgalla sensed the creature's soul. She had never been able to do that with someone so far away before. The demon…creature…seemed to be consuming the courtyard with its black cloak, or was it the creature's body? She could barely tell from where she was, but she could make out armor plating and a helm that was part of its body. She was unable to distinguish where the cloak ended and the armor began. A pair of large, black horns stretched from the top of its helmet.

All demons before the beast knelt to one knee.

Another word escaped Delilah's lips in a whisper. "Zorach."

Morgalla looked shocked. "That…is Zorach?"

"The Unholy, yes."

THEY TOOK the easy way down from the cliff with Delilah gliding to the town below. Both their stomachs rumbled. They walked through the town, down alleyways and past numerous buildings where demons were out and about doing their business.

Then Delilah stopped.

"What is it?" Morgalla asked.

"I…have no memory of this place."

The castle could easily be seen, but the buildings before them blocked their path. They sought out a different path but could not find one.

"That building is new," Delilah noted, pointing to one of them.

Morgalla spotted someone in a window and approached her, hoping she might speak her language.

"Um…excuse me…I was wondering…"

The woman ignored her but looked out the window and down the mist-covered alleyway. The female demon then stepped back and slammed it shut in Morgalla's face.

"Excuse me."

Delilah planted her hand on Morgalla's shoulder. "Shh."

As she pointed, Morgalla saw one demon emerge from the mist, then another and another. The first three had horns but many after them didn't. Their skins were all different shades of red, and they wore red leather.

From the buildings at the opposite end, more demons appeared. Some of their skins were shades of grey, others were purple. They wore black, and their bodies were dripping in gold. Same with the other group, the first few out, had horns.

One by one, demons on both sides drew weapons of all sorts.

It seemed as if the Crimson Death Crew and the Guild of the Golden Spike had a beef with each other.

Morgalla looked around and saw no exit. Delilah, with a very strong grip, took her by the shoulder and flew to the roof of a building. Two stories up, they looked down to the two tribes slowly approaching one another. Morgalla was about to leave, but Delilah stopped her. She looked at the situation with great interest.

Children had gathered on both sides of the alleyway atop the buildings to witness the goings on. There was silence throughout the area, yet Morgalla was still uncomfortable. Through the souls all around, she could feel their desire for the kill, whether they were participating or spectating. The children exchanged glances, dirty looks, and rude gestures, with each other across the alleyway.

The two sides took their places and stood with eyes intense and clawed hands flexed around their weapons. All the demons could easily feel the rage and lust for war in the hearts of either gang. After a few moments of nothing, Morgalla finally wondered something.

"Is this it?"

"Shh," Delilah snapped back.

One demon roared, and he was joined by his cohorts. The demons on the opposite end roared back. Both groups held up their weapons. Children joined in, cheering on what side they were rooting for. The sound was deafening as Morgalla covered her ears.

Like a bolt of lightning, both sides struck, their demon reflexes a blur as they moved. Metal clashed, and flesh was cleaved. Through the roars of battle, Morgalla could easily hear the wails of anguish and misery. She saw one arm severed, falling into dust, but the demon's scream was cut a moment later with another wound across his neck.

One demon's battle cry was cut short due to a mace crushing his skull. His body dropped and exploded into black ooze.

The young ones raised their fists and cheered, but it soon became apparent that the Guild of the Golden Spike was starting to lose the fight. The children on one side where Delilah and Morgalla all gave sounds of disappointment. Some even started crying. Morgalla looked at Delilah who wore a smile on her face.

A thought struck Morgalla and made her heart seize.

Will I have to do this someday...belong to a clan and fight for no good reason?

Thankfully through all the carnage, no one could sense Morgalla's terror as she backed away. Her hand clutched the center of her chest. Delilah smirked at the children's melancholy and fought not to break out into laughter.

As one clan retreated, the Crimson Death Crew all rose their fists and weapons into the air. They roared in victory.

The children, who had been cheering for the losing side, all ran off in terror. Morgalla had to avoid being knocked over as they ran past.

It was then that Delilah noticed the mood of her apprentice. Her smile was gone in an instant, but she didn't have to ask what was wrong with her. Her hands went to her hips. She took in a deep breath and breathed out a long sigh.

"Why, oh why did they make me take you off the world?"

Morgalla's breathing slowed, and her heart calmed. She couldn't look Delilah in the eye. No words were spoken during the evening meal.

FIVE

A DAY OF WAR

DELILAH HAD spent a great deal of time catching up with the allies who also flew under the banner of Zorach. Her student couldn't help but notice that many conversations ended with her in a melancholy mood.

"What is it?" Morgalla asked.

"Nothing," Delilah snapped. "I can't believe this."

Morgalla had to run to keep up with Delilah's angry stride, her long legs carrying her a great distance with each step.

"Tell me. What is it? What's wrong?"

"There are things you need not concern yourself with, child."

"Well, if it involves me, shouldn't I know?"

Delilah stopped, as did Morgalla who had to catch her breath from the exertion of running.

"Zorach's forces had lost a world. It is rare and a great dishonor to…" Delilah paused a moment, as if she would rather die than speak the next word. "Retreat."

"Well, what does that mean for us?"

"Losing one world is bad enough, but there was a rebellion on a second."

Morgalla was concerned. "Well, fine. But what does that mean for us?"

Delilah looked left and right to make sure no one was near. "It means Zorach's position among the lords is in jeopardy. And what bears ill for him, bears ill for us. That's what it means."

Morgalla's eyes widened, and she took a step back. It was then she noticed the presence of a group of demons. They saw an imposing figure at the top of a hill with a small group of demons behind him. He was dressed in garbs of dark red with black armor…a typical demon of high standing, with bright red skin and long, styled black hair. A light beard adorned his chiseled face as his lips were curled into a sneer. Black horns, small but sharp, were atop his head.

Delilah looked with curiosity as if she recognized him.

"Who is that?" Morgalla asked.

"If I'm correct, that must be Makraka."

"I take it you don't know him?"

"I know *of* him. His reputation is for being ruthless and efficient."

Makraka came down from the hill, and his people followed behind. Delilah held her ground. Morgalla copied. Since Delilah wasn't apprehensive at all, it filled her with confidence that they were not in danger.

"Greetings." The demon spoke with a deep voice.

"General…Makraka, is it?" Delilah replied with a slight bow.

"And you are Delilah, are you not?"

Delilah's heart swelled with pride. She couldn't help but smile.

"There is a dragon on the planet Gallestire Three, a pyro mare named Delilah…"

She continued to smirk. "I am named for her."

"The great romance between the dragon and the demon lord Huxar? You are the result?"

"I am their grandchild, actually."

"Remarkable." Amazingly, the tiniest of smiles came to Makraka's lips.

"This is my apprentice, Morgalla."

The young student raised her tiny hand in a little wave. "Hi."

Makraka's smile was gone as he studied the child, but it returned when his gaze went back to Delilah.

"I am headed off-world to crush some insurrection. Would you care to come?"

"Hmmm…" Delilah ran her clawed fingers over her chin then turned to her apprentice. "Care to go?"

"Crushing a rebellion?"

"Come."

Delilah took her by the arm and pulled her hard in the direction of the portal chamber. Makraka couldn't help but show his aggravation that *the child* was tagging along.

They arrived in the portal chamber. An entourage was waiting for the general; some were clearly warriors, but a few had some other function. Makraka pushed them aside as he stepped through the portal which burned like fire. The rest of them followed, with Delilah and Morgalla last. The apprentice paused a moment but felt a hard shove behind her.

Morgalla cried out as she fell through the wormhole, plummeting towards their destination. Wherever this world was, it must have been many light years away because her journey was longer than from Usta. She arrived at the journey's end, landing on a stone floor. Delilah was close behind.

An unfamiliar smell filled Morgalla's nose as she looked up to an alien sky. She was pulled to her feet by Delilah, and the two of them followed Makraka and his troupe. A new smell, one foul, carried on the air, one of death and decay. The area they walked through was a demolished city. Rubble and the bodies of the dead surrounded them.

Morgalla gave pause, seeing the dead. Their green blood stank. Delilah pushed her along.

"Don't embarrass me," she whispered.

Strange sounds carried in the air and Morgalla seemed shocked as the strangest of things came flying by. They glowed blue and gave off a strange buzz as they flew. They were not living creatures that she had ever seen, but she knew they had the souls present within them. Morgalla looked to Delilah who also looked on curiously but wasn't shocked.

"They need devices to fly," Delilah said.

"Is that…"

"*Tek-nology*? Yes."

Winged dracon came from the sky as well, swarming around the flying devices. Beams of light shot about, slaying dracon with ease. Due to their sheer numbers, the dracon were able to bring down the crafts, making them crash into the buildings above them.

Delilah grabbed Morgalla and dove under an archway to avoid the falling debris. One from the entourage wasn't so lucky as a massive piece of rubble crushed him. Makraka didn't stop for one moment as they continued on.

Delilah looked up to the sky to make sure it was safe. She pulled a shaking Morgalla from the archway.

"Come on."

They finally arrived at their destination: a cliff face that overlooked a massive battlefield. The two women came on the scene just in time to see Makraka berating some sort of subordinate. When he saw that Delilah was there, he gave the subordinate the back of his hand, making him fall to the ground.

"You disgust me," the general roared. "Allowing the rabble of this world to get the better of you."

"They caught us by surprise. It's not my fault."

The subordinate fought to his feet but was cut down by the general's blade.

"You're demoted."

The lifeless form froze into a petrified corpse as a severed head dropped to the ground with a loud thump and rolled, finally stopping at the feet of the two demonic women. Delilah didn't flinch, but Morgalla took a step back, seeing the look of fear forever frozen on the statue's face.

Delilah looked at Morgalla with clenched lips.

Makraka was shown maps and briefed on the situation. He shouted orders to the rest of the officers in charge of the armies. They did precisely what he commanded. He stood at the edge of the cliff, his clawed hands on his hips and chest out. The wind blew through his long, black hair and his cloak. He checked over his shoulder, seeing Delilah who stood with arms crossed and a smirk on her face.

Morgalla sat on a rock with an expression of disinterest.

Makraka had one more order to give. "Have the leaders of the insurrection brought to me so I might kill them myself."

Delilah smiled. When Morgalla rolled her eyes, she looked over her shoulder. "I saw that."

After a long day of violence and the crushing of a revolution, Morgalla returned to Hell with Delilah. Her head was filled with memories she was trying to process. She leaned against a stone wall.

"What is it?" Delilah asked.

Morgalla didn't answer with words but with a look.

"Your first time in the world ruled by *tek-nology*," Delilah noted. "They are capable of incredible things, make no mistake. But it turns them weak."

"Weak?"

"They rely upon it. Strip our weapons away, and we are still strong. Strip their toys away and what are they?"

Morgalla shrugged.

"Dead."

Morgalla decided to change the subject. "You know Makraka was annoyed that I was there, right?"

"Yes, of course. If he wishes to court me, I'm not going to make it obvious that I'm attracted."

"You're interested in him?"

"Who wouldn't be? Strong, powerful, tall." Delilah had a twinkle in her golden eye, but she couldn't help but see the expression on Morgalla's face. "There will be time for a mate, child. I'll teach you that too. But for now, there are more important things."

A look of disgust befell the young demon girl at the thought of mating with one of the demon males she had met so far.

Evening meal couldn't come soon enough. Morgalla usually ate quickly, but tonight she chewed and swallowed slow. Delilah noticed.

"Something else on your mind?"

"You're proud a rebellion was crushed today?"

Delilah pondered a moment. "Proud? It's unfortunate. I wouldn't necessarily use that word."

"And what would you do if you were in their place?" Morgalla asked.

"I would fight back. But I'm not them."

"But…"

Delilah interrupted. "Child, silence. The words you speak are dangerous, and there are ears everywhere."

Morgalla frowned, her soul burned with anger she had never felt. "Just because I…"

"It is the way of things. The Dark One gave us purpose, to bring order to the cosmos. It is a burden we accept gladly."

"A little too gladly, if you ask me."

They went silent as a servant approached and offered to take their empty plates. They handed them over and waited until he was gone.

"There is a word used by the lesser species," Delilah said. "God."

"Okay."

"It is a higher being they all look to for guidance, or blessings, or whatever."

"So, are you saying the Dark One is God?"

"Shh, that's blasphemy," Delilah snapped. "I'm saying the lesser species are off worshiping their false, absent God or perhaps their science, while what we have is real. The Usta, the Calamay, the humans, all of them weak and pathetic."

Morgalla said nothing, but clearly Delilah felt the doubt in her heart.

Delilah got up. "Be a loyal soldier, and someday you will hear the Dark One's call."

Delilah went back to the feast, but her student was silent and still with much to contemplate. The rumbling of Morgalla's stomach could not be ignored for long. Though she did wonder just what she had been thrown into.

IT WAS soon after the evening meal when Delilah introduced her student to the doxer races. The bronze-scaled doxer was a quadruped just barely large enough for Morgalla to ride. Its claws were large for digging through the dirt and its tail long like a whip. The bronze-colored scales made it look like the beasts were wearing some sort of armor from its snout to its rump. Small horns adorned the backs of their heads, and they had four bright red eyes.

As they walked through the archway leading to the track, they saw demons of all kinds congregating and overall having a good time. It was actually a pleasant experience. Delilah smiled as she saw her student finally enjoying herself.

Morgalla noticed a sign in a language she did not recognize. "What does that say?"

"No death," Delilah replied, to which Morgalla looked confused. "Yes, there are actual places where no killing is allowed...within the castle, for example, but that just applies to those under Zorach's banner. Anyone who comes in looking for trouble is out of luck."

"Oh."

Like a switch, Morgalla's soul was set at ease. She had the feeling she might be spending more time here.

A rumbling in the ground made her take notice. Turned out it was the charging of the doxers racing by. Though they were far from the track, their feet thumping past at great speeds were felt by them. Both women laughed.

"I missed that sound," Delilah said.

There was a crowd before them leading to the stands. Delilah instead grabbed Morgalla by the shoulders and took to the air.

"Hey, no fair," someone called.

Delilah laughed as she flew to the top of the bleachers where both women took a seat. They looked to the field. Delilah's interest was much greater than Morgalla's, but with the excitement of each race, the young demon couldn't help but join in on the enthusiasm.

"Does the winner get anything?" Morgalla asked.

"Bragging rights from the trainer and owner mostly, but they primarily have wagers against one another. But it's really the loser that people are most interested in."

"The loser?"

"They kill and roast the loser."

Morgalla looked shocked. "What?"

AFTER THE races, Delilah led Morgalla to the stables where the doxers were kept. Morgalla could tell her mistress had recognized another face and had to say hello to him. As the two talked in a foreign dialect, Morgalla took a moment to get closer to the doxers. The stable had a very high ceiling, and the compartments were of varying sizes, some very large.

She peeked in and saw a doxer nursing a litter of hungry pups.

"Awww…" Morgalla said.

Hearing a defensive growl from the mother, Morgalla backed off.

She walked down the stalls, keeping her distance from them. Sure, she was curious, but she was also cautious. She sensed there were animals within the stable, but their mood was in question. A doxer peeked out of his stall which Morgalla gave a jump. The beast's four eyes gleamed at her, but Morgalla could tell what his soul was feeling.

He's glad to see me.

Without fear, she approached the animal with her hand extended. "Hi there."

The doxer licked her hand, and she laughed. She used her other hand to pet his long snout.

Morgalla's happy mood was interrupted by a loud, booming voice. She spun around and saw a massive demon at the entrance to the stable. He was filthy from his work. His tiny, golden eyes burned at her. He roared in his native tongue, and Morgalla stepped away from the doxer, her hands raised.

"I'm sorry."

The demon continued to shout at her, his bulbous body stomping forward. She didn't know what he was saying, but it was clear he was enraged.

Morgalla was about to run away as fast as she could when another voice bellowed out. She turned and saw someone who was the exact opposite of the demon whom she'd enraged. He was dressed as a noble, clothes pressed and clean; his shirt was glistening silver, and his black vest was decorated in gold. He had light purple skin and large, pointed ears. His long, black hair was shining, and his swagger was that of a creature with no shortage of confidence, but it wasn't until he got closer that Morgalla noticed how young he was. He had to have been around her age.

He shouted commands to the demon and the servant complied, though his eyes still burned at Morgalla. The beast of a demon walked away, and her savior turned with a smile on his face, exposing his pearly whites.

"Apologies, he's rather protective of his beasts."

"Um…thanks. I was just petting one of them."

He shrugged. "No harm was done." He extended his hand. "Vex."

She took his hand and shook it. "Morgalla."

She noticed the emblem around his neck, how it was different from Delilah's.

"Are you here with someone?" he asked.

"With Delilah."

Morgalla looked around, saw her mistress, and pointed.

"Yes, with Zorach."

Morgalla stammered. "I…uh…well…"

"Relax." He chuckled. "I'm not one to start fights for no reason."

He was speaking the truth and his soul beamed with a sort of joy that made Morgalla smile.

"Finally, someone with a little sense."

Vex's laugh bellowed out through the stable. "Yes, well, it is the way of things, sadly. Say, I don't suppose you'd…"

"Morgalla," Delilah called out.

They both turned and saw Delilah running towards them. When she was in their presence, Delilah beamed a look of contempt to Vex who stood with his arms crossed, a smirk on his face.

"Well, well." Delilah started. "Looks like Vex has come from under his father's shadow."

"You know what they say about shadows, Delilah? How easy it is to disappear in them."

He smirked at her, his confidence swelled within, but Delilah didn't back down.

"Did your doxer win today?"

"My doxer always wins."

"You mean your family's, that is."

Morgalla didn't join in at all. Vex didn't hadn't tried to assault Morgalla, she couldn't understand why Delilah was so confrontational to him. On the contrary, he was actually helping her. Every comment was like a needle to either of them. Delilah didn't seem affected, but her comments were taking their toll on Vex.

"How are your brothers?" Delilah asked.

In an instant, the mood of the young demon shifted. Delilah had scored a direct hit.

"Dead."

"Really? Surprising. They were so skilled with a blade. They actually fell to a superior warrior?"

"I avenged Verik's killer."

"Yes, I heard." Delilah mocked. "Stabbing someone in the back is so courageous, isn't it?"

The rage built within Vex's soul and was written in his eyes. A soul so young was easily malleable to someone as skilled as Delilah.

"Dead is dead," Vex snapped.

Delilah smirked. "If you say so."

It was clear to Morgalla that her mentor knew more than she was leading on to the young demon. She used knowledge of Vex's family as a weapon against him. However, Vex still had an ace up his sleeve.

"I suppose it could be worse. One's soul could be…pure."

He looked for a moment to Morgalla then back to Delilah. It was clear to them all to whom he was speaking. Delilah remained unfazed on the surface, but Vex had delivered a mighty blow. Morgalla was confused.

"Now get out of my stable," Vex commanded.

Delilah smirked. "Daddy's shadow is so comforting."

Delilah commanded Morgalla to follow, and they both turned to leave. As they reached the end of the stable, Delilah had one more observation.

"By the way, your other brother was killed by humans. That's gotta sting."

There were hardly any words for the rest of the day, but Morgalla could tell that Delilah was angered by their encounter. During dinner, Delilah finally broke the silence.

"If that blue-blood snob ever touches you, you will kill him. Understand?"

"What did he mean by *pure*?"

Delilah ignored her question. "Do you understand?"

"Yes, okay, I'll do...whatever. What did he mean by his *pure* comment?"

Delilah sighed and leaned in to quietly speak to her student. "You have yet to get a kill, Morgalla. Surely you've sensed the black mark on the souls of others around you?"

"Well, maybe."

She had to think about it, never having paid attention to it.

"Morgalla, everyone can see it. The fact that you're yet to get your first kill. It is like a beacon."

"You were afraid of it."

Delilah looked away.

"Wait a minute," Morgalla added. "Are you ashamed?"

"I just knew those monks would corrupt you."

"Corrupt? Just because I've never killed anyone?"

"Keep your voice down."

"What's the point if everyone knows this anyway?"

"You just...don't get it, do you?" Delilah asked.

"Obviously not."

Delilah paused and searched for the words to help convince her. "All around you are people with the same skills as you. They can see into your very soul, Morgalla, and if they sense even a bit of weakness, they will prey upon it. You must use your anger and hate as a shield, but it can only do so much."

"And killing someone will somehow fix all this?"

"It wouldn't hurt."

Delilah turned her back, which was just fine for Morgalla who did the same. Both of them went to bed angry, camping for the night.

SIX

ARENA

MORGALLA WOKE to the scuttling of some rodents searching for their breakfast. The muscles of her hand flexed around the grip of her knife as her eyes flew open. She didn't sense anyone or anything dangerous around. Breathing a sigh, she plucked a black apple from a branch and hopped down from her hammock and found a note:

Meet me at Nathrak Castle—D

She recognized the handwriting as Delilah's and wondered why she had left early. Morgalla gathered her things and set off to the castle. Arriving, she saw that it was more of a manor, but she guessed the word castle sounded more impressive.

Several demons were playing a game of some sort. Morgalla kept her cloak concealing her arms for the time being until they saw her. They must have sensed how uneasy she felt because when she got close enough, they all looked at her. There was no bloodlust among them, and she lowered her guard though her hand remained on the blade handle.

A guard was leaning against the doorway. He saw her and did nothing.

"I think I'm expected?" she asked.

He smirked and motioned for her to enter.

The manor was beautiful with a floor of black stone lined with gold. The elegant wood had detailed images carved within. Morgalla approached one and ran her fingers over the elaborate detail. She sensed someone coming down the main staircase and saw a male who motioned for her to follow him.

Morgalla did so, walking with the demon through the manor. There was no malice with his soul or his intentions, almost as if he were a blank canvas.

"Where are we going?" she asked.

"I was not told," the servant replied. "And I did not ask."

"Of course."

"You will learn that questions are a bad thing around here."

Morgalla was led to a set of large doors at the end of a darkened hallway. The doors opened, and light filtered in, but she froze. There was that feeling again, same with the demon from before who'd tried to kill her. Bloodlust was present. She looked at the servant who was blind to what awaited, but he sensed it too.

Morgalla was about to turn and walk away, but she saw the doors at the opposite end of the hallway had closed. Under her cloak, she gripped her knife tightly and was ready to summon Hero at the next sign of danger. She saw no choice as she crept through the door and entered the arena. The ground was covered in a gravel-like substance, and it looked filthy. A high, circular stone wall surrounded her. Seats ascended like stairs all around with entrances up at the top.

Morgalla saw Makraka and Delilah at the top row talking. Their attention turned to her when they sensed she had entered. Some other demons were in attendance, but most of the seats were empty.

There was a young male at the opposite end of the arena. He was dressed in light clothes with no armor. The sword in his hand, and the fact he was warming up, made her take notice. He was fast and skilled. He had an entourage with him...many in the stands and a couple in the arena. They whispered things to him, psyching him up for what was to come.

The male was about the same age as Morgalla, if she had to guess, and the fact he didn't have horns was a clue. His skin was dark red, his hair black and tied into a tail in the back. His gaze was locked on her, the bloodlust strongest with him.

A female approached him, also young. She shot a look of contempt at Morgalla. The female had a narrow, lovely face with delicate features, red skin and orange eyes. Her black hair was tied into elaborate braids laced with gold. Small, white horns adorned her forehead at her hairline.

Seeing Delilah walking down the steps, Morgalla jumped up the wall and held on to the top. Two of Makraka's servants saw what she was doing and shoved her off. They leapt into the arena with her, weapons drawn.

"Up," one commanded. "Cloak off."

With hesitation, she did what she was told.

"How many weapons do you have?" the other demon asked.

"Only one," Morgalla replied.

The demon growled. "You lie."

She felt the slap to her face and fell back again. Morgalla sneered at them both, anger enveloping her soul. They chuckled, her anger amusing. She tossed them her knife, choosing instead to use Hero.

All in attendance took their places among the stands, and Morgalla found herself alone with the young male. Sweat already decorated his light red skin, burning his yellow eyes. Now that she had a good look at him, she could tell he was actually younger than her.

Morgalla looked up at Delilah who had found a seat in the front row.

"What the hell is going on?" Morgalla demanded.

"A matter of honor, child. For your own good."

"My own good? He's looking to kill me, and this is for my own good?"

"Makraka's last son, Harek. He has yet to get his first kill too."

"And what if he kills me?"

"I have taught you too well. But you must not hesitate."

Morgalla glanced over her shoulder. She saw Harek embrace a young woman and kiss her.

"That is Xia, his betrothed," Delilah said. "It is she who he is fighting for, his source of strength. You must find your source as well. It will keep you alive."

"Yeah, the fact that I don't wanna die..."

Morgalla sensed the coming attack and ducked. Harek's blade swung where her head had been just an instant earlier. She rolled and was on her feet immediately. Hero emerged and was in her clenched fist.

Her opponent approached, kicking some gravel at her. For a moment she was blinded. He came at her slashing. Morgalla had to use every bit of skill she had to dodge and block his attacks. Metal clashed against metal as the small audience looked on with great interest.

Sparring with Delilah was very different than this. She could feel the intensity of the kill emanating from Harek's soul. Her heart raced, and her breath came quickly. His attacks were strong, and she felt the impact of his blade send shocks up her arm.

Morgalla wanted to scream as he hacked and slashed away at her. He finally disarmed her. Hero changed back to a medallion and was lost among the gravel. The audience laughed, all except Delilah.

Morgalla rolled again, barely avoiding a slashing sword. She saw for a moment the look of disappointment on Delilah's face. Makraka stood at the top with his arms crossed, a permanent frown on his face.

The light gleamed from her medallion and Morgalla could see where Hero had landed. He was behind Harek.

"You don't want to do this anymore than I do," Morgalla said.

"It is a matter of honor, and you will not convince me otherwise."

He swung his blade and Morgalla ducked. She connected with a hit to the young demon's face. She kicked the weapon from his hand and leapt, her legs scissoring his neck. They both came down to the gravel, and Morgalla could feel the joy springing forth from Delilah's soul.

"So, you're going to fight for the entertainment of others?" Morgalla asked him.

Harek struggled to speak. "It's not amusement…but honor."

"That word again…don't be an idiot."

Harek sank his teeth into her calf, and she cried out. She had no choice but to release him with a swift kick to his face, bloodying his nose. They were both to their feet, and Morgalla saw her medallion. She dove and Hero was unsheathed in an instant, ready for action. When she turned, she noticed her foe was defenseless. His weapon was on the ground, and Morgalla stood between him and his only hope of victory. She could easily feel the fear from his soul, and they stood frozen looking at each other.

Delilah's hands clenched, her eyes intense to her student.

Do it…Do it.

"We can walk away from this," Morgalla said.

"You're not serious."

Morgalla felt the shock from the majority of the audience because she hadn't killed him, but there was one who was terrified. She could only see for a brief moment Xia in the audience, the same age as Harek.

Harek took a step, and Morgalla matched him.

"Walk away," Morgalla said.

Harek sneered and spat a mouthful of blood to the ground. "Disgusting."

The audience echoed audible sounds of disapproval. Morgalla didn't care, but Harek charged at her. With his neck and chest wide open, she could have killed him then and there, but she didn't. He attacked her, striking and forcing his way past. Morgalla fell back, and Harek had armed again.

Delilah was angry.

Their swords clashed again, and Morgalla quickly had to find a way to fight him. This battle was different than any time before. He was stronger than her and very quick. Letting his blade strike hers was a waste of her energy. She had discovered that dodging his attacks was far better, but even then she would soon grow tired. He roared with each slash and found nothing but air.

Their skills showed years of dedicated training, but Harek's dueling included more anger. Morgalla was scared. Surely they all felt it, but her will to survive was strong. She flinched at a punch to her midsection but knew it was only a ruse. Blocking his real attack, the sword came to her neck, and he punched her face. Falling back again, she felt the wall behind her.

He lunged but missed. Morgalla used his momentum to bring his face to the stone. There was a crack, and Harek's nose was broken. His back open to attack, she could finish this but didn't. She stalked to the middle of the arena, wiping sweat from her brow.

Harek held his nose. Blood flowed down his mouth and chin. Morgalla made eye contact with the Xia in the audience. The fear was written on her face as her eyes locked on Harek. The girl then looked at Morgalla, and her expression changed to anger.

"I don't want to kill you," Morgalla said to Harek, her voice almost desperate.

The audience, Delilah included, responded with disgust.

"But I want to kill you," Harek roared and charged at her.

With his anger as a weapon to Morgalla, the fight didn't last much longer as she soon disarmed him. She held the tip of her sword to his neck. Harek was terrified. He fell to his knees. Morgalla breathed the fire from her lungs, her eyes intense and showing the anger she now had for him. Delilah was overjoyed, and she clapped.

Morgalla disappointed her teacher and lowered her weapon. She turned her back and walked away. Harek looked up at his father who sneered and turned his own back, walking to the exit.

The young demon called out, "Father."

Makraka ignored him.

Morgalla hung her head, a myriad of emotions running through her. Only one emotion came from Delilah, and that was an annoyance her expression clearly showed. The solitary emotion from Harek was rage. He found his sword again and came at Morgalla. She could feel his attack coming from a mile away and held her breath.

Please...please don't.

He roared and slashed at his foe. Harek found nothing but air as Morgalla ducked and spun around. It was pure instinct, a will to survive that drove her to impale the tip of her blade into his chest. The expression of shock was frozen on both of their faces. Morgalla's jaw hung open.

"What have I done?"

The young male lost all power in his body as it went cold. His blade fell from his useless fingers and hit the ground with a clang. He fought for breath, but his lungs froze. Harek's eyes connected with hers only for a moment.

Morgalla could only manage a whisper. "I'm sorry."

Harek dropped away from Morgalla's blade. His limp form crashed to the gravel, and in an instant, changed to dust. Everyone was silent. Delilah was to her feet immediately. She turned to Makraka who was still making his way to the exit.

A scream cut through the silence and Morgalla looked to the stands. She saw the young Xia in a state of grief. Other demons held her back. The pain and her rage burned Morgalla's soul. She could only stand there, the tip of her blade stained black with Harek's blood.

All the other demons groaned in disappointment. Many of them got up and left in a huff. The young female, however, jumped down into the arena, screaming at Morgalla. Other demons joined her, weapons drawn. Morgalla held Hero up, ready to defend herself from the coming onslaught. Delilah stood in front of her protégé though Morgalla was surprised to see she had no weapons unsheathed.

All Delilah had to do was a point to the symbol of her master. She looked at the demons before her with eyes intense. Xia had to be held back by her allies as she screamed in rage.

Delilah looked at Morgalla. "Let's go."

Morgalla didn't argue with her mistress who took her by the arm and led her to the exit. Morgalla sucked back the tears building from her broken heart. Surely Delilah could sense them too, her clawed hand gripping Morgalla by the arm and pulling her away. There was also anger, something Delilah was proud to sense.

When they were alone, Morgalla fought away from her grip. "Don't touch me."

"What's your problem?"

"My problem? You put me in a death match. That's my problem."

Delilah huffed. "For your own good."

"How was that for my own good? Do you know how many enemies I just made?"

"They know you can and will kill to defend yourself. I just gave you teeth. Whether or not you know it, child…but I just gave you the greatest weapon to defend yourself."

"What's that?"

"A reputation. You really think anyone will mess with you now that you have killed?"

Morgalla yelled, "That's all shit. You did this for your ego. You were ashamed of having me with no kill."

Delilah grabbed Morgalla's arm and pushed her against the wall. "You listen to me, child. Welcome to Hell. Here, you kill, or you will be killed."

Morgalla pushed her and slapped away Delilah's clawed hand. She screamed, "I wish you'd never brought me here!"

Delilah sneered at her. "Why he wanted you away from Hell, I'll never know. It's only made you weak."

"It's weak to value life?"

"Harek wanted you dead, and you know it."

"And now his father and the entire family will want me dead."

Delilah smiled. "Relax. I've killed others in a similar way, and he never held a grudge. It is the way of things."

"What?"

"Yes. For it is better to die with a weapon in your hand than live as a coward. Today, you showed fear and compassion. Don't ever do that again."

Delilah turned and started to walk away before she looked over her shoulder. "You coming? I'm hungry, let's go eat."

"I think I'm going to be sick."

Morgalla hunched over her hands on her knees. Delilah sighed and approached her, placing her hand on Morgalla's shoulder.

"I knew it was a mistake to raise you off-world."

"It was a mistake bringing me here," Morgalla yelled, slapping away her hand.

Delilah looked angry again as if she might smack her student.

"I cannot wait until you're finally out of your teens."

SEVEN

THE SANCTUARY

MORGALLA FOLLOWED her mistress towards Zorach castle; the rage balled up within her heart. Delilah wasn't concerned, in fact, she would much rather have Morgalla be angry than sad. Sorrow would only make her a target. Rage would be her shield.

When they got to the castle, a feast had been prepared and was in full swing. Though Morgalla was starving, she couldn't find the heart to eat. While Delilah laughed at a joke some other demon was telling, Morgalla ran off. She made her way through a group of young warriors who had just arrived. She ran up a staircase, past a couple making out.

Morgalla wanted to run…run somewhere…run anywhere so long as it was away from this place. She went to the highest tower she could find but could still sense the presence of demons nearby. She climbed out the window to the ledge, needing to get away from anyone who might be close. Ignoring the height, she inched her way across the ledge.

Don't look down.

She didn't follow her own advice and regretted it. The fright gripped her soul. Normally heights didn't bother her until now…now that Delilah wasn't there. She climbed up to the roof and watched the landscape stretched all around. Mountain peaks surrounded her as far as she could see. The hot wind blew through her thick hair as she collapsed onto the roof. Convinced she was finally alone, she balled up, hugging her knees to her chest.

Then the tears came.

After pulling herself together, Morgalla climbed in through the window and made her way back down the stairs. The feast was over, and hardly anything was left. Servants were cleaning up. Thankfully, Morgalla was able to get some fruit and bread.

As she left the castle, she could see Delilah at the opposite end of the courtyard. They made eye contact, but Morgalla's mood did not change. Delilah sighed. Morgalla walked off to be alone again, resting in a garden and eating just to send the hunger away. Her eyes were still red and sore from crying, but she remembered to focus on the anger.

A pair of young males strolled by, and Morgalla hoped they might just ignore her. For a moment, it seemed as if they would, but they both stopped. Sensing they had intentions for her, Morgalla rose and was ready to summon Hero. She looked at them, focusing her anger. They turned, smiles on both their faces.

Oh, great.

Her eyes remained focused. "Having a bad day, guys. How 'bout we just call it a night?"

One of them said something to the other in a language she didn't understand.

"Look, guys, I know it's been minutes since you've killed some-one..."

They lunged at her, obvious about what they wanted. Their weapons were not drawn, but Morgalla didn't hesitate to bring Hero out to do the talking for her. She swung at them, but they dodged and laughed, drawing their own blades.

She started to fight, but it was clear she was outmatched. Morgalla ran, darting through trees and bushes, finally out into a clearing.

She was surrounded by rock, only a passage leading down a long cavern was her escape. They came out of the hedge, right on her heels.

Morgalla kept running, ignoring the fire in her legs and lungs. They were just as fast, if not faster. Her hunger was a detriment, and soon her body had weakened. Turning a corner, she was met by a large door, twice as tall as her. She tried to open it, but it wouldn't budge. Her hopes of escape were crushed.

She turned and was met by the pair of snickering goons. She focused all her anger and will to survive at them, gripping her sword tightly. They attacked. One advantage Morgalla had was they were not going for the kill. Her flesh was too valuable to them. That was clear to her now. She fought well, but it was all in vain as one blade cut across her shoulder, making her drop Hero.

They laughed, but she didn't stop fighting, punching and kicking at her attackers. It was only a matter of time before her final defenses would be crushed. One of them held her from behind as the other approached. Morgalla's legs locked around his neck, robbing him of precious air. Her teeth sank into her other attacker's arm. Biting as hard as she could, he screamed and released her, pulling her hair out of rage.

A blade came through the first demon's chest, impaling through his heart. Delilah removed her weapon, and his lifeless body dropped. Morgalla elbowed the other and proceeded to punch and kick him. He shouted in his native tongue. She didn't know what he was saying, but it was obvious he was pleading for his life.

Delilah stood, picking at her teeth with her pinky claw. Morgalla kicked the guy when he was down.

"Will you just finish him off, already?" Delilah asked.

Morgalla stopped but only out of fatigue.

"Get out of here," she said.

Her attacker looked confused, but she repeated herself, pulling him up by his tunic and kicking his rear. He ran off in terror.

"What is your problem?" Delilah shouted. "You do know that he'll only be back tomorrow and try to rape you?"

Morgalla's body heaved with quick breaths, trying to calm herself. Delilah wasn't done with her lecture as she approached, picking Morgalla's medallion up and handing it to her.

"When will you grow up? The cosmos is not a safe place, child. It's far beyond time you realized that. Unless you learn to fight back, you will be crushed under someone's boot. You will fight...or you will die."

"Why did you bring me here?" Morgalla screamed.

"This is your home. My home."

"I hate this place."

She turned, needing something to lean upon. She rested against the locked door, her arm touching the lock. Her head on her arm. There was a strange, metallic sound as the door unlocked. Delilah and Morgalla looked at each other, curious as to what was happening. It was then Morgalla noticed her blood had sprayed along the locking mechanism.

Delilah moved while examining it. "It's a magical lock. That's for sure. Look how similar it is to Hero."

Morgalla noticed too. The silver-looking metal was very similar to the style of her medallion.

"Was it made by the same person?" she asked.

"Possibly just the same species," Delilah replied and reached up to the high doorknob and opened it.

She and Morgalla stepped in. Nothing was there except for a very musty smell.

"No one has been here for a while," Delilah noted.

As they looked around, the only thing in the room was an iron bar that was parallel to the door. It was very close to the ceiling.

"The door was locked," Morgalla said.

"Until your blood touched it. The prior owner of this room must be dead."

"You mean this room will only open for me now?"

"Only you can use Hero, and if that lock works the same way, I would say yes."

A ray of hope appeared before her. This room could be a sanctuary, a place where she could lock herself in and be safe. After the horrible day she had, she needed this.

EIGHT

THE ORDER OF THINGS

HAVING NOTHING to sleep on in her new secret room, Morgalla decided to find a secluded tree to sleep in. A nightmare paid her a visit again. Harek's blank expression as he died was forever stained in her memory. She awoke starving, and her head ached from the horrible night. She found some fruit again, needing three to satisfy her growling stomach.

Morgalla made her way to Zorach castle to find Delilah, but honestly didn't know what to do next. She needed Delilah's guidance. Among some of the soldiers and other warriors around the area, she saw Xia, the young female from the prior day. The girl was surrounded by a group of primarily female demons and some males.

Great, she's got her own gang.

Morgalla froze but only for a moment, the lessons of Delilah ringing through her head. She thought of something she hated.

This place.

She focused, using the anger as a shield to hide all the other emotions. She could tell they were all looking her way, their anger beaming into Morgalla's soul. She didn't let it bother her though she remained vigilant, ready to defend herself. Best to go find Delilah, just in case.

Delilah was at the castle gate, speaking with others who clear-ly were long-lost friends. They joked and laughed with each other. When Morgalla was close enough, being around their good mood was a sudden and welcome change.

Delilah noticed her mood. "What's with you?"

"Harek's girl…"

"Ah, yes, his lover. I noticed her and the group earlier. They serve under Zorinda. You're among friends, not to worry."

"I can't hang with you all day."

"She'll get over it," Delilah said. "She can't stay mad forever."

"She only has to stay mad long enough to put a knife in my back."

"In your back? Doubtful. She might challenge you to a duel or something."

"Then what happens?"

Delilah grinned. "Then you kill her. Send a clear message that people don't mess with you."

Morgalla rolled her eyes.

"I'm trying to help you, whether you know it or not."

Morgalla felt angry still. This time it was at Delilah.

"Good," Delilah said. "Keep the anger up, and it will help shield you."

Delilah's gaze turned to the main castle gate. Morgalla could tell who was there. The four of Delilah's friends gathered around and put on a brave face. Morgalla was a little more confident, being surround-ed by a mountain of demonic muscle. Many of her entourage were almost literally twice as big as her.

Harek's lover gazed at her with pink eyes. She seemed even younger than Morgalla, her white horns barely visible over her long, black hair. With a group of nine demons surrounding her, they seemed to be ready for a fight.

"You killed my betrothed," the young woman shouted, echoing through the hall.

Morgalla opened her mouth, but no words came. Delilah nudged her.

"Say something," she whispered.

"I'm...sorry?"

"Wrong thing," Delilah replied.

The female screamed, "Sorry? I should kill you here and now!"

"Then why don't you?" Delilah shouted, taunting them.

Xia yelled, "I have ten to your six."

"Say something tough," Delilah whispered.

Morgalla searched for the words. "Um...well then you gotta go get more if you're gonna beat us!"

"Oh. Good one," Delilah said with delight.

The young woman's eyes burned with rage as she took a step forward. Her entourage followed suit. "Step out and face me."

"Um...Xia, is it?"

"It's now *Widow*, thanks to you."

Morgalla was clearly getting annoyed by the hate being thrown her way. "You mean Harek, right?"

"What?"

Morgalla shouted, "It was his fault that he sucked."

The demons surrounding Morgalla all laughed, their joy bellowed through the high hall.

"You dare mock my lover?"

Morgalla again was caught. She didn't want to mock this girl's pain, but then again, when it came to Harek, she was defending herself. She looked to Delilah, who gave her another nudge.

"Keep it up," Delilah whispered.

"I mock his skills...or lack of, anyway."

Again, laughter filled the hall. Morgalla didn't want to admit it, but it felt good to be surrounded by friends.

Widow drew her weapon and pointed it at Morgalla. "Step outside, and I'll show you my skills."

Morgalla, with the greatest of reluctance, moved out into the courtyard. Demons gathered to see the goings on. Among Widow's entourage, one male stood close to Morgalla.

"You killed my brother."

"I'm sorry," Morgalla said.

He spat on the ground. "Your sentiment disgusts me. If Widow fails, you will have me to deal with. Remember my name, Har…"

Morgalla interrupted him. "Look, I'm not gonna remember your name, so drop it, okay?"

She was still half-asleep, struggling to stay awake and yawned as Widow warmed up with her sword. Widow noticed the yawn.

"Bored?"

"No, I'm tired," Morgalla said, and Delilah gave her another nudge. "I mean…yeah, this will be quick."

Morgalla approached her mistress and spoke softly, "What are you doing?"

"Feel her anger?" Delilah whispered back. "That rage will only benefit you."

Widow took a stance, ready for the coming duel. It was then Morgalla really noticed how much taller Widow was than her. Another thing that was difficult to notice before. Since she was surrounded by demons, all of their combined souls made them blend together in some way. But with Xia…Widow…so close and her eyes burning with rage, one tiny detail came to the surface that Morgalla wasn't aware of before: there was no black mark of death on her soul.

The battle was on and Widow charged with all the fury she could summon.

"Holy crap," Morgalla shouted, dodging the attacks.

Morgalla was knocked to the ground and avoided Widow's stabbing blade. The tip came down on the stone, and Morgalla gave her attacker a hard kick. Joy erupted from the demons on Morgalla's side.

Both were on their feet, and Morgalla thought for a moment that this match was over since her opponent was now disarmed. Widow took a pendant from around her neck, and it changed into a short sword.

"Is that fair?" Morgalla asked.

She looked at Delilah for a moment. Morgalla found it curious that everyone was quiet but she had to focus back to the demon attacking her. The adrenaline took over, and Morgalla was wide awake, using every bit of skill she had to block, parry, and dodge. The widow was strong...there was no doubt, but she wasn't as powerful as Harek. If Morgalla had to guess, Widow's style of fighting was much closer to her own. The woman was a surgeon with the blade and even connected with Morgalla's leg as a sting cut through her flesh.

Widow's sword came to Morgalla's neck, but she blocked. They were in a contest of strength, but with Morgalla's weakened leg, it was doubtful she would last long.

"Where are your words now?" Widow asked, fury burning in her eyes.

Morgalla squeaked out, "Gimme a minute..."

The wound closed, and Morgalla felt the strength return to her leg. With some lightning punches and kicks, Widow stumbled back. Everyone thought the fight was over since Morgalla had a clear opening to end it.

She didn't.

Morgalla felt the anger from Delilah's soul, and it was written all over her face. Xia was able to get her second weapon, and her opponent grew concerned.

Widow continued the attack, thinking she had the advantage, but Delilah knew better. She smirked. With all the sparring sessions she'd done with Morgalla, sometimes attacking her with her arms and wings. two limbs was child's play. Both combatants attacked with professional skills. The crowd grew restless and annoyed as they had thought the fight would be over by now.

Morgalla was able to finally disarm her opponent, and she held Hero to her neck. Widow's eyes filled with fear. For a moment, Morgalla looked up and saw Harek's brother, his hand on his sword.

In that brief moment, Widow used Morgalla's hesitation to trip her. Hero fell out of her hand and Morgalla landed hard on the stone. The wind was knocked out of her and she fought for breath. Widow rolled and a blade was in her hand in an instant. She was on her feet and the demons on her side all cheered as they knew she was about to claim victory.

Delilah knew it, too. She closed her eyes, positive that her student was doomed. Widow roared as she rose her blade for the kill. In that instant a screech filled the air that caught everyone's attention. They heard the cry of dracon as they came from the sky. Something had spooked them and a flock of the beasts came through the air.

Among the confusion of flapping wings, demons scattered. Widow fell to the ground but her eyes never left her prey. Her gaze burned with fury as Morgalla fought to get away, barely avoiding the claws of the panicking beasts around her.

Through the commotion, both women felt cuts across their flesh. Morgalla's hand alone felt the sting three times as she reached to retrieve her medallion. A clawed hand came forth through the commotion and Morgalla felt herself pulled away. The last thing she saw through the insanity was Widow's hate-filled gaze.

Finding shelter, the flock of dracon flew off to the distance. Both women looked around and saw they were alone, that all others had fled. They breathed the fire from their lungs and their wounds had already begun to heal. Morgalla looked up to her mentor, sensing the relief that emanated from her soul. They caught their breath and Delilah placed her hand on Morgalla's shoulder. She would never state it out loud, but Delilah was reieved.

Later, breakfast was quiet. Morgalla forgot all table manners as she shoveled eggs and toast into her mouth. After what seemed like an eternity, the hunger pains were gone.

The entourage in her corner all sneered at her. She felt the daggers. She didn't care.

Delilah frowned. "You are aware they will see you as weak again?"

"I don't care," Morgalla replied with a full mouth.

One demon spoke in a foreign language, his voice growling as his fist came down on the table. Delilah replied with the same tongue.

"I won. Doesn't that matter?" Morgalla asked.

"Not to them and not to us," Delilah snapped.

The one demon got up, snarling at Morgalla. In broken English, she shouted, "Coward" at her. Morgalla replied with her middle finger.

The rest of the day included Morgalla being chewed out by her mistress. Delilah tried to explain why Morgalla was wrong, but the student just wouldn't listen. First time for everything.

Morgalla was confused. "So I kill Harek, and his woman tries to kill me. If I kill her, then someone else tries to kill me. Where does it end?"

"When you have the skill and the others know it, they will stop messing with you."

"And what if they never stop?"

"Then you kill them all," Delilah shouted.

Morgalla sat silent and still for a moment. Though Delilah yelled, the words didn't faze her at all.

"You are aware of how insane that is, right?" Morgalla asked.

Delilah roared to the flaming sky.

"Hey," Morgalla called out. "You're the one who brought me to this asylum."

Her attention was drawn to a couple of castle servants carrying out an old bed. Delilah continued her rambling.

"Are you even listening to me?"

Morgalla snapped out of her trance. "What now?"

"Of all the lessons I've taught you, this is the most important. That you don't hesitate, never for an instant. You must be merciless to your enemies, for they will be merciless to you." Delilah breathed a heavy sigh, and her tone changed. She sat next to her student. She spoke softly. "Everything I've done, child, is for your protection, for your well-being, for your own good. Do you understand that?"

Morgalla looked up to her and sensed something for a moment from Delilah's soul that she never had before. Was it fear? Surely not. Delilah feared nothing.

Delilah placed her clawed hand gently on Morgalla's shoulder. "Promise me you will heed my words."

Morgalla gave a huff. "I just…don't understand why they all just keep killing each other."

"It is the order of things."

"Well, it's pretty stupid if you ask me. Why did we leave Uster-on?"

"We've talked about this, and you know why. It was no longer safe for us, for our kind. The Usta drove us away."

"There are no other worlds where we could go?" Morgalla asked.

"Few other places are safe for us, and those are ruled by demon lords. It would be the same as here."

"So, what you're saying is we're truly safe nowhere?"

Delilah stood with crossed arms. "That is why I've taught you to defend yourself, child."

Morgalla still had her eye on the old bed the servants had tossed. She left Delilah's side and approached one of the servants.

"You don't want that?"

"It's not mine," the servant said. "One of the children in the castle didn't like it, so we're to have it burned."

"Burned?" Morgalla asked in shock. She walked up to the bed and ran her hands over it. It had broken stitching here and there, but she was surprised it was considered garbage. "Seems barely used."

Morgalla claimed it, and even though it was awkward to carry, she plopped it down in her new room, sending up a cloud of dust. She coughed. When the dust cleared, she ran her hands across the mattress. It seemed a little too good to be true. A real bed.

She jumped on top of it and breathed a huge sigh, and then she sank into it.

NINE

A DAY OR SURPRISES

DESPITE HAREK'S face appearing, she couldn't remember much anything else of her dreams. She'd heard roars of outrage and the scream from Harek's betrothed. It woke her in an instant. Morgalla rose, fatigue and ache pulsing through her head as she tried to wake completely. By the time she was completely awake, she noticed her horns were gone.

Morgalla gasped and jumped out of bed. Her hands ran through her hair. Indeed, not only the horns were gone, but her ears were much smaller and rounded. She found Hero. Changing it into a sword, she studied her reflection in the blade. Morgalla's hair was a dark shade of red and her skin a pale pink, almost white. Her eyes, which had been violet, were now dark green.

She screamed and started to panic before hearing a knock at the door. When she spun around, she realized it was Delilah on the other side, sensing her soul.

"Just a minute."

Delilah stood with arms crossed. She yawned as she detected the fear from her apprentice.

"Is there a spider in there with you?" she taunted. "If there is, kill it. I'm not doing it for you."

The elaborate locks on the door came undone, and the door slowly opened, the hinges squeaking. In the low light, Morgalla peeked out.

"What the hell is wrong with you today?" Delilah asked.

"I, uh…something's happened."

"Whatever it is, it's not the end of the world."

Delilah pushed in. Morgalla stepped back and froze in the center of the room. Her new appearance had obviously shocked Delilah.

"What's happened to me?" Morgalla asked.

"What indeed?"

Delilah approached and grabbed Morgalla's hair, moving her head about to examine her strange appearance. No horns. Her hair and skin changed. Her ears so small.

"Amazing," Delilah said. "And concerning."

"What are you talking about? Amazing? My face has changed. How is that possible?"

"It is a rare gift to be able to alter one's shape."

"You never told me that."

"Oh, sorry," Delilah said with sarcasm. "I thought there were more important things to teach you like swordplay and how to spell your name."

Morgalla held her sword up again to check at her reflection. "How long will I stay like this?"

"You should be able to shift back whenever you choose."

Morgalla looked up at her and expected a different mood from Delilah. Instead, she got one of concern.

"What is it?" she asked.

"Never mind. It's nothing."

Delilah reached out with her clawed hand and pinched Morgalla's ear.

"Ow," she shouted.

At the same time, Morgalla changed back to normal. She felt her ears tingle, and a buzz rattled her head for a moment. Her hands reached up to feel the horns behind her ears, and a look of relief came over her.

"There. All fixed," Delilah said. "I'm hungry, and we have business."

"Gonna make me kill someone?"

"The day is early. Anything could happen."

There was no malice in Delilah's intentions. For today, Morgalla knew she could trust her. She hadn't noticed at first, but Delilah had a brand new wardrobe, mostly made of leather. She also wore a new cloak of thick fabric. Delilah led Morgalla down into the village next to Zorach castle to the local tailor. He was a thin, tall demon whose fingers were longer than what Morgalla was used to. She also couldn't help but notice he had two thumbs, one on either side of his hands.

He had made a new cloak for her. Morgalla put on the heavy fabric that hung to the floor. She ran her fingers over it and felt the thickness. The last one had been worn and didn't protect her very well anymore from the elements. Morgalla also noticed the medallion where the cloak fastened around her shoulders. It was beautiful and was embroidered with the emblem of Delilah's master on it.

"Does this mean…"

"By wearing that," Delilah said, "it says you are loyal to Zorach and his servants. It also means you have allies."

The tailor interjected, "Zorach is a rather powerful lord. And influential."

Morgalla noticed that he too was wearing Zorach's symbol. She felt slightly trapped, but he was telling the truth, so maybe it wasn't so bad to have some friends around. Even if they might call her a coward every now and then.

Morgalla glanced at her feet and realized the cloak was a little long for her.

"Do you think she may grow some more?" the tailor asked.

Delilah pondered and spoke under her breath, "I hope so."

"Hey," Morgalla called out.

"What? It's true, your lack of height will hurt with your intimidation factor.

Morgalla frowned but then got an idea. "But...that will make opponents underestimate me, yes?"

"Perhaps, now if only you'll go for the kill without hesitation..."

Delilah sported a frown made of stone. Morgalla's smile disappeared.

"You need a new wardrobe," Delilah said.

Morgalla noted the garment was a little battered with a couple of rips and holes in it.

"Um, I guess."

"Hold still," the tailor said.

He held up the tape measure and started his work.

When they left the tailor's, Morgalla had clothes that felt nice, clean and brand new. The sensation made her confidence soar. Delilah even gave her a smile.

As the day went on, Morgalla actually was in a good mood. She was quiet for most of the time, contemplating her future. Delilah went on and on about how glorious it would be to join Zorach's army and conquer other worlds, live like queens. It seemed she had a plan for the two of them.

Morgalla, on the other hand, was thinking of the exact opposite. She didn't know what she might do or how to get it, but she wore a frown the whole time her teacher rambled on.

By afternoon Delilah was ready for another sparring session, Morgalla was far from enthusiastic, which annoyed Delilah.

Then it came time for the evening meal.

"Come, time to go to the castle," Delilah said.

"Uh, no. I'm not hungry."

"What? Well, I guess I shouldn't be surprised at your pathetic performance at practice today."

"Thanks, you're always so encouraging."

Delilah sneered at her.

Morgalla smirked. "Well, razor-sharp wit also needs to be practiced. Does it not?"

"We must meet Zorach soon and pledge our allegiance to him. Make sure that tongue of yours remains respectful."

Delilah turned and strode away. Morgalla rolled her eyes.

"I saw that," Delilah yelled back.

Morgalla made her way back down the hallway to her new secret room and was looking forward to sleeping within her vault. She passed a group of children playing with wooden swords and walked by a couple kissing under a tree. Everything seemed normal.

Her contentment was interrupted by the presence of demons nearby with nefarious intent. She froze and was ready to summon Hero. She glimpsed through the thorn bushes and spotted two of them.

Oh, great.

They burst out into the open with weapons drawn. In an instant, Hero was in Morgalla's hand and it clashed with the others' weapons. She recognized them from her duel with Harek and the second time with Widow. Someone had told her their names were Plux and Plor, brothers. She kicked one in the nose, breaking it. Then slammed another in the groin, and the beast fell.

Morgalla knew she was overpowered and would not last long with them. She ran, shielding her eyes as she crashed through some bushes. In the commotion, she didn't sense the soul of another demon waiting for her. A blade cut through the air. If it wasn't for Morgalla's sharp reflexes, Widow's sword would have ended her life in an instant.

Morgalla ducked back and did a roll to leap onto her feet. She was in a courtyard of some sort and found herself eye to eye with Widow. Her soul burned with hatred.

"Three on one is kinda unfair, isn't it?"

"Dead is dead."

"But you don't have an audience. No one will believe you killed me."

"I'm not doing this for the honor. Honestly? I just want to kill you."

Weapons clashed, and soon they were joined by Widow's companions. It took all of Morgalla's skill to avoid being struck as she ducked and weaved through the courtyard, using the statues and vegetation to her advantage.

Morgalla felt a boot hit sharply at her back and was forced to the ground. Widow stabbed but hit the stone ground as Morgalla moved just in time. Every time she tried to escape, Morgalla was met by either Plux or Plor who didn't strike with their swords but with the backs of their hands or their feet. They were keeping Morgalla within in the courtyard.

It was clear to Morgalla that she was not only outnumbered, but outmatched. She didn't care what it might do to her reputation… she needed out of there now. Plor swung at Morgalla and missed, to which she saw an opportunity to leap over his back and finally escape the yard with the trio hot on her heels.

Soon Morgalla realized she in a place she didn't recognize. *Lost.* At least, for the time being, it appeared as if she had alluded them. Her face was drenched in sweat, and her burning lungs fought for breath.

She was among some small buildings at the crossroads of many alleyways. Widow appeared at the mouth of one opening, many feet away. The demoness called for her friends, and Morgalla ran again.

The pursuit continued through alleys and crowds of demons. Morgalla sought out any friendly face, anyone who might be wearing the same symbol as her. No luck.

Just when she thought she had lost them, Morgalla noticed them catching up. She ran through a patch of thick bushes, and the vines of some plants reached out and took hold of her. She fought her way free to the clearing and almost fell off a cliff. She screamed. To her right, in the distance, were the dracon pits. On her left were the caverns that held the portal chamber where she and Delilah had entered Hell.

The pursuit forced her down the caverns and face to face with some of the guards who were there. They were in the middle of their smoke break.

Plux swung his ax, missing Morgalla by inches and striking the wall. She ducked and weaved about, screaming as the blade came closer each time. The guards protested, shouting at them both until finally Plux and Morgalla both fell through one of the portals.

They found themselves hurtling through a tunnel of light, falling out of control until they hit the bottom, skidding across the stone. From the bright light of the passage, they were enveloped in dark and cold. Morgalla lifted herself up and checked around. They appeared to be in a black stone cave. She turned around and saw the portal had gone cold and dark. Only a stone wall remained.

Plux growled at her, lifting himself up and reaching for his ax that had landed nearby.

Morgalla had thought for a moment she had lost him. "Aw, damn."

Morgalla was up and heard alien voices shouting nearby. With the echo, she could not tell where they were coming from.

She picked a path and charged down it. Surely Plux would be following. At the end of the tunnel, she nearly fell off another cliff. Her scream reverberated through the chasm below. She looked around at the torches everywhere illuminating the massive cavern. It stretched high and low hundreds of feet in either direction.

Hammers echoed as slaves worked. Ropes and chains all around carried the rock and other precious discoveries on a pulley system up to the ceiling. Morgalla turned and screamed again at the sight before her. She was gawking at a creature the likes she had never seen. It walked upright, its skin almost white with eyes sunken into its skull. The strangest thing about the creature was the fact that it had no soul. Morgalla was shocked to see it, not having sensed it coming. She pivoted around and realized there were more beasts of burden and slaves carrying full buckets and hammering away at the cave walls. The miners had dug so far that the bottom was no longer within sight.

Morgalla heard the crack and glanced up to one of the ledges. A massive demon stood there with a whip, shouting commands.

She had no time to think or contemplate what was going on because Plux had appeared in the tunnel. He swung again with his ax, cutting Morgalla's tunic as she fell back. She grabbed onto a chain and felt gravity taking over, plummeting her down to the chasm below.

Plux lost his footing. The chain was the only thing to grab onto. He also fell, but his weight pulled Morgalla back up. She pointed and laughed as it was his turn to feel gravity pulling him down. Her celebration was short-lived as she came to a stop right in front of the massive demon holding the whip.

"Um…hi."

He sneered at her. "Who are you?"

"That's a long story. I don't suppose you could just maybe let me go? I'm kinda having a bad day…"

The demon growled and reached for the chain.

"Yeah, I didn't think so," Morgalla said.

She flipped to the ledge below him and ran down another tunnel. She heard the demon shout orders and knew she didn't have much time.

Morgalla ran, encountering the beasts that walked on two legs around a corner. Their sudden appearance shocked her. She heard voices shouting down one tunnel and took off down the other.

Morgalla had to slow down because it got too dark in the tunnel to see much of anything. She heard the trickling of water, maybe a stream nearby, and slipped and slid down the rock. She clambered to grasp anything...to no avail. Morgalla saw light beneath her and was helpless as she came out the side of a cliff. Far beneath her was solid ground, and Morgalla swore as she plummeted through some pine trees headed that direction. She broke through some branches and came down hard on the ground while continuing to descend the steep hill, powerless to do anything else. The first thing Morgalla noticed was the cold, but the air was thick with humidity. Her next observation was the hill before her. Without time to react or anything to grab onto, she tumbled down the steep hill, barely missing a thick grove of trees and skidded to a halt among a bed of pine needles.

TEN

THE DEAD LEAVES

MORGALLA INHALED and took in the scent of pine. All around her the trees stretched to the sky. She coughed and managed to sit up. Thankfully, nothing was broken, but she was battered and bruised. Since demons were made of strong stuff, it would take a little more than a tumble to hurt her. Morgalla looked up at the steep cliff where she had fallen: it had been at least a hundred feet.

She brushed the pine needles from her hair and got to her feet. She checked to see if her medallion was still around her neck. Thankfully, it was. Staggering to a clearing, she spotted rolling hills covered in mist and pine trees. For a moment, she thought she might be on Usteron again.

Morgalla noted a light deeper in the valley and headed towards it. She crept closer and closer and noticed a clearing through the trees. There was a campfire and a lone, small figure by it. Whoever it was, they were clad in black with long, black hair that was unkempt. The person was working over a large, black pot. Steam poured from the top. Morgalla smelled something rancid coming from the camp.

There was no time to ponder or make a plan as she sensed the soul of Plux somewhere behind her. She spun around, eyes darting from one spot to the other, but could not see him. If she sensed his presence, he surely sensed her too.

As she stepped, her sounds attracted the attention of the creature at the camp whose gaze was now on her. Morgalla spotted a young, pale creature with bloodshot eyes. Her black lips parted into a snarl, revealing crooked, yellow teeth.

Uh-oh.

Upon command, she summoned the wind, and it lifted her from the ground. The beast picked a leaf from her hair, and she ate it. Raising her hand, she summoned brown leaves from all around. She moved her hands about like a sculptor with clay. With one command, the leaves attacked Morgalla.

Deciding not to stick around, Morgalla ran as fast as she could. The swarm of leaves was faster, and she it enveloped her, lifting her from the ground. Her arms and legs were bound, and soon her air was cut off. With Hero summoned, she cut through the leaves and landed on the ground. Morgalla hacked and slashed through the leaves. She saw her adversary hovering among the trees, approaching. The beast's attention was now on Plux who was charging down the hill at Morgalla. With his ax unsheathed, he attacked her. Morgalla ducked and dodged every savage blow. Plux's blade cut through the trees, sending splinters into the air. He stopped though when he saw the creature in black.

Through magic, the demon's adversary summoned rows that swarmed about at Morgalla and Plux. Both demons hacked away at the beasts, to no avail. A whirlwind of black feathers formed around Plux, and it was clear to Morgalla that it was more than just feathers. The sound of metal cleaving flesh came from the tornado. Plux screamed from the vortex, and when the black subsided, all that was left was his skeleton that crumbled to the ground. Morgalla was shocked and then looked to her adversary who was smiling.

"We're not together," Morgalla said.

The beast hissed again, sending the crows to Morgalla. She ran for her life, dodging between the trees, feeling the feathers cut at her flesh. Up ahead she crossed a large rock and leapt off it with the beast on her heels. Morgalla took hold of the top of a small pine and pulled it to the ground. She released the tree, and it snapped up into the face of her pursuer.

The creature roared in annoyance and continued the attack. Morgalla maneuvered through the trees down a steep hill, sensing the black soul who was gaining ground in the chase. The trees parted to show the hill ended abruptly. Morgalla tried to stop, but it was too late. She was going over.

Morgalla swore as she felt nothing but air beneath her. Far below, in a roaring river, she landed in the frigid water as if knives were being driven into her flesh. She was at the mercy of the current, tumbling about. Kicking to the surface, she gasped for air when she broke through. She fought for the shore and finally made it, clawing through the mud.

The young demon coughed so much that her chest and throat hurt. Her body shivered. She fought for breath and for the strength to rise up and took in the forest surrounding her. The clouds had parted, showing two pale moons in the early evening sky.

Her arms hugged her body, and was shocked at the white vapor that appeared with each exhale. She heard animal howls off in the distance. By sheer instinct her hand went to her neck, readying Hero in an instant. Morgalla gasped as she realized her medal was missing.

Fear gripped her heart. "Oh no."

She looked around frantically for any sign of the pendant...to no avail. Then she turned to the raging river where she had just emerged. Through the dusk, she saw the medal had snagged the branch of a fallen tree in the river. Cold water rushed past the river bank, and the branch wasn't going to last long. Morgalla scrambled down the fallen tree, fighting to keep her balance. Just a few feet more and her possession would be back in her hand.

Morgalla knelt and stretched a hand out as far as it would go while the wood creaked under her weight. *Just a couple inches more.* The branch where the medal had been snagged broke.

"No," Morgalla screamed.

She had only seconds to make a decision. Though the water was freezing and she couldn't bear to go back in, she dove into the murk again anyway. Knives drove into her flesh, and her breath left her lungs. The pendant started to sink as it was being carried away with the current. Morgalla was also at the mercy of the river and headed downstream against her will. She kicked and clawed against the water rushing past her. She stretched out for her weapon only to have it slip from her frigid fingers.

Having never been taught how to swim, Morgalla wasn't adept at this new experience. All she could do was hold her breath and fight with all her might against the cold around her. Deeper and deeper she sank, her hands paddling to recover Hero. She felt the pressure against her ears and the tightness in her chest from lack of air.

She thought the water was her adversary, but with the unpredictable swirling, it almost brought the medallion right to her hands. She reached out and snatched her prize. Carried away again with the river flow, she couldn't tell which was up or down. She sought out the light, but it was impossible.

Morgalla slowly rose closer and closer to the surface, and the pressure in her ears subsided. Through the murk, she noticed the glow of the twin moons. With what strength she had, she fought for the light. Finally breaking the surface, she gasped for breath. The roar of the river returned to her ears. She was still at the mercy of the current, and the water was getting rougher by the second. Though her muscles screamed in agony, she kicked and clawed her way to the shore just as the water had turned white and the roar deafening. She focused on the massive rocks ahead. Had she not found her way to land, she would have been in the middle of it.

Morgalla rested next to a massive rock and then fell to the ground. Her body heaved. She coughed and fought for precious breath. She opened her clenched fist and eyed the medallion. She clutched the precious item to her chest.

Shivering and spent, Morgalla made her way through the trees. She climbed a tree up to a large branch. With the medallion tight in her grasp, she rested against the trunk. She was sensitive to the creatures around her and realized only the local wildlife was near…no dark souls out to kill her. Morgalla finally breathed a sigh. Out of exhaustion, she was about to lose consciousness, but her eyes opened at the sound of thunder high above. She put up her hood and gave the sky the middle finger.

She shivered the whole night. Never before had she been this cold. At least the thicker cloak provided more protection, but she still had to huddle up, her limbs close and hugging her body. The first rays of sun over the white mountains woke her as the light warmed her half-frozen lips and nose. Her stomach was empty, and she groaned, rubbing her belly. Seeing the daylight was the only joy she felt.

Morgalla heard rustling sounds and voices that were getting closer. She remained in the tree, high above the ground but peered around below her. There was a trail, and some people were making their way with a couple of large animals that pulled a cart. She could barely see them, but they were the only signs of civilization in the area. She decided to try and get closer.

As she leapt from one tree to the other, Morgalla caught glances from the band that walked through the frigid wilderness. She must have made a sound because they stopped. Some of them drew weapons and their gaze turned up to the trees. Morgalla, standing on a thick branch, hid behind the trunk. She could feel their apprehension and fear and remembered what Delilah said about scared animals and how they were the most dangerous. She peeked from behind the trees and studied their faces. An amalgam of colors ranged from almost white, to pale pinks, light tans, and even browns. She could distinguish the females from their smooth faces. All the males had rough stubble, some even wore beards. Everyone in the group had dark-colored hair, mostly long and unkempt. Their clothing seemed primarily made from leathers and furs.

Morgalla recognized the bladed weapons, but a few of them held something she had never seen before. Some in the group held devices that appeared to be a blend of metal and wood. *Was it a staff of some sort made of metal?*

When they were apparently convinced there was no danger, they sheathed their weapons and continued on.

They can't be demons. Their ears are so small, and they don't have horns.

Following them was better than remaining out in the cold. That, and she was starving. She kept her distance just to be safe. As the group made their way through the wilderness, she realized the trees parted towards a valley. Morgalla saw a large town below. She noticed how clean it appeared. She could feel the mass of souls below.

Her wonder would be put on hold when she heard a commotion. Leaping from tree branch to tree branch, she located the group she had been following were in the midst of a commotion. Their souls were a mixture of fear and bloodlust, a sensation she had felt before. Clearly, they were in danger and in a battle for their survival. She caught up to them. They were fighting a large, hairy beast with horns. It snarled and swiped at the group with its claws. Morgalla pondered what to do. *Would they welcome the help of a demon? Are they even aware of demons? Were they friendly? Maybe. Delilah said I could change my shape. Maybe if I hide what I really am...*

The beast struck two of the party, and they fell to the ground. It slew one of the beasts of burden that had been hauling their wagon. A woman with a baby in her arms screamed as she fell off the wagon to the frozen ground. Morgalla sensed the sheer terror from the woman while she shielded her child from certain death. Morgalla had only seconds to act. She ran to the end of the branch and leapt as high as she could. In midair, she unveiled Hero and landed atop the rampaging beast. A second later Hero ceased the roaring. So did the commotion. Morgalla, atop the slain animal, watched everyone with mouths hanging open.

"Mara," a man called out, rushing to the woman who had fallen with the child.

Morgalla, just to be sure, ran her hand through her hair, feeling that her ear was smaller and her horn was no longer there.

It had worked.

Morgalla pulled her sword from the carcass. She gave a little wave to the people around her.

"Um…hi."

"Who the hell are you? Where'd you come from?"

"I uh….well…"

"You an Izari?"

She turned to one of the men. "Who?"

"Answer his question," another man demanded.

A third man stepped up. "Bill, she just saved your wife and child."

Morgalla lost her footing and fell off the animal.

A woman helped Morgalla up, dusting the frost off her cloak. "You poor thing, you must be half-frozen."

She shivered. "A little more than that, actually," Morgalla replied with chattering teeth.

"Kinda far from an Izara camp, aren't you?"

Morgalla looked up at the man. Boy, was he tall. "Yyy…eah. Pretty far."

"Damn, she killed it with one blow."

Morgalla noticed another member of the group inspecting the body of Morgalla's kill.

"L…lucky shot, I guess," Morgalla said, her teeth still chattering.

"This will be worth a small fortune, Bill."

The man, who was clearly their leader, gave his own brief inspection of the beast. "Yeah. It will make up for our losses."

"Excuse me?" Morgalla chimed. "But I seem to recall that I killed it."

"And are you going to skin it, prepare the carcass for trade in the town?"

Morgalla hadn't thought of that.

"A share, then."

Mara, holding her still crying child, stepped up. "Bill, she saved your daughter and me."

The man pondered a moment. "Ten gold marks."

Morgalla was confused. She had no idea if that was a lot of money or if they were trying to rob her. She wasn't as good at reading the souls of others as Delilah was. She wondered a moment what she might do if Delilah was there.

She'd probably punch him in the face and hold a sword up to his neck.

"Is that the best deal you can make me?" Morgalla asked.

"Not really," Bill replied.

He suddenly was confused as to why the truth just came out of his mouth. Due to Morgalla's influence, his conscience couldn't help but make him tell the truth.

"Then what is a fair deal?" Morgalla demanded.

"Closer to twenty. No more."

"Okay, twenty."

ELEVEN

FREEDOM RIDGE

MORGALLA AND the group of wanderers spent the rest of the morning traveling to the nearby town. The morning sun parted through white clouds, the buildings below in the valley were bathed in golden light. Two small moons were just about to disappear blow the horizon. Morgalla followed the group in search of this thing called money. They stopped at a trader's post, a huge log cabin with all sorts of horns and antlers on the walls. At least it was warm inside. Morgalla's eyes couldn't keep still due to the decorations on all the walls, she noticed some looked like dracon horns.

With money in her pocket, Morgalla set off for…well, what was she going to do? She arrived in this strange world she'd never seen or known about. Her only knowledge was that she could blend in with the populace and they used money. She stepped out onto the trader's porch. The weather had warmed up a bit, but Morgalla spotted black clouds on the horizon that brought her mood down.

The path was short leading into town. Pine trees parted and revealed buildings no higher than two stories. They passed through an archway with a sign—Freedom Ridge—and stepped on a street made of rectangular red brick. The buildings were also mostly made up of brick and stone with wooden rooftops. People walked around the town, from the smiles on their faces, the moods were a mix but mostly positive.

Morgalla wandered to the center of town and saw the tallest of buildings was a clock tower…maybe four stories high…if she had to guess. In front of it was a metal statue of a bird with its wings outstretched. Behind that was a red, white, and blue flag.

Morgalla pondered just what to do next.

How do I get home?

Wait. Get home? Did she even want to go back? This place didn't seem so bad, after all. But surely Delilah must be going out of her mind with worry. Her mentor was really the only reason Morgalla would even return to that horrible place. Maybe she'd do some exploration first, and see if this place truly was better than Hell. With her stomach twisting in hunger, Morgalla sought out some food. She caught the scent of something cooking and followed it to a tavern of some sort. Plenty of people milled around inside either sitting and eating. The room bustled with activity, and Morgalla had to watch out with all the movement. She watched as men and women brought out food for people sitting at tables. It smelled good, whatever it was.

A small table meant for two was pushed against the wall. It looked inviting, so she took it. *Just how does one get food around here?*

"You poor dear, you look half-frozen."

Morgalla noticed the plump woman talking to her.

"More than half, but yeah," Morgalla replied.

"Has someone taken your order, dear?"

The woman named off the short menu and Morgalla didn't know what was what. She settled on something hot and ready. The woman brought out a bowl of stew and some bread. Digging her spoon into the meal, Morgalla couldn't wait to end her hunger pains. She must have been a sight to the people around her, stuffing her face with meat and potatoes.

Soon she slowed down and savored the meal. Her situation was less bleak than when she'd entered the place, and her belly was filling up. She felt the heat return to her body as she explored the room with her eyes. Sounds of laughter filled the room. Morgalla sensed the good spirits emanating from their souls, and it was nice, almost as though wrapping herself in joy. She couldn't help but smile.

A woman walked around the room, collecting gold from people at the tables. She approached Morgalla and just stared at her as if waiting for the demon-in-disguise to say or do something.

"Six dillers please, miss," the girl said.

"Oh. Sorry."

Morgalla reached into her pocket and took out some of the gold she had attained that morning. The girl accepted the gold and counted out some other coins in her hand. She set down some different ones made of copper and some silver. Morgalla looked curiously at the metal on the table. She then noticed someone else was eyeing her collection of currency. She grabbed it up and stuffed the money in her pocket.

Morgalla grinned at the happy spirits within the room. The happiness that surrounded her felt good. That, along with the hot meal, and she couldn't help but smile. Some children sat with their parents while other adults congregated in small groups. But there were some people whose appearance confused her. Their skin had wrinkles and what hair they had stood out in shades of grey and white. Some of those bodies seemed frail and weak. One man opened his mouth when he laughed, and Morgalla could see he was missing teeth. *What were these people?*

Was that decay? Delilah had mentioned how some species aged and got weaker as they grew older. The Usta, with their blue skin, could live centuries before their bodies became frail. Morgalla wondered how old these people were.

The mood died in an instant when the main doors opened. Two rain-soaked figures entered, their boots thumping across the wooden floor. Morgalla sensed everyone's souls shift from happy to dread. The noticeable difference made her look up and focus on the figures who entered. They were clad in dark red leather. Their clawed hands rested on weapons, which, for the moment, remained sheathed. The pair of males removed the hoods from their horned heads, revealing dark red skin and yellow eyes. Their leather was adorned with golden symbols, and Morgalla recognized the calligraphy instantly. They studied the room as if predators searching for an excuse to start trouble. No one made eye contact, and Morgalla decided to follow suit. She turned her back for the moment and ate her bread.

When the demons decided on a table, they were soon served by the same plump woman. This time she appeared rather nervous. Her bubbly smile was a distant memory. Morgalla decided that maybe it was best to leave. Other people evidently felt the same way because a number of patrons got up to walk out. As Morgalla rose, one of the demons caught sight of what she was wearing. He focused on the golden runes of her new cloak, the symbol of Zorach. His fist connected with the table.

"You. Human," the demon roared.

Morgalla noticed the demon was pointing at her. "Human? What?"

"You. Thief."

The demon approached, his boots thumping along the floor. His friend was behind him with a clawed hand on the hilt of his blade, ready to unsheathe.

It took Morgalla a moment, but she looked around to all the other people...the humans who were in the room.

"You think I'm human?" she asked in shock. "I look human?"

"You steal that?" the demon roared, pointing to the metal holding Morgalla's cloak.

Oh no.

Everyone else in the room minded their business. None of them rose or approached. They wondered just what to do. Morgalla raised her hands and backed away.

"I didn't steal it. It's complicated."

"We kill thieves in Hell," one demon said in a growl.

"Yeah, that I know, guys," Morgalla said. "I'm just passing through, but trust me, I did not steal this."

She used every idea she had to try and convince them that she wasn't a thief, but so far it wasn't working.

"Someone, go get the sheriff," a woman called out.

There was no time because one demon took out his sword and lunged at Morgalla. His aim missed, and he destroyed a table instead. Morgalla ran across another table, headed towards the door. She stumbled out into the rain, tripping and falling in the mud. The demons were quick on her heels, and she was up and running as fast as she could down the street. She almost got hit by some people riding on mounted animals. She slipped in the mud again. The demons charged at her with their weapons and she unveiled Hero, ready to defend herself.

"The hoo-man is armed." One demon laughed.

She was soaked and freezing again. Morgalla glared, letting them feel her rage.

"I hate being cold," she yelled.

They attacked but soon found out that this *human* had skills. Since they were massive and strong, she didn't bother blocking their attacks but chose to dodge again and connect with any punches, kicks, or slices of her blade. She held her own. Both demons were angered that she wasn't dead. One wiped blood from his nose.

Thunder in the distance caught all of their attention, and Morgalla jumped. There was a man there, holding one of those strange staff-life weapons. He fired again, and Morgalla saw fire erupt from the end of it, making it sound like thunder. He worked a lever with one hand, and it made a strange noise. She didn't know what kind of weapon it was, but it must have been one of the many *machines* that

Delilah had told her about. Two other men approached, drawing swords with black blades.

"Enough," a man roared. "All of you, weapons down."

Morgalla didn't comply. She realized the demons still had bloodlust. She stepped back, Hero still pointed in their direction.

"She's a thief," a demon yelled. "She deserves death."

"You ain't in Hell, buddy," the man shouted back. "Now lower your weapon."

The demons complied under protest, stepping back. One of them pointed at Morgalla. "I see you again, you're dead."

A shivering Morgalla lowered her weapon when the demons walked away. The man with the *boom stick* stepped up, obviously some sort of authority figure.

"I don't want any trouble."

"What the hell are you doing, antagonizing a pair of demons? You got a death wish?"

"I...I didn't do anything to them, I swear."

"Then why are you wearing a cloak with a demon symbol on it?"

"I can explain."

"Do it and be quick," the man commanded.

Morgalla stood there shaking, searching for a good lie but none came.

"Aw, damn," she said.

"That's what I thought. Bring her."

Morgalla was taken to another building and a small room with only space for a desk and some chairs. She saw a hallway in the back where a cell was located. Her hair and clothes were soaking wet, and she shivered in the chair. She noticed fire roaring in a container made of iron. There was a metal tube of some sort that led up into the ceiling.

Keeps the room warm and sends the smoke up and out. That's clever.

There was a woman where they had taken Morgalla, she was some sort of authority figure, removed a belt from around her waist with a sword connected to it. She set the weapon on the desk. Morgalla noticed the handle and hilt. It appeared to be made by a demon.

"I didn't do it, I tell ya."

As Morgalla sat shivering, she listened to the shouts from down the hall and the banging of iron.

"Smalls, don't make me come back there," shouted the deputy. "So help me…"

The deputy took a drink of coffee from the tin cup. She looked at Morgalla who continued to shiver sitting in the chair.

"Don't worry," the woman said. "He can't get out."

"I'm shivering because I'm f-f-freezing."

The woman poured another cup and handed the tin container to Morgalla. The beverage smelled strange, but the cup was hot and brought some relief to her half-frozen fingers. She tasted it, and an expression of disgust crossed her face.

The man in his cage called out again, "I wanna talk to the mayor."

"You already did," the deputy shouted back. "Now shut up."

"But I didn't kill no one."

As she clutched the tin cup, Morgalla looked confused. "He's lying." The woman raised her eyebrow. Morgalla couldn't see the man down the hallway, but she knew and could feel the black mark of death on his soul. He also wasn't the best of liars. Morgalla found it curious though, only for a moment, that they had thrown him in a cage. She had no time or energy to ponder anything more since she was half frozen to the bone.

"Can I please go sit next to that? she asked through chattering teeth while pointing to the iron.

The woman glanced over her shoulder, then to the fire, realizing the door was next to it.

"Don't you dare leave. The sheriff will have questions for ya."

Morgalla took the chair and sat next to the fire, holding her hands near the warmth. The ache in her fingers would soon be a memory, but she still had a sniffle. She heard someone coming. As the heavy oak door swung open, a mammoth figure came thumping in. A deep, masculine voice swore under his breath at the weather, rain dripping off his heavy coat. His masculine features, carved in stone, were difficult to see clearly under his wide hat.

Morgalla looked up, teeth still chattering at the tallest human she had ever seen. He stood at least six-and-a-half feet tall with shoulders that rivaled most demons. His hair and eyes were black. He didn't realize that Morgalla was in the room at first, but she watched him shake off the rain like an animal would dry its fur. Though he wore a long, heavy coat, Morgalla spotted two weapons holsters. One she didn't recognize, but the other held a clear hint of a black metal demon sword.

The man finally noticed her and did a double-take before approaching the deputy.

"What's her story, Jel? he asked in a deep voice.

"Had a scuffle down the street, boss."

"She had a scuffle? Tell her parents and be done with it."

"She ain't no child, Dil."

The man looked at her. "How old are you, girl?"

What was that word Delilah used to describe her? "Teens." Morgalla said.

"You're rather small," he said.

"You're not the first to notice."

He smirked.

"I don't think she's from around here, Dil. I don't recognize her."

"Come to think of it, I don't recognize you, either."

Deputy Jelica Fairbrother held Morgalla's medal where the chief could see it. "She had this. She's pretty good with it too."

"Is this what I think it is?"

Fairbrother nodded, and the chief pulled up a chair near Morgalla and sat down. She wasn't as cold now, but her nervousness didn't help the shivers.

"What's your name, girl?" he asked.

"M...Morgalla."

"You one of the Izar?"

"What's that?"

He raised an eyebrow. "They're like gypsies."

"What's that?"

"Are you being a wise-ass?"

"I'm not—"

Jel interrupted, "Couple of demons came into town and claim she stole something from them."

"I didn't steal anything," Morgalla said.

"I should hope not," the chief said. "Stealing from demons is rather stupid."

"That much I know," Morgalla said. "You never told me your name...sir."

For a moment, she almost forgot her manners and remembered to add the *sir* at the end. It wouldn't be wise to antagonize someone who was obviously the man in charge.

"My name is Dillon. I keep the peace around here. Now...you mind telling me what you're doing with a shadow blade?"

"A what?"

"Playing dumb?" he asked as he held up her medal. "What do you think this is? I know for a fact you didn't steal this because shadow blades only recognize their owner."

"Then I'm not guilty of theft."

"I didn't say you were. But I will say that coming here with a concealed weapon could get you thrown in jail. Or would you prefer to have me just kick you out of town?"

"With the weather, I'd prefer neither. I already had a bad day yesterday running into someone weird attacking me with crows."

"Crows?" Dillon asked. She had caught his full attention. "This person, a woman, used magic against you?"

"Had to be magic."

Dillon turned to the surprised deputy.

"What did she look like?" Jel asked.

"Young and ugly."

Dillon frowned. "Sounds to me you had a run-in with Deadra."

"Dead-ra?" Morgalla asked in shock. "That thing had a name?"

"Deadra Greyworm. Local witch. You're the first in a while to survive an encounter with her. Folk 'round here knows not to go up on her mountain."

Dillon stood and walked over where Morgalla's cloak was hanging. He took his own heavy coat off, his holstered weapons were now clearly visible. On his left hip was a sword with a black blade. On his right hip was something she had never seen before. It wasn't a knife, but it rested in a leather sheath. From what she could see of the weapon, the handle was pearl and silver, but it had a strange curve to it. Dillon studied the medal with Zorach's symbol on it. The mark itself didn't mean anything to him, but he recognized it was a demon language.

"Did you steal this?" he asked.

"No."

"Then how did you get it?"

"It was given to me."

"Right," he said and took the cloak off the hook and handed it to her. "I suggest you take it off, so you don't antagonize anyone else, demon or otherwise."

Morgalla rose and put her cloak on.

"May I have my medal back?"

Dillon paused. He examined the medallion and pondered a moment. He held it out to her, and she took it, but his grip was tight. Morgalla figured he had another warning to issue.

"The only reason I'm giving this back is I don't want to see you unarmed. It's a dangerous place out there. We don't allow weapons like this in town. Get me?"

"Yes, sir."

She took Hero and hid him away. Throwing her hood over her head, she stepped out into the pouring rain.

Dillon peeked out his window at the small figure running into the rain.

"What are you thinking, boss?"

The chief responded with a small grunt.

"How much of that you think was a lie?" Jel asked.

"About half…if I had to guess. She's hiding something, that's for sure. Keep your eyes peeled, will ya? I got a feeling."

TWELVE

DOTTIE

MORGALLA FOUND shelter under a tree in the town square. Though shaded from the rain, her arms wrapped around her and hugged her shivering body. She contemplated what to do next.

This town wasn't much better than Hell, but at least there wasn't anyone trying to kill her...for the moment, anyway. And so long as she kept clear of any demons, she would be fine. This world was rather odd, not to mention cold. They had the strangest rules, to think someone could be punished for something that seemed completely normal to her.

Morgalla saw many people walking towards a large building. The night sky had gotten darker, and street lamps were being lit. She noticed a lot of people strolling around the streets, seemingly headed to the towering building within sight. Seemed like a gathering of some sort. At any rate, it was more than likely warmer and certainly dryer than being outside.

She ran to follow the crowd and found a secluded spot to sit. The huge room was packed with people on benches. At the front was a riser with a podium where a small group of men and women were sitting. One woman stood at the podium and called the meeting to order.

She spoke in a loud voice. "Our first order of business..."

"And the last if we're not careful," a man called out.

Some laughed, but the woman at the podium banged a gavel. "You'll have your chance to speak, Mr. Sudderth. You've been warned before. Now, as you all know, Lord Makaro has made another offer."

"Which will mean the death of us all," another voice echoed.

The woman at the podium had to bring the room back to order again. "Lord Makaro has given his word that the truce will stand."

Sounds of disapproval rumbled within the room. Someone shouted, "And you trust him?"

One man stood with his hand raised. After the room had been brought to order, the woman gave him the floor. "Mayor Rasper, I'd like to point out that it was Lord Makaro himself who has lived with us for over a hundred years."

"Mr. Davis, he was not the one who enslaved us," the mayor noted.

"He's his father's son," Sudderth shouted.

Davis, keeping a calm demeanor, continued with his questions. "Another concern is that you refer to him as a demon lord when he isn't one."

The mayor ignored the second question. "We must give peace a chance to prevail. He is our neighbor."

A woman rose from the crowd, and the mayor gave her the floor. "Miss Ramirez?"

"Why wasn't the new ordinance put to a vote?"

Sounds of approval echoed through the audience.

"The city elders and I all agree that allowing demons into town, so long as they're peaceful, is a step in the right direction."

Miss Ramirez appeared a bit annoyed but kept her composure. "But…we had an incident earlier today. Everyone is talking about it."

There were rumblings from the audience.

A voice called out, "Two demons attacked some girl."

Morgalla sank in her seat.

Pleasedontnoticeme, pleasedontnoticeme, pleasedontnoticeme…

"What does the sheriff think?" another person asked.

"Sheriff Dillon assures me it was just some sort of misunderstanding."

"We wouldn't have this problem if you didn't let demons in town."

Again, grumblings of disapproval came from the townsfolk. The mayor raised her hand. "We feel that peace with Lord Makaro can be achieved."

"At what price?" Ramirez asked. "What are we giving up, and what is he offering?"

"He offers protection."

Another man rose with his hand in the air. "Protection from whom? He's the only one we have to fear."

"Makaro has never declared war or attacked us in any way." The mayor spoke with clarity.

"But…if we allow those who follow him and only him into town, that might be a prelude to an invasion."

The people applauded the man speaking. Morgalla wanted to stand and tell them of her experiences, but good sense kept her silent and still.

Morgalla detected the apprehension of the mayor. She kept a calm demeanor on the outside, but the demon-in-disguise knew better. The audience was quickly becoming a mob.

The mayor had to wait for them to calm down again. "We cannot let fear rule our lives. Since before any of us were born, the inhabitants of this town have let the shadow of Dracon Peak rule their lives with fear. We must give peace a chance."

Morgalla was uncomfortable being in a room full of souls who were all skeptical and borderline angry. She felt her heart race and tried to keep calm thinking about guavas.

The meeting was adjourned, and Morgalla noticed at least it had stopped raining. With wet clothes, she still trembled under her cloak.

Night had fallen, and she wasn't looking forward to the possibility of sleeping in a tree again. As her teeth chattered, she felt fear course through her because of the uncertainty. This was the first time being away from Delilah…who always knew what to do.

"Are you okay, dear?"

Morgalla turned and saw a frail woman with white hair. She was shorter even than her, and that was saying something.

"Oh…uh…yeah. I'll be okay," Morgalla replied.

"You don't look okay. I saw what happened earlier today with those horrible demons."

"I'm…well, I've faced worse."

"I feel so bad for you Izari sometimes. You won't be able to get back to your camp in the dark."

Again with that name. What were these Izari? Why did so many people think Morgalla was one of them?

"I'm not…"

The small woman interrupted her. "Do you have a place to sleep tonight, dear?"

Morgalla looked confused. "What?"

"You look like you've been sleeping outdoors and for too long, too. I have plenty of space in my home."

Morgalla looked a bit surprised by the offer. After having so many beasts trying to take her life in Hell, an act of such charity seemed alien. One thing was for sure and that the woman's motives were completely honorable, Morgalla could clearly see from her soul.

It took little convincing for Morgalla to go with the woman because she was offering a warm, dry bed. They walked slowly. The woman could only move so fast. Morgalla thought for a moment that maybe she might need some help, but with her spirit, she seemed as strong as any of the younger people in town. As they arrived at the woman's home, Morgalla realized she didn't even know her name.

"Oh, by the way, I'm Morgalla."

"My name is Doretta, but please call me Dottie."

Dottie's home was small and humble, but it was clean and warm. After helping her build a fire, Morgalla was shown to a bedroom.

"This belonged to our daughter years ago, but it hasn't been used for a while. Hope it's okay."

Morgalla's heart lifted, and she couldn't help but smile. "It's perfect, thank you."

She hung her wet clothes around the room and slipped under the thick, warm blankets. Exhausted from the day's activities, Morgalla found sleep easily.

Morgalla was awakened by the rays of the morning sun. She rubbed the sleep out of her eyes and climbed out of bed. She ran her fingers through her hair and noticed her ears had grown much larger, and her horns had returned. Surprised, she rushed to the mirror on the wall and saw the demon face again. She'd changed back overnight. She closed her eyes and concentrated, hoping maybe she had some sort of power over this transformation. When opening her eyes again, the human disguise had returned. Breathing a sigh of relief, she walked to the window and watched Dottie outside gathering kindling and firewood from a woodpile. Morgalla dressed in her britches, tunic, and boots and ran outside. Dottie was having some trouble lifting some of the logs, so Morgalla insisted she carry them inside.

The old woman was overjoyed. "Oh, thank you, dear."

They built a fire in the kitchen stove, and Dottie made some breakfast. With a rumbling stomach, Morgalla was thrilled by the smells that filled the room.

"Why are you so nice?"

Dottie glanced over her shoulder, confused. "Why wouldn't I be? See, that's the problem with some people in this or any other world. Why shouldn't we help each other?"

"I'm sorry. I didn't mean to sound so suspicious."

"Well, you Izari have faced some troubles, I know. But you have a lot of supporters here in town. More than you may think."

Hearing the word again made Morgalla roll her eyes. Thankfully Dottie didn't notice.

"How come they don't want Izari in town?"

"Your parents never told you? Well, if you ask me, it's due to the whole witchcraft thing. Maybe also because they're children of nature. But some might still hold a grudge for being brought here against our will."

Dottie served breakfast, and Morgalla shoveled the food into her mouth. "Against your will?"

"Oh, it happened long before even I was born. We were all brought here from a planet called Earth."

"Brought?"

"Abducted for slave labor to work in their mines. Damn demons."

Morgalla swallowed hard and frowned. "Yeah, um…damn demons."

"A wizard and his followers tried to fight them and get our people home, but unfortunately that didn't go over too well. We won our freedom from that bastard Makaro and his father, but with the portal here so small and only leading to Hell, we weren't going anywhere."

"And you've been trapped here ever since?"

"Well, trapped is a strong word. Remember this happened long ago and no one is alive anymore who remembers the great revolt. Ever since then some people went with the wizard and his clan… your people…but the majority of us stayed here to build the town. They must not talk about this among your clan."

"No…no, we don't."

"Well, now that bastard Makaro lives up in his castle on Dracon Peak with his followers. Pardon my language, dear, but there's the constant fear that he might come down and try to conquer us again.

Some of our own people have gone up and joined him. I guess they felt he could offer them a better life."

Morgalla had more questions, but they were interrupted by someone entering the house. It was a woman dressed in heavy clothes, middle-aged if Morgalla had to guess by her appearance and her soul. The woman seemed surprised she was there.

"Hi."

"Uh…hi," the woman replied with a note of apprehension. "Mother, a word please."

Dottie excused herself and went into the next room with her daughter. The women thought Morgalla couldn't hear them, but little did they know the demon in disguise had great hearing. Dottie's daughter was aggravated for sure, not just from her soul but from the sound of her voice. The women tried to keep their voices down, but she was still able to hear some of the words.

"Alek said you brought an Izari girl home?"

Dottie's command was immediate. "Keep your voice down."

Morgalla felt uncomfortable but she ate every crumb on her plate quickly as the two women had their *discussion* in the next room. Morgalla searched around the kitchen and noticed the sink and the area where clean dishes were put to dry after she had washed them. By the time she was done, Dottie had walked back in.

She snapped at her daughter, "My breakfast is cold now, Sera. Thank you." Dottie noticed Morgalla had done the dishes and was holding the last clean plate. "Oh, sweetie you didn't have to do that."

"Well, I…" Morgalla started, but Dottie reached for the dish and put it in the cupboard.

"I'm amazed she even knows how to clean anything," Sera said as she left.

With a slam of the front door, Morgalla felt the embarrassment from her benefactor. "Sorry about that."

"It's okay."

"I just don't know why she's so untrusting. Don't let that make you think this isn't a good place to live. Really, it is. We stand by our neighbors and have done so for generations."

"That's what I like about it."

"I'm sure there's a place for you here."

"Well, where I'm from is a little difficult at times to live. There's only one reason why I would stay."

"Is it because of someone close? Family perhaps?" Dottie asked. Morgalla nodded. "Why not bring them here too?"

"I don't know if Delilah would fit in here."

Dottie took Morgalla's hand and squeezed it as much as an old woman could. Morgalla managed a smile.

THIRTEEN

THE FOREST OF IRON

DELILAH REMAINED on Morgalla's mind over the next couple of days. Dottie was more than accommodating, and Morgalla even offered her money as compensation for giving her a place to stay. She took every moment to help around the home, primarily cleaning up.

Most mornings Morgalla woke to a mist among the surrounding mountains. On this day the air was cool and crisp, and the fog cleared up before midday. People went about their business. Where demons had sneers on their faces, and their souls hid dark emotions, these humans were actually quite happy and weren't afraid to show it.

One afternoon, Dottie was standing on a footstool in front of the fireplace, trying to reach for something that hung above it.

"Want me to get that?" Morgalla asked.

"Oh, thank you, dear. Even when I was as young as you, I'd still have trouble reaching it."

Morgalla stood on the step and stretched to reach the object Dottie wanted. It was long and rested on a rack made of wood. Her delicate hands grasped the cold metal, and she lifted the heavy object down.

Now standing on the floor, Morgalla looked curiously at the item made of heavy metal and wood.

"What is it?"

"It's a rifle."

"Oh, I thought it was a gun."

Dottie laughed. "A rifle is a kind of gun, dear." She set the heavy weapon on the coffee table. Morgalla noted that she had already laid out a large cloth and a pile of small tools. "Even though this hasn't been fired in a while, we still gotta keep it clean."

Dottie's hands, weak and arthritic, struggled to hold and open the device. Morgalla gladly did the heavy work, and her elderly companion showed her how to do it. She also couldn't help but notice the name Robert Haven engraved into the metal.

Morgalla pointed to it. "Who is this?"

Dottie paused, and Morgalla sensed a slight shift in her soul. "He…was my husband." She then nodded to the framed photograph of a much younger Dottie with a man and two young girls. "It's been difficult without him. This weapon hasn't been fired in almost two years, but it needs to stay clean. Just in case." Morgalla continued to wipe the weapon. "You don't talk much, do you?"

Morgalla looked at her. "I…well, I guess I don't have much to talk about."

"Please, you're more than welcome to say something here."

Morgalla smiled. "Yeah, I know."

"I take it you've never fired a gun before?"

"No."

"Well, I could teach you, but I don't know how good a teacher I would be. But if you're as handy with a firearm as you are with a sword, you would be an asset to the community."

"How did you know?"

"The sheriff told me," Dottie answered and pointed to the pendant hanging around Morgalla's neck.

"Well, it's just for defense…"

"Don't need to explain anything to me. The world is a dangerous place. We all need to know how to defend ourselves."

LATER IN the day, they went shopping for groceries. Morgalla contributed some money and carried the bags home. Morgalla helped in the kitchen and was even doing some things by herself thanks to Dottie's teaching.

Dottie had noticed that Morgalla's clothes were a little dirty and torn, and she offered to take her to their local retailer to buy some new attire. Dottie offered to pay, but Morgalla insisted that she use her earnings for them.

Walking back to Dottie's home, Morgalla couldn't help but hear a slight rumbling in the distance, and it wasn't thunder.

"What's that?"

"What's what?"

"That sound, it's coming from over there."

"My goodness, you have good ears. I don't even hear anything. You must be talking about the river and the new electric station."

"What's electric?"

"Electricity," Dottie said as she pointed to one of the tall street lamps. "They're gonna light all those up with electric power. Can you believe it?"

Morgalla could only stare with confusion.

"Why don't we go take a look, if you're curious," Dottie suggested.

The rumbling got louder the closer they got to the station. As they reached the entrance to the massive brick and steel building, a man and a woman appeared in front. Morgalla guessed they were guards because of their weapons and the same gold star she'd seen on the sheriff.

Dottie waved. "Hi, Suzin. Hi, Rik."

They smiled at Dottie and nodded politely to Morgalla. She returned the gestures.

"My friend Morgalla here was just curious about the station."

The female deputy looked at her companion and then back to the old woman. "Well, we have strict orders from the mayor herself. The station is going to be under guard twenty-eight, seven."

"Oh, that's a shame."

Rik interjected. "I suppose if it was just a minute or two…"

The iron doors parted, and the two women entered the massive structure. What had been a light rumbling on the outside was a grinding of steel and a hiss of steam. Morgalla's jaw dropped at the massive machines all around her that rocked and turned. Wheels with teeth spun at different speeds. Some were small, but others reached as high as the ceiling.

Dottie found a seat to rest her weary bones, but Morgalla explored this strange man-made forest before her. She soon lost herself in the scene and didn't even notice the group of people touring the facility. When she froze as if she had done something wrong, they all looked at her. Someone asked her a question but she hadn't heard it.

"I didn't touch anything, I swear," Morgalla said.

The mayor stepped up and laughed. "I asked what you thought of our new achievement."

"Um…well, it's certainly impressive. I can honestly say I've never seen anything like it."

"You don't work here?"

Uh-oh.

Morgalla's eyes grew wide. "I…I'm here with someone."

"She's with me." Dottie stepped forward. "We were just curious about the station, is all."

"I see…" the mayor replied.

"We should be going, dear."

Dottie took Morgalla's hand, and they left. As they walked out, Morgalla had to take a peek over the iron railing and watch the mighty river that flowed past the station.

"What does it do, actually?"

"Oh, the station? Well, somehow the river runs by, makes all the gears in there turn, and we get power for all the new electric lights." The old woman shrugged. "I have no idea more than the basics, but they say it will light up the town at night, and soon it will heat our homes during the winter."

A single whispered word escaped Morgalla's lips. "Wow."

They were making their way back home when a procession met them in the street. Dottie hadn't seen it at first, but when she did, she stopped and made a strange gesture to Morgalla.

"I forgot Deni Santamaria's funeral was today."

Morgalla was silent, clutching the paper bag of to her chest. The procession walked past. A group of six people were carrying a large wooden box, and a crowd of people trailed behind them. Morgalla felt her heart start to race. She took a few steps back, feeling the black cloud of people in mourning.

Morgalla noted the size of the box.

It looks big enough for someone to fit inside...

Her hand then went to her mouth due to her epiphany.

She tried her best to hide her reaction to the procession, but her sweating forehead was a giveaway.

"You okay, dear?"

"Y...yeah, I'm all right."

Dottie took her by the shoulder and led her away. Morgalla felt a lot better when they got home.

"What will they do with her?" Morgalla asked.

"Oh, they have to burn the body. Otherwise, that witch who lives up in the mountain will bring her back."

"What?"

"Why yes, sweetie. She brings back the dead to work in the mines of that bastard Makaro."

Morgalla's hand went to her mouth in shock.

"Believe me," Dottie continued, "what we wouldn't give to get our hands on that witch."

"Why haven't you? There's thousands of people living here."

"Over the years we've tried. Not only is she slippery but also nearly impossible to kill. Best we can do is avoid her."

Morgalla wished she could do something about it. The more she heard about Deadra and Makaro, the angrier she grew. She pondered that maybe if she could find a way to help the town, she would curry favor with them.

Dottie clearly saw how disturbed Morgalla was. Her answer for all problems was tea. The kettle whistled, and she poured two cups as the young woman hunched in the chair…silent and still.

"How did that woman die?" Morgalla asked.

Dottie set the kettle down and took a deep breath. She pulled up a chair next to Morgalla. She still hadn't made eye contact as she sought out the words. "She was murdered," Dottie said, and she was answered with a confused look. "She was killed by a man named Camron Smalls."

Morgalla pondered over the word Dottie had used. "Murder?"

"When someone kills another with no warning or reason. It's a great offense here." Morgalla contemplated the new word as she clutched the hot teacup in her hands. Dottie took a sip. "They don't even have a word for it where you're from?"

Morgalla snapped out of her trance. "No, they don't."

"A lot of people in town are torn over what to do with him since the crime was so brutal."

Morgalla noted another word *crime* that she had never heard before. But she said nothing. "Torn?"

"This hasn't happened in years, not since my children were young. What do we do with him? What punishment would fit the crime?"

"If this has happened before, what punishment was given then?"

"Death."

Morgalla was unfazed by Dottie's answer, but she remembered something: A man was in a cage the day she'd arrived in town. She remembered the name the deputy had said. She also recalled sensing his soul. The black mark meant little, for the mark of death would still be present if someone killed another in battle. But he had lied to the deputy when he'd said he hadn't done it.

"What do you think?" Morgalla asked.

"Well, Deni Santamaria was a wonderful person. I wanted to see justice. Somehow I would have felt...soiled...if we were to execute him. But on the other hand, keeping him locked in a cage didn't seem right, either. Almost everyone was in agreement though that he should not be let loose."

"Almost?"

"There is a very vocal minority who feel he should be allowed to make amends somehow. But what is a human life worth?"

Morgalla was silent for a moment as both women drank their tea. "Do you consider life precious?"

Dottie's reply was immediate. "Of course, I do."

Morgalla smiled.

NOTHING MORE was said for the next couple of days. Morgalla started each morning bringing in firewood and helping Dottie however she could. She learned a lot...even how to cook eggs and various meats. As night approached, Morgalla, still in disguise, looked out over the surrounding hills and mountains, bathed in glorious light in different shades of orange. Dottie approached. Morgalla noticed she had dressed in her best outfit.

"Dear, you're not going?"

"Going where?"

"Why, the celebration, of course. I thought I told you. Why do you think I've been doing all that baking?"

Dottie pointed. Then it hit Morgalla why she had baked ten pies.

"Oh," Morgalla said. "I thought maybe you were preparing for winter or something."

Dottie laughed. "Come, it will be a good time."

Morgalla pondered a moment. "Um…well maybe…"

Dottie had mentioned a celebration of some sort, but with much on her mind, Morgalla had forgotten.

"It will be a big party. You can wear your new clothes."

Morgalla hesitated a moment. "I don't know…"

Dottie gave her a slight nudge. "They'll have lots of food."

Morgalla tapped her chin. "I sure could go for that." She checked her cloak, which technically new, had seen better days. Already it was tattered with mud stains. "I don't know if I can show up in this…"

Dottie smiled. She had a solution. The elderly woman hobbled to the closet and rummaged through some clothing. Morgalla watched over the woman's shoulder and noted that a lot of the clothes were men's and had dust on them. Dottie reached for something and pulled it out, handing it to Morgalla.

"This belonged to a much younger woman."

Morgalla didn't ask but accepted it. She slipped out of her cloak and replaced it with the new item: a dagged hood made of worn, brown leather. Morgalla pulled it over her head and checked in the mirror. She tied her raspberry hair back into a tail.

Morgalla smiled. "I promise I won't mess it up."

"Don't worry about it," Dottie said and patted Morgalla's shoulder.

FOURTEEN

SOMETHING TO CELEBRATE

MORGALLA PULLED a small wagon filled with the pies that Dottie had made. As they got closer to downtown, Morgalla noticed the coming mass of souls, an amalgam of smells carried on the air, each of them wonderful. Tables were set up with a cavalcade of delicious looking and smelling dishes made by people all over town. Morgalla stared with wonder, her eyes wide at the different foods before her. Each kind of food had its own section: one for meats, one for vegetables, and one for desserts.

"Who made all of these?"

"Everyone contributed," Dottie replied with a smile.

Her words brought a smile to Morgalla's face too. "I don't know where to start."

They put the pies among the other desserts. Morgalla wasn't sure what some of them were, but they were all different bright colors and smells…the smells that hit her nose were almost overwhelming.

"Make way for beer."

Morgalla almost got run over by a group of men coming through, rolling barrels past her. They were setting up casks on the other side of the street, taking up an entire section of the party area.

When evening came, the town square was lit with oil lamps. Banners and other decorations of red, silver, and blue were raised everywhere. Morgalla had no idea what they were celebrating—nor at that moment did she really care. By then the band was playing, and people were dancing.

Morgalla had a difficult decision to make with all the food on display. She sniffed along the area reserved for the various cooked meats and picked up something unfamiliar.

"What is this?"

"That's bacon," someone said.

Morgalla nibbled at it for a moment.

She and Dottie found a place to sit. Dottie had a small portion of food on her plate, but Morgalla's was overflowing. Half of it was bacon.

The two of them were content sitting and watching the people dance, but Dottie's soul was shifting.

"Oh great. Here comes Lindon."

"Who?" Morgalla asked as she noticed the familiar tall, lanky human approaching. His red hair and sideburns were quite easily spotted. He was dressed quite proper with polished shoes on his large feet flopped about as he strode through the crowd. He stopped a moment to look at himself in the shop window, straightening his tie.

"Don't look," Dottie noted. "Maybe he'll walk on by."

They weren't so lucky.

"Hello, Mrs. Haven. I see you're enjoying yourself. And your young friend."

"He-wo," Morgalla said with her mouth full of food.

"This is Morgalla, Lindon. She's new in town."

"As I've heard. Teaching her some naughty habits, too I see."

"Hmm?" Morgalla asked as she crunched on some bacon.

"I've been trying to educate the savages of this town that eating the flesh of animals...our brothers...is beneath us."

"But it's so yummy," Morgalla said as she took another bite.

The young man stood with arms crossed. His eyes closed, and he shook his head. Morgalla thought maybe she had seen him before, and finally, it hit her. He was at the meeting the first night she'd spent in town.

"Aren't you going to enjoy the party, Lindon?" Dottie asked.

"I'm enjoying it enough."

Morgalla sensed annoyance from the young man.

"Want some bacon?" Morgalla asked, holding up a piece to Lindon who took a step back, covering his nose.

"Oh, God no," he replied with disgust. "I refuse to partake in the murder of innocent creatures of nature."

Morgalla crunched on the bacon and ever so slowly chewed in front of him. "Mmmm...so yummy."

Lindon's hand went to his mouth. His eyes closed. Morgalla stood and approached him.

"Cooked animal flesh," she continued. "Yum yum in my tum tum."

Lindon gagged and ran off through the crowd, his body hunched over and his hand still over his mouth.

Dottie chuckled as her friend sat down. "That was good. I'll have to remember that next time." They loved the scene, surrounded by the happy people enjoying the food and music. "You should go out and dance, dear."

Morgalla wiped her mouth clean. "Um...well I wouldn't wanna hurt anyone's feet."

Dottie chuckled. "Oh, if only I were you..."

"Why don't you go?"

"My old bones haven't seen a dance floor in a while."

Morgalla happened to see the sheriff and his wife on the dance floor, their souls intertwined in joy. She watched children running around playing, their souls also joyous.

Morgalla caught a glimpse of a woman with her daughter. The child was barely old enough to walk on her own. The unity of their souls was something Morgalla found curious; it was a binding that seemed as strong as any metal, and the bliss glowed from their hearts as they embraced. She couldn't help but smile, but only a little.

As the evening continued, Morgalla spent most of the time at one of the large wooden tables, a safe distance away from the festivities. She had another plate in her hand, this time sampling something called cake. With her lips and mouth littered with crumbs and frosting, and her stomach aching, she sat back and enjoyed the bliss and dealt with the misery.

Dottie hobbled up to her. "Morgalla, look at all those handsome boys over there." The old woman pointed, and indeed there were gentlemen dressed in their best. "Why not go ask one of them to dance?"

Morgalla groaned. "If I get up...I'm gonna throw up."

Dottie chuckled and took a seat next to her. "Are you afraid?"

The young woman wiped her mouth. "Um...well I wouldn't want to hurt anyone's feet, is all."

"Yes, I'm sure that's it." Dottie had a coy smile on her face. "How old are you, dear?"

"I'm not too sure. I think maybe nineteen?"

"Really? I'd have guessed younger."

Morgalla chuckled. "Yeah, you're not the first to say that."

"Have you given thought to what you're going to do?"

"Here? Well, I'm not sure I can stay."

"Of course you can, dear. You're a hard worker and a good person. Surely there's a place for you and the rest of your people."

For a very brief moment, Morgalla thought that *your people* meant demons, but she had to remember that Dottie and everyone else thought she was one of these Izari people. She had so many questions but didn't know how to word them.

"I thought everybody here was cautious of outsiders," Morgalla said.

"Nonsense. We'd welcome all the Izari if they'd only drop their distrust of us. It's long past time for both groups to bury the hatchet."

Morgalla paused and contemplated her words. The phrase Dottie had used was confusing, but she had a feeling she understood. "Yeah...I agree."

The music then stopped, and all attention was on the stage. Mayor Rasper stepped up to the stage that was filled with many people, including Lindon who was still looking a little green. She took the podium, and the crowd noise died down to silence. She spoke loud enough for all to hear.

"Four years ago, we made a promise. Tonight we keep that promise. We take our first steps into a bright future. No longer will we cower in the dark. Soon every home and business will have electricity surging through it.

Night in Freedom Ridge will be as bright as day."

After a round of applause, the mayor continued, "We all give thanks to our engineering department and the dozens of men and women who brought our community into the light."

More applause erupted, and the mayor and city council all led the crowd in a countdown from ten. Morgalla noted that only half the throng joined in. Many of the people standing in the back were old-timers and skeptics. Another thing the demon-in-disguise noticed was that the mayor and all the members of the city council appeared afraid of something.

When the countdown was complete, a man took hold of a giant lever and strained with all his might to pull it back. Morgalla noticed nearby the ground was littered with a series of cables covered in black rubber. A strange humming sound came from them and the lamp posts. What happened next left everyone in a collective gasp as the posts lit up with electric power. They dimmed at first but soon stabilized into a warm glow that illuminated the entire town square. When people seemed to regain their breath, everyone erupted into applause.

The effect of the demonstration was a strange sensation to Morgalla; the crowd's mood had changed in an instant from a mixture of curiosity and skepticism to a sense of wonder. On stage, the emotions had gone from fear and dread to relief.

Everyone marveled at the town square. Up and down the main street was ablaze with electric light. Even the old-timers were in a shock as the amazing modern-day lights lit up the town.

"Good Lord," Dottie said. "Imagine these in our homes."

Morgalla was astounded too. In Hell, gems lit up caverns and darkened hallways. She didn't know which she preferred, but since she hated the dark, either was better.

Soon both women were yawning. Dottie thought it was time to call it a night even though the party was still going on.

"You stay, dear. You're young and can stay up late."

Morgalla rubbed her aching belly again and yawned again. "Naw, it's okay."

They were about to leave when Morgalla sensed something disturbing from behind. She knew someone was watching her. She looked and spotted the mayor, still on stage speaking with Sheriff Dillon and Lindon.

"What is it?" Dottie asked.

Mayor Rasper and Lindon approached. Morgalla couldn't determine what their intentions were.

The mayor spoke first. "Pardon me, but you're the Izari girl, yes?"

"Uh…yes."

The woman extended her hand. "Mayor Tora Rasper, it's a pleasure."

Morgalla accepted it. "Morgalla."

"I would love to discuss with you the possibility of having your people meet with ours."

Morgalla's eyes were wide, and she was turning white. "Well, I don't know about that…"

"See, that's something I'd love to discuss. It's time to become one big family." The mayor then referred to Lindon who was still looking a little weak. "My associate, Mr. Alma, is the one who drew up the negotiations with Lord Makaro."

"Feeling better?" Morgalla asked Lindon.

Lindon swallowed hard, his face sweaty. "I believe all people of this land should live together in peace."

"That would be great," Morgalla added.

They must have sensed her skepticism because the duo frowned slightly.

"You disagree?" Lindon asked.

Morgalla pondered a moment. "The...Izari I cannot speak for. But demons?"

"Surely they cannot all be bad," Mayor Rasper added.

Morgalla smiled. "I know for a fact they're not all bad. But it is their way of life, their very culture that concerns me."

Lindon added, "Makaro has shown no aggression to us. If anything, it's been a century, long before anyone here was born, that demons attacked us."

Morgalla held back a fury within her heart. She wanted to shout at him, that he didn't know what he was talking about.

Sucking back the rage, she was able to speak softly. "Have you lived with them?"

"Have you?"

"Perhaps," the Mayor interjected. "We should wait until our next meeting to discuss such things."

Dottie's hand went to Morgalla's arm. "It's getting late."

"Please, keep it in mind," Mayor Rasper suggested. Morgalla's answer was simply a smile.

When they got back to Dottie's home, Morgalla headed for the bed and practically collapsed onto it. She let out a groan as her hand ran over her bloated belly.

Worth it.

FIFTEEN

THE SHROUD

THE YOUNG demon was up most of the night, just lying in bed and staring at the ceiling. That word *murder* kept ringing in her head and its meaning. Delilah and the monks had taught her many things, and they'd expanded her vocabulary, but they'd never mentioned that word. Morgalla had remembered only one death in the forest while growing up, but it wasn't because someone had murdered him. His death was natural.

It became clear to Morgalla on her first day in Hell that death was something of an everyday occurrence. If demons even knew the word murder, they would probably scoff at it, and if she told them about the meaning, she imagined them laughing.

The presence of multiple souls outside of the house caused her to wake. Morgalla got up and walked to the front of the house and checked out a window. People were walking past, headed towards downtown. She tiptoed past Dottie's bedroom and realized her friend was still sound asleep. Morgalla got dressed and decided to see what was going on outside. She had to check the reflection in the mirror before heading out, making sure her demon visage was gone. Yup, only pale skin, green eyes, and dark raspberry hair.

The closer she got to the downtown area, the more crowded it became. Through the mass of humanity, she saw signs that had sprung up like trees in a field of tall grass. The signs had messages on them. One thing was for sure, some of the locals disapproved of whatever was happening.

Morgalla had a gut feeling about the source of the commotion. The mood of the crowd was mixed; some people were actually happy, others were sad, still more were angry. Being in a group like this almost felt as if she were helpless in the river again, being tossed around and at the mercy of some outside force. She chose a place and leaned against a building.

Morgalla studied the curious structure that was built in the center of the town square. It was a wooden platform that stood higher than everyone. Steps led up to the top with a tall arm that stretched high. At the top of it hung a rope with a strange loop at the bottom.

She overheard some conversations and, much like the souls around her, they were of varying subjects and emotions. Some people even started to argue their points.

"He's a murderer," one man shouted.

"He deserves a fair trial."

"He got his fair trial."

Morgalla also noted someone she recognized as Lindon among the crowd, holding a sign up. Lindon made eye contact with her for a moment before turning up his nose and walking away. She smirked.

After some time, Morgalla noted that more and more people with badges were surrounding the area. Some rode out on horses, and even Dillon himself stood outside his post, giving the crowd a hard look with his dark eyes. He issued some commands, and his subordinates charged into the crowd to enact them. The people obeyed, except for one. Lindon stood before the wooden structure, his hands on his hips and his chest out.

Dillon chuckled and stepped forward, his boots thumping on the brick street. "Move."

"I refuse," Lindon proclaimed in a loud voice. "This is an immoral act, and I'm here to..."

The sheriff wouldn't tolerate the insubordination as his voice thundered across the silent crowd. "I said move your ass."

"I'm not scared of you."

Dillon was about to shout again, but he was cut off by uproarious laughter. He slowly glanced over his shoulder and saw Morgalla leaning against the building. Her face had turned red, and her sides were sore from the joyous sounds she was making. She hunched over, never having heard anything so funny.

Morgalla pointed at Lindon. "He's scared shitless."

Though the red-haired human had put on a brave face for the crowd, his soul was an open book for the demon in disguise. His ego was deflated, and he stood there with hunched shoulders.

"Enough," Dillon commanded.

Morgalla fought hard to suppress the laughter, and soon it stopped completely when Camron Smalls was brought out in chains. The crowd erupted in boos at him. Deputies swarmed around the prisoner, convinced the masses might attack. Dillon displayed his large weapon and fired into the air. With a tremendous boom, the crowd was silenced.

"I will have order."

Even though she saw it coming, Morgalla still jumped at the sound from the rifle. Through the silence, a woman shouted.

"This is wrong. He didn't do it."

"He got his trial," Dillon shouted back. "This debate is over."

Though the black mark was on Camron's soul, Morgalla was still concerned. She studied Camron...who stood less than twenty feet from her.

"Did you do it?" she asked.

Camron's answer was immediate. "Yes."

The crowd erupted again. Those who had been objecting to the proceedings were silent. Some even froze in place with their mouths hanging open.

Camron was the most surprised that his soul had been an open book to the young woman. The deputies escorted him through the crowd and up the wooden steps.

A man proclaimed in a loud voice, "Camron Smalls, after being found guilty of the murder of Deni Santamaria, on this date you are to be hung by the neck until dead."

Another man slid a black hood over the prisoner's head and wrapped the rope around his neck. With a pull of a lever, the platform beneath Camron fell open, and his body dropped. An audible gasp erupted from the crowd, and some women screamed. For a brief moment, life remained in him, and then it was over.

To Morgalla, who stayed in the back, she could barely see what had happened and was unable to watch the body drop, but she knew from the absence of his soul, that he was dead. One moment the flame was there. Like a candle, it was snuffed from existence.

After the collective gasp from the crowd, the only sound remaining was that of wood creaking as the body swayed from the rope, motionless. Morgalla watched as many people bowed heads and placed their hands together. They spoke under their collective breaths.

Dillon spoke out for all to hear. "Okay, that's all, people. Go home."

A black cloud seemed to hang over the group. Morgalla threw her cloak over her body and wrapped her arms together tight. She felt her heart beat a little faster, pounding in her chest. She recognized the knot in her stomach, cueing her that it was time to leave. As she strolled away, the group became silent. In a collective state, they were apparently in shock at the happenings of the morning.

Dottie was awake by the time Morgalla had returned to the house. "Where have you been, dear?"

Morgalla found it difficult to speak. "I uh…"

"You didn't go to the execution, did you?"

Morgalla said nothing.

"Why did you do that?" Dottie asked.

"I…I guess I was just curious, is all. And then when I saw why they were all gathering around, I just had to know…if he did it or not."

"How could you tell?"

Morgalla was quiet a moment. "I asked him."

Dottie frowned. She noticed Morgalla's mood and placed her hand on the young woman's shoulder. Being away from the melancholy mood of the townsfolk made Morgalla feel better, though.

MORGALLA LAY in bed listening to a strange sound coming from outside. She rose and walked to the window. Opening the curtains, she was shocked to see the sky was on fire, just like Hell. She almost fell back from the shock. The room around her had disappeared, and she was back in Hell, surrounded by red stone. She heard the sound of dracon coming from somewhere, getting closer by the second.

She ran as fast as she could, but the dracon were faster and gained ground. Morgalla tripped and braced herself for the worst, letting out a scream. The dracon, however, ignored her and ran past. Morgalla looked up and realized she was in the middle of town. The beasts of Hell tore through it and the streets filled with the screams of the townsfolk. Morgalla shut her eyes and covered her ears, but she still heard the sounds of terror all around.

"Get up."

Morgalla looked and saw Delilah above her, weapons drawn and in the middle of a battle. She wore the black armor of Hell's army.

Delilah yelled. "I said get up, child. I need you."

Morgalla grabbed Hero in her hand and found the strength to rise. She was shocked to see that she too was wearing the black armor. Back to back with her only ally, she noticed demons were attacking from every angle. Delilah laughed at the joy of battle but it was clear with the two of them surrounded by enemies, their cause was hopeless.

It went dark, and Morgalla felt her arms and legs constricted, a pair of strong hands around her neck, choking the air from her. She struggled with all her strength, but it was no use. She could not break free.

Get up...wake up.

AFTER WHAT seemed like an eternity of suffering, Morgalla awoke for real. Her heart raced. She even felt it in her chest and ears. Soaked with sweat, she stood and looked around the darkened room. She caught her breath. Her mouth was dry, so she walked downstairs for a drink of water. Morgalla was about to sit down, but she sensed fear from above her. She marched back upstairs and noticed Dottie's bedroom door open. Though asleep, the woman let out a moan and mumbled. Morgalla felt the fear from her friend's soul.

Morgalla pondered what to do. Should she wake her? Would Dottie be offended that she was in her bedroom? She grew concerned for her benefactor.

"Dottie?"

There was no answer.

Morgalla repeated, this time with more conviction. "Dottie."

Through Morgalla's special influence, she was able to reach out to Dottie's soul and wake her. The old woman was shocked as her eyes flew open. She found her bearings, and her hand went to her chest to try and coax a sense of calmness over her.

Just a dream...it was just a dream...

Dottie sat up and focused on the doorway. Though barely any light in the room, she could see the look of concern on Morgalla's face.

"Are you okay?"

"Yes…yes, sweetie. It's nothing."

"I don't think so."

"How come you're up? Don't tell me I woke you."

Morgalla frowned. "Looks like this is the night for nightmares."

They went downstairs. Dottie brewed some tea, and they sat in the silence and dark of her living room. Morgalla knew the sorrow from her companion's soul. She didn't want to pry, but at the same time, she cared about the woman's feelings. As her frigid hands clutched the hot mug, she noticed Dottie staring at a photograph on the table.

"Who are they?"

Dottie paused. "He's my late husband, Robert…the girl on the right is Sera when she was twelve."

It might as well have been a sting to the woman's soul. Morgalla hung her head and frowned. "I'm…I'm sorry."

"It's okay, you didn't know. Robert and I had more than fifty years together. Just been difficult, is all, having the house empty."

"Sera still comes 'round."

Dottie set her tea down and took hold of the framed picture. She ran her hand down the glass. Morgalla could feel the dam holding back the emotions that wanted to come pouring out. It would take little effort to do so.

"Dottie I…"

Dottie pointed to the other girl in the picture. "This is Sera's twin sister, you know. We lost her just a few months after this picture was taken."

Morgalla's jaw dropped.

"They were by the river, and Sera fell in. Mari did everything she could to save her, and she did…but Mari was swept away."

The tears flowed. Dottie's weak and elderly hand shook as it went to her face. Morgalla felt the woman's sorrow and found it hard not to cry herself. The teacup shook in her hands, and she had to set it down to avoid dropping it.

Dottie continued, "Robert and I arrived too late...but I can still hear her..."

Morgalla didn't know what to do, feeling a lump in her throat and twist in her stomach. She stepped to the end of the couch and put her arm around Dottie, joining her in misery, but she also remembered Delilah's words ringing her head.

Never cry...never.

In the dark of the living room, Dottie finally cried herself to sleep as Morgalla tried to comfort her. The demon had found the simple act of embracing her friend was enough to bring some solace. Though she didn't understand how.

SIXTEEN

THE SAVAGE PEAK

WHEN MORGALLA rose the next morning, Dottie asked if she might be able to help out at the local stable a couple of blocks away. She stepped out the front door to feel the sun shining on her face and closed her eyes and smiled. The heat felt good.

She located the stable easily enough and was surprised to learn that Dottie's daughter worked there. Morgalla still got frowned at with contempt from some of the locals, but it wasn't as harsh as before. She hung her cloak on a hook and did whatever she was told. The person in charge put her to work doing manual labor, which was easy enough for Morgalla since she was stronger than the average human.

Morgalla was taught how to feed the beasts called horses and strapped the feed bag over each of their snouts. Though animals, she could still sense the happiness from their souls. Morgalla smiled as she stroked the muzzle of one of the horses. She felt the glare of someone watching. Turning to the stable entrance, she saw Dillon standing there. He had taken a bucket, turned it upside down and sat. Morgalla knew he was doing more than just relaxing.

"Good morning," Morgalla said.

"Good afternoon."

She hadn't realized that it was mid-day. No wonder she was so hungry. She took a seat across from him in the hay.

"Dottie has a good heart," Dillon began. "She's also a good judge of character, but you'll excuse me if I'm a little protective of my mother-in-law."

"Your what?"

"My wife's mother. I didn't expect a demon to know what that was."

Morgalla felt as if someone just stabbed her in the heart, and her stomach twisted. She was ready to summon Hero.

"I don't know what you're talking about."

Dillon's eyes and voice were intense. "Drop the bullshit. Makaro has sent spies before but hasn't done so in years. And they were far better at hiding than you."

"How..."

"Shadow blade for one, that and the cloak. Your boots sure weren't made by human hands. You also really hate the cold as all demons do."

Morgalla glanced at Dillon's sword, which still remained in its sheath. "You all have demon weapons."

"Remnants of the great rebellion. The only way one can kill a demon is with a magical blade or black metal."

"Your people have kept them...just in case."

He nodded.

Morgalla sighed and swallowed hard, hurting her throat. "Why not confront me right away then?"

Dillon smirked. "You're really terrible at hiding. What are your intentions? Your *real* intentions?"

"I wound up here by accident. I have no allegiance with any demon lord, Makaro especially. Never even met him."

"Accident, huh? You plan on staying?"

Morgalla's mouth opened, but nothing came out.

"I don't know what it's like where you come from," Dillon continued, "but if it's better than this place, I don't understand why you don't go back now."

"Well, it has its ups and downs, for sure. Tell me, Sheriff, were your men going to come in here and attack me if necessary?"

Dillon smirked. "You can sense their souls."

"Their apprehension. But they're not afraid."

"Can you blame me for being cautious?"

Morgalla didn't reply. Dillon made eye contact with one of his men standing on the other side of the yard next to the barn. He waved him off, and the other three deputies followed.

"Now, what are *your* intentions?" Morgalla asked.

"You were at the meeting the day we met."

"Yeah."

"There's a lot of fear going around, always has been, living under the shadow of Dracon Peak. We don't know what Makaro has in mind or what his plans are…if any."

"And you want me to find out. What makes you think he would trust me?"

"You stand a much better chance of getting close to him than any of us. You have a skill that no human being does, the gift of sight. Something we've never truly understood."

"Demons can see people's souls, judge them at a glance, and know their true intentions. We can also influence them, like bringing out the truth."

"The truth part? That much I knew as well."

"So, am I to gain his trust or something? Have *you* even met this guy? He might kill me at first sight!"

"Like you said, judge someone at a glance and find out what their true intentions are. If you're uncomfortable…"

"Yes, yes I am. He'll be able to see through me, and you know that."

"Makaro is no fool, but I think he's grown over-confident like his father did."

"Seems to be a trait among most demons."

"Do you not even know your own kind?"

Morgalla frowned, getting back to the subject at hand. "What's in it for me, Sheriff?"

"Ah, now you sound more like a demon."

"No, more like someone who is taking a great risk."

The sheriff smirked. "Some people hold a grudge against the Izari, but many prefer the idea of just letting them into town."

"What do they have to do with this?"

"If everyone still thinks that's what you are, then it's best. You might even be able to stay here. Does that sound appealing?"

Morgalla knew he was telling the truth.

"And will you tell anyone else?" she asked.

"Not unless you want me to."

He's telling the truth.

"And what if I don't do this?"

"I'm not giving you order or an ultimatum. But Makaro is still a threat to this town and everyone in it. If you're going to live here, he's a threat to you too."

Dillon stood and walked to the exit.

"Answer me one thing, Sheriff. Does Dottie know?"

"Not that I'm aware of. I haven't told her. She's a sweet lady."

"Yes, she is."

"Just how many people know what I am?"

"Me and me only...for now."Morgalla pondered more later in the day as she helped at the stable. In the late afternoon, she made her way back to Dottie's home. The elderly woman was wearing heavy clothes, ready to go out.

"Oh good, you're back, dear."

"Yeah, what's going on?"

"My daughter invited us over for dinner."

"Us?"

"Yes, us."

Her first lie. Morgalla could easily tell. Sure, Dottie's daughter probably made dinner, and she had invited her mother, but with Dottie's lie, Morgalla guessed she did not invite both of them.

Morgalla frowned. "I actually…have something to do."

"What could be more important?"

"Well…I think I need to find out whether or not I can make this place a home…a real home."

"Are you going back?"

"Yes."

"Will you bring your friend here?"

Just the thought of Delilah in this town made Morgalla think *hell no.*

"I…don't know. But I wanted you to know that if I don't come back, it's not that I don't want to because I appreciate everything you've done for me."

"Sweetie…"

Morgalla felt Dottie's weak, elderly hand go to her cheek. Never before had Morgalla felt such affection for someone. She literally did not have the words. Was this normal among humans? She thought. There was an emotion coming from the elderly woman's soul that Morgalla had become familiar with: fear. She knew she had to give some sort of comfort to her.

"Please, don't be afraid."

Morgalla left Dottie's home with a lot to think about. As she was walking away, she stopped. She could just tell that Dottie was there in the window looking at her. Morgalla looked over her shoulder one more time and gave a smile a wave. Dottie returned the gesture. As she walked away, she sensed someone else watching. Looking over her shoulder, Dottie's daughter was inconspicuously standing at the corner. Though Morgalla frowned, she didn't blame the woman for being cautious.

THE MORNING was chilly and foggy. Morgalla put up her hood. As she walked through town, her eyes were on the ground, pondering just what to do. She hated Hell, but this place wasn't much better.

Pros of Hell: never cold, plentiful food, Delilah was close by. Oh, and her new room locks.

Cons of Hell: everything else.

Pros of this place…

Morgalla had to think. Since they didn't like demons, it was dangerous, but at least the people seemed to be a friendlier…a little. She'd really have to work at making friends here, but if they were anything like Dottie, that should be easy.

Cons: It's cold. But, if it were one of those worlds with changing seasons it would be warm at least half of the year. Then she thought about how she could never show her true face to them. Even Dottie, what if someday she discovered by accident? Dillon knows, and he seemed like an honorable man who would never tell, but what if it suited him to hold it against her?

Out of curiosity, Morgalla climbed a ladder on a building to take a look around. Most structures were only two stories tall, and they stretched to the horizon. She wouldn't be able to guess how many humans lived here, but it certainly had to be in the thousands. It could be a good place to disappear.

But Delilah…

Morgalla owed her everything, and she knew she cared about her. To just leave Hell without explanation or even a goodbye…maybe there was a way to have the best of both worlds. There is a portal to Hell here, though obviously small, where she might be able to come and go as she pleased.

She made up her mind on one point: She had to go talk to Delilah. There was one hurdle, and that was getting back to Hell.

The morning was still foggy as Morgalla made her way out of town and followed the path back. She had to retrace her steps, where she encountered that *Deadra* person and then back up the cliff to Dracon Peak. Through the forest draped in fog, she saw the cliff face leading upwards into the mist. She took a deep breath and started her ascent.

Using every bit of her strength, Morgalla climbed the rock face until she got to the top. Her energy was spent by the time she got there, but the fog still hadn't let up. She could tell there were souls somewhere around, but couldn't determine who or precisely where, or if they were the kind of people she might want to avoid. Through the mist, she saw towers of a castle appear and get clearer as she approached. Now on the highest plateau of the land, it appeared as if the mountain was wearing a crown.

Morgalla froze as an image appeared in the clearing. A figure approached slowly, its boots thumping on the rock. When near enough, the armored creature removed its helmet to reveal a demon underneath. He watched her curiously, wondering how and why a human girl would be in their presence. Was she brave? Was she stupid? What might she want?

She seemed to know he was looking at the demonic symbol that held her cloak in place. His eyes squinted. He awaited her next move, to state her intentions.

Morgalla started the conversation. "There is a portal here."

"Indeed," the beast replied. "What is it to a human who is clearly hiding something?"

Couldn't get anything past him. Surely his skills could see into her soul...the same as she could for him.

His hand was resting on the hilt of his sword with claws wrapped around the grip, ready for action. Pondering what to do, she wasn't sure what to tell him. *He'll see through a lie for sure.* Morgalla revealed her real face to him, her ears growing large and horns appearing from her hair that changed from dark raspberry to orange.

The demon raised an eyebrow. "It is best that you change back. The fewer people who know, the better." He motioned for her to follow him.

She did as he commanded and resumed her human disguise.

As they walked, more of the castle was revealed to her though still mostly shrouded in morning mist. It was strange to see a fortress in the demon style of architecture among a grey sky and pine trees. Through the main gate, they entered a courtyard and approached the massive front entrance. The doors groaned as they entered, the sound echoing through the high ceiling laced with gold. Thick, ornate columns lined the long hallway. She noticed the carvings in the stone, depicting acts of violence…typical art for demons. The floor was inlaid with gold and precious stones. On the walls hung all types of precious pieces of art. Morgalla was no art critic, but she could easily tell they were from different artists and eras.

At the end of the hallway, there was the biggest painting yet. It was dozens of feet high and depicted a demon standing proud, a sword in his hand. His posture displayed his strength, and his face had the expression of a conquering hero. Morgalla stopped to look at it. Her eyes danced up and down to soak it all in. She looked up to the guard.

"Yeah, I know," the guard said with rolling eyes.

SEVENTEEN

THE WOODCARVER AND HIS MASTER

MORGALLA AND the creature continued on to a hall with a large staircase. It was grand with elegant carvings from stone and wood. The marble floor was lined with gold. At the base of the main staircase, she noticed one of the statues was unfinished.

"Wait here," he said.

Morgalla did as she was told and waited. She was nervous due to the fact that she didn't know this *lord* or what his reaction to her might be. But the guard showed no malice in his soul, so she had that going for her.

She felt a presence enter the room and spun around to check the entrance. A young human male stood there, and he seemed surprised to see her...but only for a moment. He averted his eyes to the floor.

The boy was younger than her, barely a teenager, if she had to guess. His brown hair was messy, and his hands were that of a crafts-man: filthy. He wore plain clothes with kneepads and heavy leather boots and apron. All of his clothes were used and worn, the leather especially. Goggles hung around his neck.

He approached but kept his eyes on the ground. Morgalla sensed apprehension in his soul and deep concentration. When he reached the bottom of the steps, he knelt and took out a series of woodworking tools. He put on his goggles and went to work on the unfinished statue.

"Did you do all of these?" she asked.

He stopped what he was doing, sliding the eyewear off and looking up to her. He was surprised she was speaking to him. "Uh…yes."

"It's amazing," she said.

"Thank you," he replied with a blush.

"You're very talented," she said.

"Again, thank you," he replied as he averted his eyes. He looked around. "Why are you here?"

"I…well, I'm seeking help from Markaro, I suppose."

"From Lord Makaro?" he said with a chuckle.

"Did I say something funny?"

He checked around to see if anyone was listening. "Well, first off, he's not really a lord. Too young, as I'm sure you know.

"Of course," Morgalla replied as if she knew.

"And I hope you have something to offer if you want his help."

Morgalla sighed. "Great."

"You must be good with a blade."

"What makes you say that?"

"If you're able to survive alone in this land? You must have skill with a weapon."

She offered her hand. "I'm Morgalla."

He hesitated, almost surprised at her gesture, but he took her hand nonetheless. "Mylo."

"Why are you here, Mylo?"

"Better than living outdoors in the wilderness."

Morgalla thought a moment as he went to work on carving.

"You're an Izari or from the town?"

Mylo nodded. "I was an Izari. They banished me. Here at least I have a shelter from the elements."

"Yeah, I can see that," Morgalla said and walked up to another wood pillar and studied the carvings on it. "You seem to be doing pretty well for yourself."

"When you have a skill such as mine, you find that you end up being rather pampered. For a human, anyway. The only downside is that one must have patience with the lord of this manor."

"Where did you learn to do this?" Morgalla asked.

"A local artist. I took over for him after…"

Like a switch, his mood went somber.

"Say no more," Morgalla said.

Morgalla was piecing together a puzzle. This world was strange for sure and for now, she hoped maybe keeping a low profile might be best. She glanced around and saw the demon guard standing in the chamber. He motioned for her to follow him.

"Good meeting you," Morgalla said to Mylo as she walked away.

"It was…yeah, same to you," the young man replied with a hint of confusion in his voice. He went back to work.

Morgalla was led through the flamboyant castle. Even the manors and castles of Hell didn't live up to this place. Tapestries of fine silk and elaborate designs hung from stained-glass windows depicting the visage of Makaro. The same marble and gold floors were beneath her feet, and the artwork again seemed to be from many different cultures, different worlds.

She heard laughter coming from behind a set of doors and noticed the set of golden handles. When opened, a private chamber, mostly white marble, was revealed to her. It was a bathing area of some sort. The fixtures and statues were gold. Morgalla looked at the figure in the large circular tub before her. Makaro, the lord of this land, was up to his waist in bubbles. His red, hairy skin shined, covered in oil. His scraggly beard was unkempt, a large crumb of food rested within view. His horns were decorated with gold rings, and his long, black hair was braided. Human females stood on either side of the tub, laughing with him.

The guard stepped to the side and spoke with a loud voice but without energy. "Presenting his lordship, the Magnificent Makaro."

Makaro frowned at him. "You were more than a little unen-thused there, Bruk." His lordship's smile was then aimed at Morgal-la, revealing the food stuck between his teeth. "Greetings, my dear."

"Um, hello."

"What brings someone like you to my humble home? What message do you have?"

Morgalla knew that lying to a demon as old as him was point-less. "Message? I don't represent anyone."

He seemed confused for a moment as one of the females fed him a piece of fruit. "Really? Looking for a master to serve then?"

"Not exactly."

"Humph. You are difficult, child. I don't like that. Speak plain-ly. What is it you want?"

"Passage back to Hell."

Makaro appeared even more confused. Bruk leaned in and whis-pered something in his ear. "Oh. A demon who can look human? A rare gift indeed, child. There are those who might pay handsomely for the use of such a skill."

Morgalla's eyebrow went up at his words.

Pay handsomely?

Her reaction made him chuckle, and he sensed the intrigue from her soul. "Oh, she likes that idea. So, I'm confused, child. Just where did you come from?"

"I've been in the town for a past few days."

Makaro's jaw dropped. "And they didn't suspect you were a de-mon? Well, you do come off as the pacifist type."

"They thought I was something called an Izari?"

"Amazing."

Morgalla thought Makaro was overjoyed, and it wasn't lost on her that if he was this excited, she might have a bargaining chip.

The demon lord shifted as the bubbled water splashed over his bulbous body. Morgalla made sure not to look down, afraid she might see something she would not want to. One of the lord's servant girls offered him another piece of fruit.

"Hmmm…me thinks there is something else on your mind, yes?" he said with a wink. "You want more than just passage back to Hell."

"I was actually hoping that maybe…you would allow me to come and go."

He laughed. The females joined him, and so did his guard, but their laughter was incredibly fake. "Come and go? As you see fit? My dear, you will need to offer me a lot more than a *please* if you want access to my portal."

"One-way then."

Makaro yawned. "You are boring me, girl. You have nothing I could possibly want."

He rose from the tub. There weren't enough bubbles to cover him. Morgalla looked away.

Guavas. Keep thinking of guavas. God, I wish I was anywhere but here.

She made eye contact with Bruk, the guard, who was rolling his eyes again.

Makaro's bulging body walked to one of the females who held open a case. He selected some rings of various shapes and styles, and his servant girl put them on his clawed fingers. The other servant girl dressed him in a silk robe.

Thank God.

Hiding her disgust became a challenge. She didn't look at him. During her silence she had to think fast. *Surely there must be something…*

"I suppose," she started. "That it depends on what one either wants…or needs."

"And sometimes they are one and the same," he replied with a wink.

"I suppose."

Makaro chuckled as he approached a little closer. He was taller than Morgalla, but not by much, another exaggeration of his portraits.

"I'm a demon of many...desires, my dear. I can make your stay a pleasant one."

He winked at her. Morgalla struggled to hold back the disgust. She had to think of something happy and fast.

Guavas. They're very tasty. Wish I had one right now.

"Gosh...sure is tempting."

He ignored her words and dragged a claw down the symbol of Zorach on her medallion.

"One of Zorach's underappreciated minions, I see. He's so boorish, isn't he?"

"I haven't had the pleasure of meeting him yet."

Makaro chuckled. "Oh, pray that you don't, my dear. Are you looking for a new employer, perhaps?"

"I guess it depends on the job."

"I would promise you a life of luxury like you never have experienced before."

Morgalla stared blankly at him. Sensing the desires of his soul, she could tell what *job* he had in mind for her. She continued thinking of guavas and the forests of Usteron...the sunsets and the sunrises... Dottie's lovely smile and warm nature.

Makaro grinned. "I see you are drawn to the possibility."

Well, at least he believes I'm thinking about him.

Morgalla remained still.

He wasn't done with his interrogation. "You aren't here because of Zorinda or Zorach, are you? Makraka perhaps?"

"None of the above."

With Morgalla's words spoken in confidence, Makaro was overjoyed. "Oh, how delightful. Delicious. That's just what I wanted to hear."

"My dear, plans are in place to finally secure my kingdom."

"Secure it from what?"

A clawed finger, clad with a large jeweled ring, went to his lips. "Shh! All in due time." His bulbous body went to a large chair and collapsed into it. "See, there are treasures beneath my palace here, a mine filled with riches!"

"You seem to be doing well."

"Well, there is the risk of being discovered, you know."

"You want to be left alone permanently."

He smiled at her, but when another door opened, his face lit up. One of his servants, a human male, came in gripping a chain. At the end of the last link was a collared, wingless dracon who pulled at the leash. Makaro had to use all his strength to lift himself out of the chair to greet the beast.

"There's daddy's little devil!" Makaro crooned, leaning down and kissing the beast on its snout. The dracon returned the affection by licking his master's face with its long, black tongue. "That's my good Dante! Who's daddy's Pookie? Who's daddy's widdle Pookie?"

As Makaro laughed, Morgalla looked up to the demon Bruk whose annoyance was bubbling over in his soul. He watched her and shrugged.

Makaro rose and approached his ladies again. One had a bottle and spritzed a fragrance on her master. Morgalla smelled it from where she was standing, and it wasn't unpleasant. The demon approached Morgalla again, and she felt his eyes all over her body.

"Listen, female. You are in my domain, and my word here is law. I have many warriors, and your sword will be an asset to me. I expect everyone here to remember one thing: I am the master." He turned to Bruk. "Isn't that right, Bruk?"

Bruk's response was immediate. "Yes, Master."

Makaro then faced the women. "Isn't that right, ladies?"

"Yes, Master," they said in unison.

Makaro then focused on the human who had entered the room, still clenching the chain leash. "Giles?"

"Of course, Master."

Makaro chuckled and smirked at Morgalla with a wicked grin. There was an intensity in his eyes that Morgalla could almost feel physically in her very heart. She took a step back.

"And what say you, child?"

"I..."

Morgalla fought an urge. It was as if his very gaze was trying to make her soul submit to him. Her heart raced, pounding in her chest as sweat formed on her forehead. She couldn't stop breathing quick and shallow.

"There is strength in you, I see," he said with a grin. "Fine, return to Hell. Return to Zorach and his iron fist. Avoid the gangs of demons looking to rape a young female like yourself." His words and his grin sent chills along her flesh. "No matter, the town will submit to me sooner or later. Giles, why not show our new friend to one of our guest rooms so she can think it over?"

Giles bowed to his master and guided Morgalla away. As soon as she exited the chamber, she felt her heart slow back to normal. She had to take a moment, leaning against the stone wall, and she spun around to face Giles who returned an emotionless gaze.

EIGHTEEN

THE MASTER OF NO ONE

MORGALLA FOUGHT for breath. "He's…good at that."

"He's the master."

Morgalla was led up one of the many staircases to a lavish, yet small, bedroom. Giles escorted her inside, but she hesitated, sensing he had other intentions. He seemed meek enough, and she knew she could take him with ease especially since he was unarmed.

"You will wait here," he said.

Morgalla checked around the quarters. It was certainly more opulent than any room she had ever been in but still rather humble in comparison to the rest of the castle.

"Wait for what?"

Giles smirked. "Demon or not, you will learn that you do as you're told around here."

Morgalla cocked her head to one side, and a smirk came to her face.

Giles had a smile on his. "You don't like that, girl? I represent of the lord of this castle and this land. I can tell any demon what to do. You'll soon learn that.

Morgalla became a ball of caged fury at his words. It was more than just what he'd said, but his very gaze annoyed her. Behind his exterior, she saw the truth of his soul. He thought he was better than her. In his eyes, she was nothing.

Giles walked out, and she heard the lock latch. She tried the handle, but the door was bolted. It was thick wood, and the handle appeared to be a thick metal. She might be able to break the door down, but she could hurt herself doing so. Any thoughts of escaping that way were crushed as she felt the presence of two soldiers on the other side. Break the door down, and they'd be on her in an instant in close quarters. She heard Delilah in her head.

Always look for the best path through a problem.

She looked out the window and saw that it was a long way down. No wonder it was unlocked. Morgalla realized there was no real way to climb down. She paced the room, her hands clutched together, and she bit her lip.

Before she had time for another thought, the door opened, and two tall women entered. They were dressed in lace and gold. Morgalla smelled their perfume from across the room. Their hair was done up in elaborate hairdos, and both faces had been painted to accent their lovely features. Their lips shined red, and Morgalla squinted at the gold in their eyelashes.

One woman set a bundle of clothes on the bed. The other had some bottles and towels with her.

"I am Rey-chell, head mistress. Lord Makaro wishes that you be bathed and prepared for tonight."

"Prepared? For what?"

"Listen, demon or no…"

"…*I still do what you say*, yeah the other guy told me that. It's just a question."

"Girl, one command and I can have the guards outside come in and teach you a lesson you will not soon forget. Might I add that we know you can heal quickly from any injury and not leave a scar or bruise? Shall a good beating teach you some manners?"

"What are humans doing working for a demon?"

The woman stepped closer, her eyes burning with anger at Morgalla's defiance. "The master lavishes his loyal subjects. Better than living in the cold down in the filthy town."

Morgalla was bewildered. "You're from the town?"

The woman snapped back," Yes, I was from that shithole. Now, girl, you will learn your role here, and you will learn mine."

"Oh, it's pretty obvious what your role is here."

Morgalla saw the coming attack from a mile away, yet she did nothing to stop it. The woman wound her hand back and with all of her strength, brought it across Morgalla's face. The demon hardly flinched, in fact, she barely felt the strike. Rey-chell held her hand in pain, caged fury burning in her soul. Morgalla smirked.

Rey-chell's eyes continued to glare. "I look forward to seeing you on your knees before our master."

"Something you do very often, I wager."

"You are lucky the master wants you tonight and soon."

A male voice interrupted. "Is there a problem here?"

Both women glanced at the door and saw Giles standing there.

"We were just teaching this young woman some manners."

"Why is she not prepared? The master, as you know, does not want to be kept waiting."

Rey-chell had no explanation. The women were ordered out, and they slammed the door behind them. Morgalla rolled her eyes as Giles approached.

"Your stay here can be pleasant or miserable, girl. Pick one."

Morgalla said nothing.

Coming here was a huge mistake.

Giles walked to the bed and took the clothing the women had brought. He held up the...the...

What the hell is that?

Morgalla saw an item made of metal, gold, and lace, barely enough to cover anything.

"You are to wear this," he said, and he dropped it at her feet. He crossed his arms and soon became annoyed when Morgalla refused to move. "I'm waiting…"

"You expect me to put that on in front of you?"

"I can have the guards come in here and do it for you."

Morgalla held up her hands. "No, no. That won't be necessary."

The two human guards waited outside. One of them yawned. They both snapped out of their trances when they heard a knock at the door, loud and fast. They could have sworn that they heard the word *help*, but it was muffled.

Not to leave anything to chance, the guards opened the door. Their jaws dropped when they were greeted by Giles hanging from the ceiling, tied and gagged, his shouts muffled. They also noticed the clothing that he had intended for Morgalla to wear was instead now being worn by him over his clothes.

Giles struggled with the restraints and the gag as he dangled from the ceiling like a freshly caught fish from the river. As one guard tried to help him down. The other noticed the window was open. Sheets and curtains had been pulled down and turned into a make-shift rope that hung out of the opening. Shocked, he ran to the window and looked out. The rope Morgalla made only extended ten feet or so, but he saw nothing below.

He should have looked up.

Morgalla had been standing on the ledge above the window. With the guard distracted, she leapt in, kicking the him in the face. She ran at full speed to the other guard and struck him. He fell to the floor. With her three opponents dazed, she took the opportunity to run out the door and slammed it shut as she escaped. The guards were trapped.

She didn't have much time, so she rushed down the spiral staircase, ducking into shadows or behind a tapestry whenever she heard someone's voice. She hoped it wouldn't be a demon because they would be able to sense her even if she were physically hidden.

Morgalla made it to an exit only to spot some guards were there. She overheard a conversation. They were talking about a girl who escaped. The entire manor was now on alert.

Damn.

NINETEEN

THE PRISM OF AKUBAR

NOW THAT she was on the lower levels, maybe escape through a window was possible back to…

Wait, back to Freedom Ridge? Or did she want to go back to Hell? See Delilah? She saw the path that led down into the mines and the portal back to Hell. She had seconds to decide.

Morgalla ran down the staircase towards the mines. She turned a corner only to be met by four demons who were standing in front of the portal. Just the fact that she appeared like a criminal caught in the act was enough for them to draw weapons. The slave master himself entered from the mines and grinned at her.

He shouted some orders to them, and they all approached her for the attack. Morgalla didn't draw a weapon but used her smaller stature to avoid the coming onslaught. She ducked and weaved past the attacks and ran down the tunnel to the mines.

Ignoring the burning in her legs and lungs, Morgalla continued into the darkness. She bumped into walls and even tripped, falling hard onto the stone. She ignored the pain, realizing that demons were still hot on her trail. By the time she stopped at an intersection, her face was soaked with sweat and her body heaving, trying to calm herself. She breathed fired from her lungs and for a moment she thought she had lost her pursuers. She then sensed their souls and heard the sounds of their voices from deep down the tunnel from which she came. There were multiple paths to follow, and she contemplated which one to take.

In her apprehension and building terror, she was too preoccupied with her pursuers to realize that Mylo had come around the corner from one of the other tunnels. He could barely see her but was startled nevertheless.

"What are you doing here?" Morgalla asked.

"I could ask you the same."

They both looked down the tunnel behind them and heard the voices. Morgalla looked back at the young man.

"Is there another way out of here?"

Mylo was terrified and conflicted. He knew he couldn't lie to the demons, but if he just turned her over to them, it might mean her death. He took a hard swallow.

"This way," he said.

Mylo escorted Morgalla down another tunnel. They reached a dead end.

"What is this?"

"Shh."

Mylo climbed the wall to a ledge and Morgalla followed. The two of them rested at the top of the passage out of sight. They still heard voices echoing through the tunnels, and Morgalla wondered just what species the guards might be. She and Mylo focused on the lights of lanterns approaching. The hiding demon could sense their souls but couldn't tell what species they were until they stepped into view.

Humans.

The guards weren't demons and could only rely on their eyes and ears. Morgalla and Mylo remained silent and still as the others shined their lanterns around the passage.

When the pursuers noticed a curtain made from an old cloth, one of them pulled it back. Mylo's sleeping space…a simple hammock. They wondered what it was but only for a moment. Since their quarry was not around, they turned back.

Both Morgalla and Mylo let out a huge sigh. They hopped down, and Mylo fumbled around in the dark cubby hole for a lantern. When he was able to light it, his humble abode was only dimly illuminated. He had very few personal possessions besides a makeshift curtain and the hammock.

"What is this?" Morgalla asked.

"My home. Where else did you think I slept?"

"Makaro didn't give you a room? But the castle is huge…"

"I'm not worthy, I suppose."

Morgalla frowned. "Sorry about that."

"Why are they after you, anyway?"

"I refuse to be his sex slave."

"Oh."

A frown crossed Morgalla's face as a horrible epiphany struck her. "Wait…they'll know you helped me. Makaro will. He's really…"

"Yes, he's really good at seeing into the souls of others, and manipulating them."

Morgalla felt the fear from his soul and saw it on his face. He was sweating.

"Why did you help me?" Morgalla asked.

"I…" Mylo started and then pondered. "I don't know. I don't have many friends. I suppose if people don't need a reason to be cruel in this world, I don't need a reason to be kind."

"I…I'm sorry. You shouldn't have helped me."

"It will be okay if we can only find the prism."

"What?"

Mylo continued explaining but with a lowered voice. "Makaro is looking for something besides the black metal in the mines. It's a prism of some sort…"

"Magic?"

Mylo nodded. "And I think he's close. It's why Makaro is here in the first place."

Morgalla was confused. "I thought it was because of all the metal his slaves are mining."

"That's just a front so Hell won't look closer into what he's really doing. So long as he provides them with their precious metal for weapons, they leave him alone."

"It's my understanding that it's magic based and stronger than steel."

"And more valuable than gold," Mylo added, "but the prism is worth everything. He thinks it's his ticket away from the Dark One forever."

"Is it?"

They both jumped to the sounds of soldiers nearby in one of the tunnels. They knelt down and lowered their voices. For the time being, it seemed as if they were safe.

"Wait a minute, you're hoping you can make some sort of deal with him if you find it."

"The master enjoys making deals."

"Mylo, don't be a fool. He'll kill you if you don't hand it over right away."

The young man turned his back. He wanted to punch the wall but remembered it was made of stone and decided against the idea.

"If you do find it, why not take it to the town? Can they use it? If you're gonna make a deal with anyone, make it with them."

Mylo spoke under his breath. "It's not fair…"

Morgalla approached with her hand outstretched. She was about to place it on his shoulder when their attention was drawn to a sound farther away in the tunnel. Then there were voices.

"Uh-oh," Morgalla said. "I think they're demons." She looked to the young human and saw the fear written on his sweat-soaked face.

"How can you tell?"

Morgalla had forgotten she was wearing a human disguise and Mylo didn't even know about her true form. "I...the language they're speaking." She hit it lucky. Indeed, they were speaking a demon dialect. "Is there another way out of here?"

"Our only other option is to hide in the woods."

Mylo promptly led the way. They snuck around corners and hid in the dark, avoiding the undead slaves who were lumbering around. Just as Mylo was about to go down one passage, Morgalla took him by the shoulder.

"No," she whispered. "There's someone down there."

"How do you know?"

Morgalla didn't answer because she sensed the presence of souls in one passage.

She pointed down the tunnel. "We're better off this way."

Even though she knew there were soldiers in the tunnel, she was positive they were human...or at least easier to deal with. Strange... she knew the difference from a distance between human and demon souls. Demons somehow had more jagged hearts where humans were, for the most part, softer.

The pair hurried down the passage, but the voices were getting louder. Mylo froze in his tracks, and Morgalla pushed him up against the wall. She looked around and figured there was nowhere to hide.

Oh, damn.

As the soldiers rounded the corner with weapons drawn, Morgalla unsheathed Hero in an instant and clashed with them. She pushed Mylo onto the ground for his safety. From his perspective, he saw her professional skills in the low light of the cavern. Every attack the humans threw at her was parried and dodged. She could have easily killed one but gave him a sharp kick and knocked him out of the fight.

With only one opponent left, Morgalla dealt with him easily. She was driven back to the wall and Hero came around to his neck… but stopped.

She held the blade in place. Both combatants breathed the fire from their lungs, their hearts pounding in their ears. Their faces were soaked with sweat. Morgalla's eyes, intense and committed, met with the human's whose were filled with terror.

Morgalla took a deep breath and with the hilt of her sword, struck the soldier unconscious. She fell back against the wall, a hand on her chest while she tried to slow her heart.

"Wh…where did you learn to fight?" Mylo asked. "I've never seen anyone move like that before."

She said nothing, not sure what to say. "Come on!"

They ran down another tunnel and thought for the moment that they were safe. They were wrong. Morgalla heard soldiers coming as she spun to the passage they'd just left. These guards were demons.

"We need to get out of here, now," Morgalla said.

"We'd have to double back."

They had to think fast what to do because the duo was heading their way down the cave and quickly.

Mining equipment, including chains, pullies, and swivel arms, were everywhere. Mylo and Morgalla looked out to the massive cavern but saw nothing. Falling hammers echoed throughout the stone walls.

The fugitives froze for a moment while their minds raced for an idea, any kind of advantage they might have. One came too late as they turned around and spotted two demons approaching them. Mylo froze. The young man saw two beasts with weapons drawn.

Morgalla, fighting the terror within her heart, drew Hero again and clashed with the aggressors. She was soon outmatched with strength and found herself on her knees and disarmed. The demons stood. One said something to the other in their native tongue, and they both snickered.

Mylo, with all his strength, took hold of a swivel arm. The massive iron tool creaked as it came around. The demons didn't see Mylo as any kind of threat and were caught off guard. As the iron connected with the demon's face, he stumbled back. Morgalla took the opportunity to run and drop-kick the demon into the cavern. He roared as he came crashing down on one of the catwalks far below.

Dodging the other demon's attack, Morgalla took Hero again in her hand and slashed at the beast's legs.

"Run," she shouted.

Both she and Mylo hightailed it back down the route they had taken. They stopped a moment among the labyrinth of rock. Mylo had to think about where they were.

"Down this way."

He pointed to another path, and they were about to run that way when another demon came around the corner, grabbing Mylo and tossing him. He went flying out of cave opening into the massive chasm. He screamed. Out of desperation, he grabbed a chain and swung down, landing hard on a catwalk.

"Mylo," Morgalla screamed.

There was no time to see if he was okay because she was in the middle of a fight of her own. Her opponent swung a massive mace in a circle, smashing rock but missing his prey.

The beast was powerful and full of rage, smashing through rock as if it were nothing. The walls and ground shook, and soon Morgalla and her attacker found it hard to stand. An entire section of the wall was coming undone.

Mylo checked his location and realized the wall in front of him was coming down. He ran for cover as rock rained over him and down into the abyss below.

The ground gave way beneath Morgalla, and she fought to keep from falling over into the void. Her adversary had seen an opening. With a wicked grin on his face, he raised his weapon and took a swing at his helpless prey. She had no choice but to fall back into nothingness.

With a flip, she was able to land perfectly on the catwalk near Mylo. She looked up and watched the demon roaring out of the cave in anger and striking the stone walls, trying to collapse them on top of his enemies.

"Holy crap," Morgalla shouted and dove for cover, bringing the young man with her.

She and Mylo stared at black rock crashing down around them, including the demon who caused it. The stone had given way, and he was the cause of his own demise as he plummeted into the pit below.

The avalanche of boulders struck the iron walkway where Morgalla and Mylo had been. They struggled to keep their balance as the metal footings shook beneath them. Then everything went silent. Both of them coughed from the dust and debris in the air. Peering out through the haze, they saw rock strewn about on the iron.

After the dust had started to clear, they heard voices from high above them. Clearly, the other soldiers, both human and demon, had been summoned due to the commotion. Morgalla noticed something in the haze; a bright light shone like a beacon.

"What's that?" she asked.

Mylo, his face filthy and his coughing fit subsided, peered into the cloud and saw the light. At first, he was shocked, but his heart was suddenly lifted when he realized the source of the illumination.

"Fate is with us," he said while running towards the entrance.

Morgalla grabbed his ragged cloak, afraid the soldiers above them might see him.

"Wait. I'll go."

As she snuck out, she knew that any demon present would sense she was there, but at least she was cloaked in dust. She got closer and closer to the light and realized that near the rock was some sort of diamond, almost the size of her own head. Its glow was blinding. She reached out and took it, marveling at the magnificence of the gem as it glowed.

She looked back and saw that Mylo had approached, an expression of shock on his face. "You...you're one of them."

"What?" Morgalla asked, confused. Seeing her reflection in the gem, she knew she was no longer in her human disguise. "I...I can explain."

TWENTY

THE IZARI

THE BOY roared, "You liar!"

"Mylo, wait."

The young man took off running as fast as he could, but Morgalla was quick on his heels. She still had the glowing gem in her arms. She looked around and found an old, dirty cloth to wrap the gem up.

Mylo thought he had lost the demon girl, but she could easily track his soul so long as she stayed close enough.

Through the labyrinth of black rock, Morgalla crept as quietly as she could. Thankfully there were no soldiers close, but she could still hear them. Through the darkness, she thought she could smell the familiar scent of pine. She followed it and her eyes adjusted to the low light. She felt a breeze coming from a crack in the mountain. Morgalla squeezed through the narrow passage and nearly fell out. She grabbed onto the stone ledge with one hand, the prism wrapped in cloth in the other.

Cool, outdoor air rushed over her, and the bright light of the coming dawn nearly blinded her. Twenty feet down was the forest floor. She jumped, landing on a pile of decaying leaves. Mylo was standing among the trees. Strange. She should have sensed his soul before she saw him, but it was as if he wasn't there. One moment he was normal, and then his soul was gone, covered in some sort of shroud.

He must have heard her landing on the leaves, but he didn't react. She didn't even try to mask her sounds as she approached, yet the young man remained silent and still.

"Mylo?"

Morgalla kept her distance as she stepped around in front of him. A strange look appeared in his eyes as he stared off into the wilderness. He started walking.

"Mylo, what is it?"

He neither answered nor stopped.

Morgalla didn't understand what was happening to Mylo.

"Mylo, stop."

After no response to any of her commands, she finally took hold of his shoulder. Still, no reaction. All she could do was follow him. Clearly, something strange had bewitched him.

She was about to follow when a feeling overcame her. She didn't know exactly why but her instinct was to leave the gem where it was before continuing.

She found a large rock and kicked it over, digging into the soft earth with her hands. When the hole was big enough, she put the gem inside and covered it up. She positioned the large rock on top of it. Before continuing, she checked around for any major markers. From her vantage point, she could only see a large insect hive high in one of the trees and made a note of it.

During their whole journey, Morgalla had kept her senses sharp, on the lookout for any wildlife or enemies. They were in luck…none.

Morgalla heard the roar of a massive river up ahead. When they arrived at a huge, fallen tree that spanned the river, she noticed nothing was below it but white water that rushed passed. Mylo climbed up on the tree, and she followed. She called out his name again but couldn't even hear her own voice because the swiftly moving water was so loud.

She didn't like the idea of crossing. If either of them fell, they'd be doomed. The memory of her nearly drowning to retrieve Hero was still pretty fresh. Still, she followed, scaling up the fallen tree with Mylo. The boy didn't waver. He had no problem keeping his balance. Morgalla, on the other hand, did her best not to look down.

The tree had seen better days and must have been there awhile, the wood decaying over time. As Mylo walked, she noticed some of the wood was so rotten it was crumbling beneath him.

"Mylo!"

He didn't try to save himself as his body fell over the side. Morgalla ran and dove for him. She lost her balance too, grasping what was left of a branch with one hand, gripping his tunic with the other. She cried out. Mylo was silent and showed no emotion as his body hung over the river.

Morgalla dug her boots into the rotting wood and realized the branch she was hanging onto wasn't going to hold their weight for long. She climbed and clawed up to the limb, dragging Mylo behind her. As soon as they reached the top, he stood up and continued on his way. Morgalla had to catch her breath before following him.

"You're welcome!"

As the remaining glimpses of sunlight extended shadows between the trees, she grew concerned because she didn't like the idea of spending a night in the forest.

When thunder rumbled in the distance, her only thought was *oh great*.

There was light, bonfires up ahead and Mylo was headed straight for them. Morgalla was about to continue, but she stopped a moment. Her senses told her they were not demons, more humans perhaps? But were they friendly? She had little time to ponder but decided to take a chance and follow Mylo into the camp.

Morgalla ran to catch up to Mylo, who had entered a camp of some sort. People had gathered around him as he stood still in the center of camp.

She quickly ran her hands through her hair to make sure she had put on her false face. No horns. Ears still small…good.

The group of people noticed her enter, and she felt the daggers of their eyes staring. Some of them held weapons but didn't draw them.

Morgalla raised both hands above her head in surrender. "Hey… take it easy."

Confusion was written on their faces. The one who seemed to be in charge gave orders to check the area. His subordinates complied and sprinted off into the woods.

"There's no one else," Morgalla said.

"We'll see about that."

Some men and women with weapons scattered about in all directions. They had lanterns and searched the area. Random questions were shouted at Morgalla: "Who are you?" "Where did you come from?" She clearly could not tell them the truth. They were distrustful enough.

"Hold."

Everyone turned and focused on a figure approaching. He was the oldest human Morgalla had ever encountered. Her jaw dropped as to how feeble and weak he seemed. His flesh had atrophied and was wrinkled. His hair, what hair he had left, was long and a mixture of grey and white. He wore furs and leather. Multiple talismans hung from his neck. He ambled with a staff, and it appeared that all of his weight was centered on it.

The old man apparently caught the expression on Morgalla's face.

"She must be from Freedom Ridge," one man yelled.

The old man looked at Mylo. "What's her story?"

Mylo, whose expression remained blank, finally spoke in a voice with no emotion. "She's a demon."

Morgalla's jaw dropped, and so did everyone else's. The old man approached and held up his hand. He started an incantation, and Morgalla's disguise was gone. People in the crowd drew weapons and pointed them at her. Morgalla had Hero out in an instant, ready to defend herself.

"Back off," Morgalla shouted.

"Wait."

The old man's words were taken as gospel, and they all froze. Morgalla saw Mylo whispering something into his ear. He smiled and looked to the demon girl.

"You found the prism? The Prism of Akubar?" His skeletal, shaking hand extended. "Give it to me, girl."

"I don't have it," Morgalla replied.

"That would be very bad for you."

The old man's eyes squinted and a fury burned in his soul as intense as anyone Morgalla had ever encountered.

"Explain to me what the hell is going on."

He took a deep breath and smiled.

"Put your weapon down, and come with me."

With reluctance, Morgalla did as she was ordered, but she kept her eyes on the people around her.

The man hobbled along, gripping the wooden staff. Mylo and another human accompanied them into a large tent. Books and scrolls were piled up in all the corners. The tent wasn't large, but it was clear to Morgalla that it wasn't intended as a permanent residence. A strange smell curled her lips into a sneer.

"Sit."

The old man sat. His two companions stood on either side of him. Morgalla complied, an uneasy truce of sorts in play, but she went along. For now, anyway.

"So," the old man started, an uneasy smile on his face. "Why would Makaro be so foolish to send one of his minions yet again into our camp when he knows I can see through them?"

"Makaro didn't send me."

"Really? That's damned strange. Then who did?"

"No one. I'm here by accident."

"Where is the prism?"

"Buried under a rock far away."

Morgalla appeared confused, realizing that she had just told him information she wanted to keep secret for the time being. The old man chuckled.

"Not wise to enter a wizard's domain, young lady. I put a charm on this tent that prevents people from lying. You know, I thought you were cute the first moment I saw you."

Morgalla's eyes widened. "I take it the charm also works on you?"

"One of the drawbacks."

"You're really creepy, and I wanna leave now."

A guard spoke up. "Believe me I don't want to be here, either."

The wizard laughed. "My name is Wulfric Armand Zuccaris Smy…"

Morgalla interrupted, "Any way we can shorten that? I'm not gonna remember it."

"Pardon?"

"Wulf the Wizard," Morgalla said, pointing. "That will help me remember it."

"Fine, whatever."

"You're the Izari, aren't you?"

"Yes, we are."

"I've been mistaken for one of you for the longest time now. You're not very well liked in town."

"Or by Makaro and his ilk. As for the people of Freedom Ridge, I guess they're all a little bit sore about what happened years ago. If you ask me, they're ungrateful. After all, our ancestors were trapped here too, and we helped them win their freedom."

"So why even let a demon into your tent? Aren't you afraid I'm going to kill you?"

"Are you going to?"

"Not unless you try something."

"Yes, well Mylo also told me you saved his life at the river. I'm curious why you did that."

"I didn't want to see him drown. Mind explaining to me what's wrong with him?"

"It's part of the spell I placed on him."

"He's working incognito for you?" Morgalla guessed. "You can't just have someone working in secret in the castle."

"Makaro and his minions can spot treachery quite easily. Mylo is the perfect mole because he doesn't know that he is one. Every now and then, I have him report to us and tell us what he has seen and heard. As far as he knows, he's been exiled from our village."

"Just in case they ask him?" she said. Morgalla was annoyed. Normally she would hold her tongue, but the magic surrounding her must have had some influence. "You're using him."

The wizard didn't reply.

Morgalla grew more concerned. "What if they discovered him somehow? They'd torture and kill him."

Again, the old man didn't reply.

"You do know that someday, out of the blue, they might just kill him for amusement."

Still nothing from the old man.

"Do you even *care* if he lives or dies?" Morgalla asked, the annoyance clear in her tone.

Finally, the wizard's male companion spoke up. "It's not that we don't care about him…"

"Seems like you don't from where I'm sitting," Morgalla snapped. "You're no better than anyone in Hell."

The young man was about to speak again, but Wulfric held up his hand. "Erald, silence."

"You know," Morgalla continued, "why don't you and Freedom Ridge team up and fight Makaro?"

The old man chuckled. "Child, it would take a miracle to defeat Makaro. We don't know how many forces he has. And look around you. How many warriors do you see? How many warriors does the town have?"

"Yeah, why not ask Mylo?"

"He's told us," Erald said. "Makaro convinced some humans to join his…cause. That and he may still very well have reinforcements from Hell."

Wulfric interjected, "No, no. Our best bet is to find the gem and somehow…somehow make peace with the town."

"We don't need those bastards," Erald said.

"Oh yeah, you're doing great by yourself."

Erald shot a hateful gaze at Morgalla.

"Oops, sorry. That was the tent talking."

People outside of the tent heard the raised voices and shouts. Without warning, thunder and lightning stopped the conversation in the tent, and rain poured down. When Morgalla exited and looked up, the water was striking an invisible barrier. Within the Izari camp, the ground was completely dry. The rest of the Izari had surrounded her, but their weapons were not drawn. She gave them all a dirty look.

"Get out of my way."

They did not comply.

Wulfric stepped outside with his two companions. "Let her go." Upon his order, the crowd parted to comply. Wulfric had more to say. "That gem can free both the people and us of Freedom Ridge.

Makaro is not to be trusted, and if you think you can make a deal with him, you're wrong."

Morgalla spun around. "Neither are you."

"More trustworthy than Makaro, I assure you of that, girl."

Morgalla shouted. "Makaro can come down here and slaughter all of you for all I care. I'm done with it."

"Do you really mean that?" Wulfric shouted back.

Morgalla spun around. "You're no better than the bastards in Hell *or* Makaro! You're using Mylo and don't give a damn!"

"And what about the town?" Wulfric yelled back. Morgalla had turned, but his words made her freeze. The old man hobbled forward. "Ah, yes, the town. The gem is the key to their future too.

Morgalla stared at him. She didn't hide her anger. She approached, pointing a finger. "You have to promise that Mylo won't be harmed."

"A demon cares about a human?" one of them asked. "What for?"

Morgalla didn't answer, only glaring at Wulfric. "Promise."

"I cannot promise he'll be safe. You're asking too much. But you could keep an eye on him."

It was late, and the weather was too poor for Morgalla and Mylo to head back where they'd been. The Izari gave them shelter for the night. As the thunder and lightning continued around the camp, the tent remained dry and free of the wind. Morgalla was sitting on one bed, looking at Mylo who just lay on the other. His eyes were still wide open. She reached over and closed his eyes.

Morgalla tried to sleep but with all the apprehension around them, and the guards outside with hostile intent, she found it hard to doze.

She stepped outside the tent and watched as her keepers held their swords a little tighter.

"Relax, will you?" She yawned.

A fog had rolled in, and she saw a long figure standing through the mist on the outskirts of the camp. Even before she could see him clearly, she knew it was the old wizard. He approached, her guards keeping close by with their hands gripped tightly on their sheathed swords.

Morgalla stopped a moment. Rolling her eyes, she turned to them. "You mind?"

They didn't stop as she approached the wizard who remained motionless in the midst.

"Can't sleep?" the old man asked.

"I was about to ask you that."

"I hardly ever sleep. When you're keeping your eyes open due to the danger around you, I guess it's tough to close them, even for a minute."

"You mind calling off your people?"

Wulfic took a moment and gave a slight wave of his trembling hand. The guards stepped back into the camp but kept their sight clearly on Morgalla. To avoid antagonizing them, she decided not to get too close to their leader.

"I understand," the wizard continued. "That's what it's like in Hell. Always looking over your shoulder."

"You could say that."

"I don't blame you for wanting to leave it."

"How do you know that?"

"Oh, I've got you figured. At least for that, anyway."

A small smile crossed his wrinkled face.

"Then why not trust me?" Morgalla said.

"I think all the demons up in Makaro's castle wish to leave too. But they're still untrustworthy."

Morgalla's mouth opened, but no words came out for a moment. "Okay, you've got me there." His words had made her ponder the situation.

"What is it?" he asked.

"Well, what if other demons are more like me up there?"

"You're not suggesting that we...lead a rebellion of some sort?" Morgalla's eyes widened. Could it be that simple?

"What if Makaro were to die?" Morgalla thought aloud.

Wulfric chuckled. "Even if you can get close to him, there's no guarantee the rest of the demons around him feel the same."

"So what's your plan? Just get the gem and hope the town accepts us all with open arms?"

"You've been there. What is the general consensus of the people?"

Morgalla shrugged. "Tough to tell."

"How many people are there?"

"Few hundred, at least."

"Damn. How many demons?"

"Maybe a third."

"Really? Only that?" The wizard caressed his scraggly facial hair. "That many people still there? The powerful really do have an appeal, I suppose."

"Wow, really? Those people used to live in the town, and they left?"

"Yeah, I guess they felt life under Makaro was better."

Morgalla looked over her shoulder to the wizard's guard. Their souls were still apprehensive as they gripped their swords. She was annoyed, but part of her didn't blame them.

"You must forgive them," Wulfric said. "They've...we all have had some bad experiences with demons. They enjoy giving us scars."

"I don't doubt that."

"My people are dying, Morgalla. They can't live like this anymore. Our only hope is to assimilate into the town. If they'll let us, that is."

"And if you had the prism, promising them protection and freedom, that would go a long way to convince them."

"Indeed."

Morgalla sighed. Her thoughts went to Dottie and all the other people who had been so nice to her in the town. "You judge them too harshly. They're good people."

The old man smirked. She could feel his skepticism, but there was a bit of hope within his soul. If she could only help make it stronger.

"Everyone there thought I was one of you."

"Everyone?"

"Okay, maybe one person saw through it."

"And you're still alive?"

"See? Isn't that proof that maybe the town will accept you?"

He turned his back. "You will excuse me if I'm cautious."

Morgalla had nothing else to say. She was exhausted from yet another trying day. Maybe his mood would be different tomorrow. She found a place to sleep in one of the tents, next to a motionless Mylo in his trance. Sleep would not come easily.

AFTER A restless night, Morgalla and Mylo made their way from the Izari camp. The boy again was in his trance-like state. As he made his way into the wilderness, Morgalla gave one final glance at the old wizard. His face was plain, and he held an apple in his hand. Morgalla turned and approached him. The others continued gripping handles of their weapons, ready to draw them.

The old man polished the fruit on the lapel of his coat and was about to take a bite when Morgalla snatched the it from his hand and took a bite out of it. She spun around and walked with a grin on her face.

TWENTY-ONE

A PLAN IS FORMED

THEIR JOURNEY through the woods was uneventful throughout the morning. He took in a deep breath, feeling the cool morning air fill his lungs. He looked around, wondering where he was. When he noticed Morgalla, he fell back.

"Stay away from me."

It was a shock when Mylo came out of his trance. "Relax. Relax."

As best she could, using any ability she had to bring him to a sense of calm, it was all for not.

Mylo shouted, "You lied to me."

Morgalla raised her hands and confessed. "You're right. You're right. I did, and I'm sorry."

Mylo looked around, still confused. "Where are we?"

"The wilderness, somewhere close to Makaro's castle. We're on our way back there now. Listen, I'm not going to hurt you, I swear. You're looking for a gem, a magical gem called the Prism of Akubar."

Mylo rose, trying to collect his thoughts. "You…you found it. Where is it?"

"It's safe. But we need to get back to Freedom Ridge."

"They hate Izari there. There's no way I'll be able to stay. And they'll kill you."

"Then why do you live with Makaro in his castle?"

"My people banished me. Told me never to come back."

Morgalla frowned. He was a young man who was homeless and whose talents were limited. He used what skills he had to survive.

She sighed.

"Look, I can relate to not knowing what to do, that you think you don't have any options. It's a terrible feeling. I'm not asking you to trust me completely. Just trust me for now, okay?"

Mylo checked the area and realized they were alone. He looked into her eyes and saw her sincerity, but she could tell his soul was still skeptical.

"You go first," he said.

He pointed into the wilderness, and Morgalla took the lead. "You know the way back, right? Make sure we don't get lost."

They were on their way and approaching the large tree that spanned the river. Morgalla told Mylo about it but he wasn't afraid. By the time they reached it, however, and saw how rotted the wood was, they decided to take the long way 'round. The journey was virtually uneventful, though Morgalla was able to appreciate the scenery around them. Mountains surrounded the valley of tall grass and pine trees stretched up and down the slopes. Morgalla noticed that Mylo was rubbing his stomach and wasn't keeping up very well.

"What's wrong?" she asked.

"I'm starving."

Morgalla reached into one of her pockets and handed him a biscuit. His cautious hand snatched it from her. Hunger kept him from arguing.

"So where did this prism come from?" she asked.

"Some ancient magic. They used it to defend against demons."

"If it's meant to be against demons, could Makaro even use it?"

"He seems to think so. He's an arrogant being."

"That I know all too well," Morgalla said.

They continued through the forest just in time for the sun to break through the clouds.

"As you know, the mines are blessed with veins of black metal that demons use for their weapons. Makaro provides Hell with the metal, and they leave him alone. But he knows the prism is there too."

"He's able to search for it incognito?" Morgalla asked.

"I don't know how many people actually know what's really going on."

"How do you know? About the prism, I mean."

"I've listened as long as I've been there and kept my mouth shut."

"They haven't asked you anything?"

Mylo answered her question with a question. "Why do you care so much?"

Morgalla frowned. She was starting to wonder.

Morgalla thought she knew the way back, but Mylo suggested a longer but safer path. She didn't argue. Morgalla found that Mylo was often lagging behind, and he seemed to have a tough time breathing. He stopped and rested on a log.

"What's wrong?"

"I'm tired, that's what's wrong. We've been walking for hours."

"Sorry."

She looked around for any vegetation but found nothing to eat. Morgalla looked curiously as Mylo tore off a large root from the tree. He started to eat it. Out of curiosity, and a rumbling stomach, she did the same. A look of disgust crossed her face.

"This tastes like crap."

"Would you rather starve?"

"Lemme think about that."

They sat and ate the root. Morgalla could feel the anger in the young man's soul.

"Why do you hate me?"

"I need to answer that?"

"Okay, I get that you're sore about me lying. I already apologized for that."

"It's more than that, and you know it."

"I don't know what else…"

"You're a demon. All you know is death and conquest."

Morgalla remained calm but the hate Mylo beamed at her was starting to take its toll on her own heart.

"I'm not going to deny that, Mylo. All I can say is that I've never…"

Mylo rose to his feet. "Never what? Killed a human?"

"No, I haven't."

Morgalla didn't know what to say that would change his mind. All she could do was not say anything and maybe not make things worse.

The safer path ran through the plains. Morgalla was walking fast now, and Mylo had to sprint to keep up.

"What's your hurry?"

"Gotta get back. I do not want to spend the night out here."

"Can you at least slow down a little?"

Morgalla stopped and let him catch up. They continued on with her trying to walk at a slower pace. She didn't understand. It wasn't as if his legs were shorter than hers…if anything they were longer. Mylo stood an inch taller than her.

All around was tall grass and a herd of grazing paolos. In the distance were hills covered in pine trees. Beyond the jagged cliffs, Makaro's castle stood alone, a fortress that seemed out of place.

Mylo and Morgalla were hungry again by the time they reached the woods. Thankfully they passed by a brook with fish swimming near the surface. Mylo knelt next to the water and submerged his hand. A fish swam by his palm, and he tried to snatch it, but it slipped out.

Morgalla noticed another one and with lightning speed, impaled it on the tip of her sword. She did it a second time and held her catch out to Mylo.

"Dinner time."

Mylo took out some tools from his bag. He rubbed two together, and sparks formed. Morgalla was impressed how fast he was able to build a fire.

He noticed her look. "You don't know how to make fire?"

"Yes, I do. It just takes me a little longer. That, and I happen to know someone who can breathe fire, so she usually starts it."

Mylo stared at her with no shortage of curiosity.

"She's part dragon."

"Dragons are real?" the young man asked…wonder in his eyes.

"Yeah, apparently so," Morgalla replied with a shrug. "I've never seen one."

They held their fish over the fire. Morgalla was silent, deciding that small talk wasn't called for. Mylo was also quiet, but she could feel the turmoil in his soul. He finally spoke.

"What is it like?"

"Pardon?"

"To see the souls of others?"

Morgalla raised an eyebrow. "Well, I've always known it, so I guess it's tough to put into words. I mean, try to describe music to someone who can't hear."

"I've always been jealous of your people. To know what someone is feeling, to understand what their true intentions are."

"It can come in handy, for sure. Especially in Hell. It's probably been my best ally, figuring out who to trust."

"What did it tell you when you met Makaro?"

Morgalla rolled her eyes. Mylo laughed.

"My second sight told me I could trust you too. But I'm also scared, Mylo."

"Scared of what? What are you not telling me?"

Morgalla pondered a moment. She knew that if she told him the whole truth, it would be dangerous to him.

"I think we need to get the Prism of Akubar to the people of Freedom Ridge and soon."

"Makaro knows where the town is, though. What if his witch—"

"Damn, forgot about her." Morgalla cut him off and went back to pondering, but the only option on her mind was an all-out war between Makaro and the people of Freedom Ridge. Maybe Dillon had a better idea.

"What are you thinking?" Mylo asked.

"It's nothing. We just gotta come up with a plan, that's all."

"Either way, I end up in the cold."

"What do you mean?"

"The town won't accept me, and my own people banished me…"

"The town isn't too bad," Morgalla added. "What made you think that? They thought I was an Izari. Besides some dirty looks, there were plenty of nice people there."

"Makaro told me he's the only one who would…"

"Oh, forget that bastard," Morgalla snapped. "That's him manipulating your fear, something he's very good at. He doesn't want to lose your skill, so if you think he's your only friend, that you'll die without him, that you'll stay…it's not true."

"But…"

"It's a lie, Mylo. He's the same as the rest of them in Hell. Just one of many monsters, trust me."

"I'm very well aware of what they're capable of," he said and pointed to a scar on his arm, then on his cheek. The gash on his ear appeared as if someone had cut a piece of his flesh away long ago.

Morgalla was silent, Mylo took an angry bite out of his fish.

"I…I know you're afraid, Mylo."

The boy scowled. "I'm not afraid. You are."

"Of course I am. Only a fool wouldn't be."

"How do you hide it from your own kind?"

Morgalla calmed down and took a deep breath. She remembered Delilah's training that had kept her alive up until now. "I…I use my hate as a shield. They can't see past it."

"But what if they think the hate is directed at them?"

"They don't take offense, believe it or not. Don't ask me why because I barely understand them. Look, there's no greater enemy than one's own fear. You may feel like you're helpless against them, but you're not."

"He's too strong."

"Yeah, he's strong. But there's something he can't…that he hasn't completely destroyed in your soul yet, Mylo."

"What's that?"

"Hope."

"I can't…"

"Look, I…we have a chance for a future. Help me fight for it."

The only sound was that of the fire crackling. Morgalla couldn't tell whether or not she was reaching him. Years of doubt and Makaro destroying the boy's soul had taken its toll. One thing she was sure of: This was going to take some time.

"Why do you even care?" he asked.

Morgalla thought a moment for the proper answer. "Because I feel it's the right thing to do. Do I really need a reason?"

With their bellies full and the fire extinguished, they continued on. The sun was setting in the west, and the twin moons were rising in the east. Morgalla noticed the young man's pace had quickened. *Must have been the meal.* She also realized he was now walking side by side with her. It made her smile.

The castle was within sight and they made their way through the forest. Morgalla found it difficult to retrace her steps, but up ahead she could see the cliff face, the wall of stone where the secret entrance was. The Prism would be close by. As they approached the cliff face where the secret entrance was, their hearts sank. Morgalla froze and held up her hand to signal him to halt.

"What is it?" he asked.

"Shh."

When they both heard voices, they ducked behind a large tree. In the distance through the foliage, some figures moved about. They wore Makaro's clear red uniform. One of them, due to his sheer size, was clearly a demon...Krug, the slave master.

Morgalla muttered under her breath, "Damn it."

"What do we do?"

"The town, that's our only option."

"They won't..."

"Mylo, you have to trust me. That's our only option, okay? Head to the town, now."

Morgalla gave him a shove. She looked back to the group behind them and realized they were around the area where she had hidden the gem. It was best that the boy not know it, she felt. *What if they got their hands on him? They'd be able to coax the truth from him.*

"I'm not leaving," Mylo whispered.

There was no time to argue because Krug had sensed their presence. With an order, the soldiers made their way towards Morgalla and Mylo.

"Run!"

It took no coaxing at all for Mylo to take off with Morgalla hot on his heels.

"Don't stop," she shouted.

Morgalla's influence worked on the young man's soul, and his fear worked to her advantage. He took off down the hill, tripping and falling on a bed of leaves. He was up in an instant, ignoring the pain to his knee and chin. He looked over his shoulder only to notice that Morgalla was missing. Terror gripped his heart, but when he heard the voices of the coming soldiers echoing through the wilderness, he panicked. A tear came to his eye, but his instinct for survival took over. He ran in the direction of the town.

One of the demon soldiers saw Mylo running, and he was about to give chase but stopped when he heard a voice.

"Hey."

He turned toward the voice and saw Morgalla.

The demon was confused to see another of his kind standing there…an unfamiliar face. She was ready to defend herself though she didn't have her sword in hand. She had hoped that maybe—somehow—she could confuse him.

"You."

A man's voice called out, and Morgalla saw Giles running down the hill.

Oh, great.

He was enraged and shouted orders at all the soldiers to apprehend her. His voice cracked, and his hand trembled as he pointed her direction. Morgalla did find it both strange and amusing how the soldiers around him did nothing. She smirked, but it was short-lived as she felt a slap across her face from Giles.

"Ow," he shouted, and his entourage laughed.

Morgalla barely felt it. She kept her ground though her face barely flinched at the smack. She glared back at him and thought she had an angle for the situation.

"Awww, look. The human's feelings are hurt." She mocked and then with a powerful boot to his midsection, Giles was driven back to the ground. "Now the rest of him hurts."

As she pointed and laughed, the other demons joined in. The entire area filled with a joyous mocking as Giles clutched his stomach, hunched over in the pile of fallen leaves.

Giles held his stomach and groaned in agony. He looked to his comrades. "Help me!"

"Why?" One demon asked. "We're too amused by your pain."

"Hello, Morgalla."

She looked and saw a familiar face standing on the high ground looking down. It was Widow.

Uh-oh.

The woman's eyes were locked on Morgalla like a predator who had found its prey.

Morgalla had little time to react or say anything as Plor, the brother of Plux, struck Morgalla in the back of the head. Her world went dark.

TWENTY-TWO

IN THE MOUTH OF EVIL

FREEZING COLD clung to Morgalla's face and head as she was forced into the ice water. Instantly her flesh went numb. She fought for breath. Her lungs seized. Her hands fought for freedom but they were bound behind her back with chains.

Just when the fear got the better of her, and she thought she might suffocate, she felt her hair pulled and out of the water she came. She coughed, trying to draw in precious air. When her vision was no longer blurry, she saw Widow there with her sword, practicing. She spun the blade with lightning speed around the room, slicing at the air. The woman's companion tossed her an apple, and she cut it in half mid-air. She proceeded to do the same to other fruits of varying sizes. It was really then Morgalla realized the woman was not practicing.

She's warming up.

Morgalla looked around the darkened room. They had struck her so hard in the woods that she lost consciousness for a bit. She guessed she was in the castle and they had been using a well of some sort to dunk her head in. Morgalla recognized Plor as the demon holding her. He was strong, far stronger than her.

"Hold her here," Widow called.

With her arm twisted behind her and her hair pulled, Morgalla fought—to no avail—for release. The massive demon was too strong for her. She was presented to Widow, and Morgalla felt a blow to her midsection. As Morgalla coughed on the floor, Widow knelt to her. "I've been keeping my skills sharp. Can you say the same?"

"Yes, you truly are the terror of fruit everywhere."

Widow put on a blank stare, but Morgalla realized that within her was an erupting volcano. Morgalla felt another strike, this time to her face.

"Where are your snide comments now, Morgalla? Nothing to say?"

"Gimme a minute."

"Put her in again," Widow commanded.

Her companion, Plor, responded and dunked Morgalla's head into the water again. She struggled as hard as she could, but it was no use.

Hold your breath. You can do it.

Morgalla was held under even longer now, and it seemed for a moment the water might claim her. She heard voices, sounding as if they were arguing. She was slipping into unconsciousness. Just as it seemed like the end, she was pulled from the water and air filled her lungs again. She gasped and coughed, thrown down onto the floor.

"I had hoped for more of a fight," Widow said. "You know, Plor here is sad you killed his brother."

Morgalla couldn't help but notice that her medallion was hanging around Widow's neck, just out of reach. "I didn't kill him. A witch did."

Widow frowned because she knew Morgalla was telling the truth. "Well…I suppose you could tell him, but he doesn't speak English."

Morgalla had another comment on deck but decided another route. "You…loved him. Harek, I know it. And I'm sorry."

Widow spat to the floor. "Your sympathy…"

"I know," Morgalla interrupted. "It disgusts you. But…this whole system, if you can call it that, is just doomed to fail."

"We are strong because of it."

"Did you see how Makraka turned his back on his own son? I was forced to kill him, and I didn't want to."

Plor shouted something in a different language. Widow replied to him with the same ferocity.

Morgalla wasn't done. "We fight amongst each other, and most of the time it's for revenge or for a reputation." As Morgalla spoke she could feel the shift in Widow's soul, the rage starting to subside. *Was she finally reaching her?* she wondered. "After you kill me, Delilah will come after you. And you know her well enough to realize she'll enjoy fighting all of you."

Widow's companion continued to roar out in his native tongue. Widow's soul was shielded from his words, they did not affect her at all.

"He had no choice," Widow said.

"Neither did I," Morgalla replied. "I know you would trade me for him in a heartbeat, but what's done is done."

Widow got in close to her, the rage building within again. "Delilah would never know that I killed you. You'd be gone, and I'd be a hell of a lot happier."

"We both know the only reasons to kill someone in Hell are either for revenge or to build a rep. Harek will still be dead. The man who put him there, your real enemy, Makraka, will still be alive." Widow's rage burned in her heart, but her fury wasn't at Morgalla. "Remember who really dumped Harek inside that pit to fight me."

Plor shouted something, the fury building. He didn't wait for Widow's orders, dunking Morgalla's face back into the cold water. She struggled. Morgalla didn't know if she could hold out this time.

Without warning, but thankfully so, she was pulled from the water. She coughed and fought for precious breath.

Morgalla looked around and saw Makaro with his soldiers, including Krug with his whip. A frail figure emerged from the group. Deadra threw off her black cloak and held out a small knife.

"She's mine," Widow roared.

Deadra hissed and Widow and then took hold of Morgalla's hair and cut a lock from her head. She grinned, exposing her crooked, yellow teeth.

Morgalla felt the moods of those around her. They were all like caged beasts, fury begging for release. But release to whom? They sure didn't like her, but with some luck, the hate for each other might be greater.

Makaro wagged his finger at Morgalla. "Young lady, you've been super naughty. You took advantage of my hospitality and hurt the feelings of my poor Giles."

Morgalla sat on the floor, finding it hard to breathe. She could only mutter one word. "I…"

"Oh, don't be too hard on yourself." Makaro went on with a chuckle. "I actually found what you did to Giles rather funny."

"Hey," Giles called out.

"Oh, silence. Human bitch…" Makaro grumbled. "But I'm willing to forgive you, girl. That is…if you're a little more friendly."

Morgalla's heart sank. Makaro could easily tell.

"Oh, come now," Makaro chimed. "Don't be like that. Come… this way."

Morgalla stretched her arms past her feet. Her bound hands were now in front of her.

Plor and Widow did not approve, but with Makaro's orders, they wouldn't dare disobey. Morgalla thought for a moment she might reach out and grab her medallion from Widow's neck, but Plor stood between them.

Morgalla followed the master of the castle. Two guards marched on either side of him. She couldn't help but notice that everyone else was following. She checked over her shoulder and spotted Deadra switching between jeers and smiles at her.

Looks like she can't decide which side to join.

Soon they were in a large chamber, as opulent as the rest of the castle. She almost bumped into a statue on top of a pedestal.

The floor was dark stone with golden circles that extended all around. Curtains were drawn, and Makaro motioned for Deadra to step forward. The witch held out an amulet and spoke an incantation. From the floor came green and blue light. Images appeared all around Morgalla. There were pictures of demons conquering other worlds, other races, their flags atop hills on worlds that Morgalla had never seen.

"Do you know just how many worlds in which the Dark One's influence is felt?" Makaro asked. Morgalla shook her head. "Too many. Commanding billions of soldiers and other minions, must get rather difficult to keep track of them all, yes?"

"I…I guess."

"Sure it is. But, I would never venture into anything without a little insurance." Makaro approached, his hands clasped together in front of his bulging belly. "You look like the kind of girl who doesn't want to be part of…all of this."

His clawed hand waved around at the images. Morgalla didn't answer with words, but he could see into her heart with ease. All the images disappeared and were replaced with what looked like planets. They moved around in orbits. Some worlds were barren rock. Others were lush green, and one was as white as snow. Another glowed red with molten lava. Some of the spheres were blue and green, blessed with land and water.

Makaro continued, "Well, you know what? Neither do I. Despite what some might say, I'm actually a very non-violent person."

A look of disgust came over his face. "I hate soiling my hands with such things."

He's telling the truth...sort of.

"Just look at what I've done with the people of Freedom...well, whatever they call their silly little town. Other demon lords would have slaughtered them all. Have I? I don't wish to kill anyone, not unless they make me."

Morgalla couldn't tell if he was telling the truth. Dante, Makaro's pet dracon, sauntered into the chamber. His claws clicked against the stone floor. His tail gave a wag at the sight of his master who returned a kiss on the beast's head.

"What do you want from me?" Morgalla asked.

The lord snickered and wagged his index finger at her. "Clever girl, getting to the point. I like that. See, all other demons always want to conquer each other, dominate and take what they have. Me? I want to live in peace. Co-exist with one another."

"With you in charge?"

His voice bellowed. "Who better?"

Morgalla felt all eyes on her. She had never been this uncomfortable in her life. She looked slightly to her left and saw Deadra standing there smiling. Morgalla glanced over her shoulder to all the minions at Makaro's command.

"I have a dream, Mor..." Makaro thought a moment, snapping his fingers. "Remind me again?"

"Morgalla."

Makaro looked at an imaginary thing in front of him. "I see before me a chess board. You ever play chess?"

"No."

"Human game. It's where you have a board and game pieces, and your opponent has game pieces. Some are worth nothing." He studied some human soldiers against the wall. "Like them, for example. They all have a function. Some are rather valuable."

Morgalla motioned to Deadra. "Like her."

"Oh, indeed," Makaro replied and then returned to his rant. "I forget what the goal of the game is. I've never played it, but I see my own chess board. I have Deadra, Krug, Dante...and with some mentoring...you on my board."

Morgalla had noticed that Rey-chell had entered the room, giving the demon a dirty look.

"And my...function?" Morgalla asked.

Makaro chuckled and so did some others in the room. The snark in her comment raised more than one eyebrow.

"Well, you have a sharp wit. You make me laugh. But you're also quick on your feet and with your blade, I understand. However, and this is just a minor observation, you have no lust for the kill."

"I fail to see how that's weakness."

Morgalla's comment was met with a thunderous round of laughter by the demons and humans in the room. Her lips clenched.

"Child, please," Makaro said. "You didn't grow up in Hell, did you? You know how I can tell?"

"I know how."

"This is nonsense," Widow spouted as she stepped forward. "You want her on your...chessboard when she doesn't even want to be."

"You may have the desire to kill, girl," Makaro noted. "But you don't have a kill on your soul, now do you?"

The cauldron that was her soul bubbled over with rage. Makaro chuckled.

"Oh, I see the two of you in a little...*audition* for this job."

Morgalla's response was immediate. "She can have it. I just want to go back home."

Morgalla felt her air cut off in an instant and a string around her neck. Krug was quick with his whip as he pulled her down to the hard floor.

Makaro approached, standing over the helpless demon girl. "I'm afraid I cannot let you do that, girl. See, you've seen and heard too much of my operation here. I can't allow you to let the lords back in Hell know."

Morgalla fought for the words. "You...mean the real lords?"

The sting to his soul was as clear as day to all the demons in the room. Makaro's eyes burned at her, and he gave a slight kick to her face. He motioned for Deadra to approach.

The witch held up her hand to Morgalla's face and recited an incantation. The demon girl felt a rush through her head, recent memories flashing before her eyes. It made her head spin and ache. Deadra smiled again.

The witch approached Makaro who knelt near her. She whispered something into the demon's ear. He frowned.

Makaro grinned at his minions. "Find the woodcarver and kill him."

"No," Morgalla screamed.

"He is a spy for the Izari," Makaro said. "Oh, and we have to find all of them and slaughter them too. They've been quite the annoyance long enough."

Morgalla fought her way out of the grasp of the whip.

"Mylo didn't know," Morgalla begged. "I swear to you, he was being used by them."

Makaro scoffed at her words. "Girl, I don't care. Your only hope to avoid a horrible death is if you hand over the Prism of Akubar to me...now."

Morgalla climbed to her feet, but she still hung her head. She took a couple of quick breaths, her head still swimming as to what to do. She watched Makaro picking his teeth with his pinky claw.

"Well?" he asked. When Morgalla didn't answer, he sighed. "Listen, girl. You have only two choices: You will die quickly, or you will die slowly. The prism will shield me from the Dark One's gaze."

Widow looked on with curiosity. "It will?"

"Yes."

The woman caressed her chin in contemplation. "Hmm…what if I could get her to talk?"

Morgalla's somber mood dropped even lower.

Oh, no.

TWENTY-THREE

BATTLE IN THE PIT

WIDOW APPROACHED with her weapon in hand. Morgalla didn't have time to think of a plan. She needed to get Hero back and escape, but for the time being, seeing the blade before her and feeling the iron grip of her captor, options were limited. She leapt up, her horn connecting with Plor's eye. The beast roared, falling back as his hand went to his wound. Widow swung her sword around, trying to connect with her prey.

The widow charged again, and Morgalla retreated to the window. Both women crashed through it and tumbled down the roof. As she rolled, Morgalla stretched her arms as far as they would go, her hands gripped the ledge just in the nick of time. Widow was able to hold on with her free hand and slash at Morgalla, barely missing her. They both leapt to ledges and ran along the castle walls. Makaro and his entourage watched as Morgalla, with bound wrists, made her way to the ground. He shouted orders for pursuit.

Morgalla scrambled around the courtyard, avoiding guards and servants. She sensed Widow's soul through the brush and tried to avoid it, to no avail. The angry demoness swung her sword in a circle, hitting nothing but air, but she could feel Morgalla's fear and knew she could use it. Morgalla used one of the slashes to finally cut the bonds that held her wrists.

"Ha," she shouted.

Widow swung, again and again, barely missing her quarry who flipped over her. While in flight, Morgalla saw the medallion hanging from her opponent's neck and was able to snatch it.

Morgalla didn't hang around. She was off again and escaped but was cut off from the exit that would lead her to safety. When she saw the swirl of leaves coming from the sky and realized it as a sign Deadra was making her way to the fight, Morgalla saw few options. She remembered the secret passage that led out of the mines.

She ran to the opening, which led to the caverns below with demons and human soldiers hot on her heels. She avoided a sword being swung at her and connected with a punch and a kick to any adversary she encountered.

Morgalla ran through the tunnels and got lost a couple of times. She had to remember just where the passage was that would take her outside. Several times, she thought she had found the right exit but was cut off when she felt the sting of a whip to her leg. She fell to the rock floor and turned to see Plux and Krug standing there. Krug chuckled as he flicked his wrist again. This time the whip wrapped around Morgalla's neck. The air cut off, but she fought against it. She summoned Hero while Plor kicked the sword from her hand. The two demons mocked her in their own language, laughing at her pain.

Plor kicked her in the stomach and reached down. He lifted her with ease from the neck. Morgalla struggled, but the demon was too strong.

Plor spoke in broken English. "You...die."

He continued to laugh, but his joy was cut off in an instant. Morgalla had reached into her boot and took out her knife. She summoned all her strength to drive the blade through Plor's temple.

"You first."

The demon wasn't able to react because he was dead in an instant. His flesh changed to stone, and Morgalla kicked away from him. Krug was surprised but yanked on the whip again. He dragged his prey along the rock. Morgalla tried for Hero, but he was just out of her reach.

With the whip still tight around her neck, Krug drew her close, his foot on the center of her chest. His eyes burned with rage as he peered down at the demon girl who was slowly being suffocated.

A tremendous boom rang out, and the demon staggered back. Morgalla coughed as she felt the air return, fighting her way from the whip's grip.

She was on her feet with Hero in her hand, ready to fight the beast. On the opposite side of the chasm, Dillon had set up with his deputies, all of them armed and ready for battle.

The sheriff's weapon did little but annoy Krug, but it was enough to free Morgalla who didn't stick around since the demon's friends were showing up. Morgalla leapt into the abyss and grabbed a chain, which she used to swing to the other side.

Morgalla was on a ledge above Dillon and his cohorts, who had opened fire at their enemies across the gorge.

"Get out of here," Morgalla shouted.

With all the commotion, Morgalla made her way through the tunnels. Makaro's human soldiers were cut down by the barrage of bullets, but there were still demons to deal with, and bullets weren't going to be enough.

Morgalla tried to make her way to Dillon, but when she turned a corner, she was met by Widow who swung the sword at her. Both women dueled in the close quarters. Due to her surprise attack, Widow had the edge on Morgalla. They fought to a ledge and with a sharp kick, Morgalla was thrown back into the abyss. She fell a long distance before grabbing onto another chain, coming down hard on one of the wooden catwalks below. Widow jumped from ledge to ledge, the fire burning in her soul for her opponent's death.

Krug was also going after Morgalla. Dillon noticed the beast and ordered his men to continue the fight. He ran to Morgalla's aid.

Widow took a leap into nothing and landed safely before Morgalla. They fought along the catwalks.

"Give me the prism, and I'll let you live."

"That's the biggest lie you've told so far."

There was a sudden thump on the ledge behind Morgalla. She didn't need to look to see who it was. Krug drew his sword and was ready for battle. Widow grinned.

Dillon took a bounding leap. Grasping one of the chain pulleys, he swung down. He braced himself, and with all of his might brought both feet into Krug. The strike was just enough for the demon to lose his footing and fall off the catwalk, tumbling down to one of the stone ledges. Dillon felt the chain give way and became the victim of gravity. He fell down on a catwalk, many levels beneath Morgalla. Body aching from the impact, he rose only to be met by Krug's sneering face, eyes burning.

"Oh, shit."

Dillon's hand was on the grip of his sword, but just as he was about to draw it, Krug's foot slammed hard to the center of his chest. He grunted, and the wind was knocked out of him as he tumbled back.

Morgalla got knocked on her back, and Widow struck in an instant. Morgalla blocked, and they were in a battle of strength. She looked down and saw Dillon was in trouble, but she had her own problems to deal with at the moment. She was able to kick Widow off her, and the women were back fighting, their skills sharp. The widow was clearly going for the kill, but like before, Morgalla hesitated in her strikes. She disarmed her opponent, but just as it seemed victory was hers, she felt a strike from behind.

Morgalla screamed and collapsed to her knees, fire being driving into her upper back. Widow grinned wickedly as she took her time getting to her feet. She looked up to one of the upper levels and spotted Deadra. The witch had something in her hand and was stabbing it.

Morgalla was desperately trying to reach behind her to find the blade in her back, but to her shock, there was none. It was then she saw Deadra too and realized that the witch was also attacking Morgalla with her magic.

Widow kicked her opponent, and she fell back. She proceeded to strike her with her fists and feet.

Dillon was not much better off. He was up, and his weapon was out. Krug appeared amuzed. The human blocked the first strike and was thrust back against the wall. Krug laughed. Dillon knew he was no match for the beast's strength, so he had to change his strategy in a hurry. He dodged the attacks although his body screamed in pain.

Morgalla was also fighting through her own pain as Widow laughed, tormenting her foe. Deadra removed the needle from the doll in her hand, and Morgalla's pain subsided. She connected with Widow again, knocking her opponent off balance. Both women struggled to their feet, taking weapons in hand again and continuing their duel.

Wulfric finally arrived, overlooking the scene with Mylo next to him. He had to put all of his weight on the wooden staff, but it still wasn't enough. Mylo had to help him. He looked below and saw the battle raging. He saw Deadra and knew what she was doing. Just as Morgalla got the upper hand again, ready to bring Hero down for the kill, she felt a sharp stab in her hand. She screamed and dropped Hero, staggering back. She looked up to Deadra who was hysterical, laughing.

Wulf pointed to Deadra, to the device she was using to torture Morgalla. "Go. I'll distract her. You get the doll."

The boy ran off as the wizard grabbed a handful of dust. He held out his hand, said an incantation and blew the powder from his palm.

Deadra felt the dust and debris around her swirl like a whirlwind. She dropped the doll and shielded her eyes, roaring in rage. She spoke an incantation and Wulf's spell dissipated. She saw Mylo, who had reached the doll, taking the needle out of its hand. Deadra hissed and shot a jinx at the young man who barely dodged it. He dropped the figurine and fell onto one of the catwalks.

Mylo jumped to his feet and ran for cover as the witch and wizard both exchanged spells. Explosions erupted throughout the mine. Wulf deflected an incoming spell and barely missed Morgalla and Widow by a hair, instead striking a group of demon soldiers who exploded in a shower of dust.

ELSEWHERE, MAKARO was enraged. He shouted profanities and orders at all his subordinates who cowered before him.

"Intruders? Intruders in *my* kingdom? I want them all found. Killed!" He slapped one of his subjects with the back of his hand, knocking the man down to the ground. "I want all of them dealt with."

As Makaro glanced around the area, he noticed not many demon soldiers were available to assist. He ordered the human reserves to deal with the problem. They did as he commanded.

All soldiers were on alert as they ran throughout the castle. They entered the chamber with the portal. It appeared as a normal stone wall until it came to life. They all gave a jump as the stone turned to liquid and ripples shot through it. A hooded figure emerged, and they took a step back. The woman removed her hood to reveal crimson skin, long white hair, and white horns. As most demons out and about, she was dressed with light armor and bladed weapons sheathed at her hips. Piercing golden eyes glared around the chamber at them.

"I'm looking for a girl," Delilah stated and held up her hand about the same height as Morgalla. "She's about yay high, has orange hair, horns, and hates short jokes."

The guards shrugged.

"What do we do?"

"You heard the master. She threatens us."

She drew weapons as they attacked but stood little chance against Delilah's skill. With a blade in either hand, she hacked and slashed at them. She left one alive on the floor, nursing a wound.

"Care to answer my question?"

"I…I do not know where she is."

"Then what good are you?"

Delilah's blade spoke, and the soldier went silent. She continued on her way up the steps. She looked back and saw the soldiers entering, scattering about on their mission. She left them for her mission was different. More of Makraka's soldiers were coming with her as they charged through the castle. It was only a small battalion, a hundred at best, but their ferocity and skill was more than enough. Any demons were given a chance to join them or die. Humans didn't get the choice. Delilah was merciless with her search, striking down whomever rose a blade to her.

Some put up a fight, and she used every combat skill she had including breathing fire. Makaro's minions went running, some of them engulfed in flames. She was all business, searching through the castle for her student.

THE BATTLE wasn't going well for anyone within the mines. Deputies of Freedom Ridge were overpowered by Makaro's demon soldiers. Deadra had the advantage of youth over the elderly Wulfric who was nursing a cut on his head. Morgalla was tiring against Widow, and Dillon was no match for Krug's raw power.

Morgalla's constant distractions gave her opponent an opening time and again, giving her a cut and hard strike constantly. The widow was able to disarm her, and she thrust her blade to Morgalla's neck. Morgalla was able to grasp her opponent's hands and they were in a contest of strength for the weapon.

Mylo made it to the lower catwalk where the doll had landed. Deadra, unfortunately, had also seen him, and she levitated down to the boy. He was frozen in terror. A simple spell raised the young man off his feet and sucked the air from his lungs. He gasped for breath, unable to even call for help. Morgalla noticed him.

"Your compassion makes you weak, Morgalla," The Widow said with a grin.

She kicked Widow off her and noticed her medallion, picked it up, and leapt down to the catwalk near Deadra. The witch dropped the boy and picked up the doll. Morgalla charged as fast as she could, but Deadra already had a knife in hand, stabbing the doll again.

Morgalla fell to her knees, dropping Hero from the lacerating pain in her abdomen. Deadra laughed as she twisted the blade, causing the demon girl to writhe in agony. Widow took her time coming down to the catwalk to her opponent. She stood above Morgalla, ready to bring her sword down.

"This is for Harek."

Mylo, with his breath restored, drew his own knife. The next thing Deadra felt was his blade being driven between two ribs. The witch's hands flew open, and she gasped. The doll had fallen from her grasp. In an instant, Mylo snatched the doll and removed the knife from it. By the time Widow had noticed what was going on, Morgalla was on her feet and had already struck the widow, Xia.

Morgalla winked at Mylo. "Thanks."

Delilah would be proud of the lack of mercy that Morgalla showed her adversary. Though she didn't have a blade in her hand, she was still a weapon. She used every move she knew: punches, kicks, head butt, and even a thumb to Widow's eye. She screamed and fell to her back.

Morgalla again spotted her medallion on the floor. With one foot, she flipped it up to her hand and Hero was back. It was time to end this. She looked back to Deadra, making sure Mylo was safe. The witch hissed at them both, and with a wave of her hands, the dust in the cavern swirled around her, and she disappeared. Morgalla realized Widow was up on her feet.

"Mylo, get your people out of here."

With a new furor in her heart, Morgalla used every skill she knew against her opponent. She looked around and saw on the upper levels that the Izari had arrived to assist the fight against Makaro's horde.

The women fought, Widow roared with every slash of her blade and Morgalla easily dodged or blocked her attacks. Thanks to her opponent's rage, Morgalla soon disarmed her and with a hard kick, the widow fell back hard. Morgalla stood with Hero ready for another attack. Xia looked up and saw that her sword lay behind her enemy, at first she looked concerned but then Morgalla did something she did not expect: she stepped back. Slowly she walked backwards until finally the sword lay between the women.

"Walk away." Morgalla said.

Xia, with the greatest of speed, snatched her weapon from the ground. "I'd rather die!"

"Have it your way."

The women continued their duel.

Dillon had an injured breastplate and bruised ribs, trying to dodge the attacks of the slave master. Both warriors were out for blood. Rage and hate fueled them in their battle. Krug had the upper hand in strength and skill, but his human opponent wasn't giving up. Just when he thought his sword might connect with his demon opponent, Dillon found nothing but air or the clash of metal.

Krug laughed with every swing against another sword. With a hard strike of his weapon, he disarmed Dillon. The human felt the hard punch to his face. He was on the ground, Krug standing over him, his sword ready to finish the sheriff off. Instead, the demon reached down and took him by the neck, lifting him with ease, his fangs on display through a wicked smile.

Dillon saw a chance. His enemy had made a mistake by getting in close. He wasn't near enough to his neck, though. He'd have to settle for any target. The demon didn't notice until it was too late. Dillon had drawn a knife from his boot and stabbed the monster on the side of his abdomen. The beast roared and dropped him. Dillon fought across the stone ground with his sword. He was up on his feet again and sought out an escape. There was none. The only way was through Krug who was fighting to remove the blade from his side.

The human roared as he charged at him. He did a spin and brought the blade up to the demon's face, only to have Krug step away. The edge cut the demon across his face and nose, his black blood spraying on the cave wall. With the back of his hand, Krug struck his opponent. Dillon tasted his own blood and fell to one knee. The demon tried again to remove the knife from his side, only to have Dillon reach up and drive it deeper. The beast roared, striking the human again.

The sheriff spat a mouthful of blood and one tooth. He saw double. His eye was swelling shut, and he looked up to see Krug bringing his sword down...again. Dillon, with all the strength he could muster, brought his weapon up and took the beast's hand. The monster roared as his severed hand turned to dust. He dropped his own blade with a clang. Dillon wasn't done, drawing back and impaling the demon. Even with metal through his body, Krug punched his opponent again, and Dillon went down, coughing up blood. Krug staggered back, nursing the wound.

Dillon knew Krug's wounds would soon be completely healed. When that happened, he'd be doomed. Krug pulled the steel from his body and tossed it aside. Dillon, his vision still blurry, caught a glimpse of his adversary's sword on the stone. He fought to get up, taking the blade in his hand and roared and charged at Krug. The two connected and fell over the side into the abyss. Due to their momentum, Dillon was also cast into the pit. With his own weapon embedded into his body, Krug's now lifeless form plummeted, nothing but a shower of dust into the pit far below.

He noticed dozens of chains hanging above and reached out to grasp one. When he swung, it came down hard on one of the catwalks.

Mylo went to the sheriff's aid as Morgalla continued to battle Widow. Dillon fought to his feet with Mylo's assistance.

"Get moving," he shouted.

Part of the catwalk was giving way and crumbling beneath them. Behind Widow, the catwalk fell away inch by inch as she stepped near the edge. Widow looked at her and started to panic.

Morgalla fought to keep her balance. The structure she was standing on was wobbling and breaking apart. She ran. Widow was close behind her. Morgalla jumped just in time as the catwalk crumbled completely. She grabbed the stone ledge. Widow was able to take hold of Morgalla's ankle.

Morgalla's fingers dug into the stone, clawing away and searching for anything to grip onto. She felt the weight of her adversary hanging on her leg. Finally, dangling from the rock, stable for the moment, Morgalla looked down to Widow.

Their eyes met, both unsure. After a moment of contemplation, Morgalla extended a hand to her. Widow didn't reach for it.

"Don't be a fool."

Widow fired hate at Morgalla with her eyes. Her fangs were exposed, and her face contorted in rage. The young woman let go.

"No!"

TWENTY-FOUR

BOOM

SILENCE FILLED the cavern as Widow plummeted into the darkness.

Morgalla felt herself slipping. She tried to claw her way up and felt the strength leaving her fingertips. Mylo's hand seemed to come out of nowhere, and he grabbed her wrist. Their bodies weary; both had to summon what strength they had left to pull her to safety. They embraced, glad to be alive.

The friends gawked at the ledge, staring out into the void.

"Why did she do that?" Mylo asked.

It took Morgalla a moment to find an answer. "I don't know."

Morgalla turned and realized that Dillon was barely conscious. What was left of his deputies had arrived and assisted him. The Izari were with them, along with Wulfric who had hobbled, all of his weight on his cane. Mylo went to him, concerned about a cut his the wizard's head.

"Don't worry about me," the old man said.

Just the sight of him with Mylo made Morgalla angry because she knew the truth.

Jel helped Dillon up. "It's all set, boss. They got the charges set and are ready to blow this place to kingdom come."

"Plan?" Morgalla asked. "What plan?"

Jel replied. "We got our people up top planting dynamite."

Sheriff Dillon groaned. "Where are they?"

"Three levels up."

"They should have been done by now. I'll go check on them."

Morgalla spoke up. "No, I'll do it."

Without any time for debate, the demon girl sprinted down the tunnels. She heard Dillon protest, shouting something, but she ignored it. She ran up three levels, past the dead bodies of Izari and deputies from Freedom Ridge. She stopped and concentrated, searching out any souls who might be in the area. Were any deputies still alive?

Finally, she sensed the heat of battle down one tunnel and sprinted in that direction. The closer she got to them, the louder the shouting became. There were a couple of dead humans. Two others were fighting off a group of demons. With surprise as a weapon, Morgalla charged into the fray, cutting down two with ease. The other two put up a fight, but they were confused as to why a demon was coming to the aide of humans. Soon the two were down, but the humans were in just as bad shape. She checked on one who had clutched a wound, falling over, his body now just a husk with no soul.

Morgalla helped the other human who was coughing up blood. He clutched his wound and fought to get the words out.

"L...lever..."

He pointed to something, and Morgalla saw a strange device. It was a small box with thin pieces of metal that stretched out down the cavern where she had just come from. There was a handle on it. She picked up the device, examining it.

"What is it?"

"Twist...the lever."

The human coughed out his final words. She sensed the intensity of the human's soul, how important the device was and that his mission, whatever it might have been, had to be accomplished.

Having no idea what its function was, Morgalla followed his instructions.

She grew concerned when she heard a booming below throughout the mine. The stone shook with dust and debris falling from the ceiling. With no way to help any of the humans who had fallen, she ran back up the tunnel, retracing her steps.

Throughout the fight, the deputies of Freedom Ridge had set up various human inventions; they had devices whose purpose was to bring great destruction through fiery explosions. She felt the ground shake as one by one the objects exploded. She turned a corner only to be face to face with one of them. Morgalla was greeted by what appeared to be a bundle of red sticks with the word *dynamite* written on one of them.

Her eyes grew wide, and the air was drawn from her lungs in terror. She ran and leapt off the stone ledge, a wall of fire trailing behind her. She cried out of terror as the thundering boom came from above just as she fell into the mine.

Catwalks and bridges started to collapse, crashing down into the mine. The pulley system also was coming undone. Morgalla grabbed for anything within reach but everything was falling down around her, all of them victims of gravity.

Finally, one chain remained stable enough to keep her from plummeting to her doom. She was still helpless due to the momentum as rock and debris thundered down above her. She swung into one of the openings that led to a tunnel and slid across the rock and rolled out of control until she struck the wall.

The entire mine seemed to shake from the tremendous booming from the levels above. Morgalla fought through the pain and clawed her way up the wall to her feet. She knew that had she stayed, she'd be dead.

Morgalla couldn't see where she was going, coughing through the smoke but saw a light up ahead and found herself inside the chamber with the portal…and six demon soldiers.

There was no time to be shocked or scared as she felt a slap on her face and she was pulled by her hair into the center of the chamber. The soldiers all drew weapons. Morgalla looked around for an ally. Her adversaries all chuckled at her fear.

"Excuse me."

All eyes turned to the sound of a woman's voice. Morgalla's face lit up, and her heart was overjoyed to see the crimson-skin and golden eyes of her friend Delilah.

"That would be a very big mistake," Delilah announced.

The six attacked. One was dealt with Delilah's speed and efficiency. She leapt into the center. Now back to back, the women fought their foes. Morgalla sensed the overwhelming joy of the battle emanating from Delilah's soul, or maybe it was because she was glad to see her. Surely not, the sentiment had never been one of Delilah's virtues.

While Morgalla was more of a surgeon when it came to the use of Hero, Delilah was the brawler, hacking and slashing away at her enemies. The two together seemed unstoppable.

Finally, the remaining five were able to separate the women, but they were no less deadly. She found herself battling three of the demons. Delilah was impressed by the skills of Makaro's minions as they struck and cut here and there. Two fell to her skills, but the third was a massive beast wielding a hammer.

Delilah felt the hard stone at her back as she was struck. She saw the monster coming at her, already in full swing with his hammer. Morgalla was up and charged slashomg with Hero across the back of his legs. He roared but only for a brief moment. His voice was cut silent by the rebound of Delilah's weapon.

Both women breathed fire from their lungs; they were surrounded by the dust and muck of their dead enemies. All was silent.

"Good to see you not hesitating," Delilah said.

A smile broke through Morgalla's fatigue. "How did you find
me?"

"Persistence." Delilah rose and took her by the arm. "Child, we
must leave."

"No, there's something I need to do first."

Delilah's clawed hand grasped her student's arm tighter. "Don't
be a fool. After all I went through to find you?"

"Trust me, I'll meet you in the courtyard."

Delilah found something different in her student, a new form of
confidence that wasn't there before. She had always asked Morgalla
to trust her, maybe it was time to do the same.

Morgalla fought her way out of Delilah's grasp, and she ran back
down into the ruins of the mines. Delilah followed but stopped at the
entrance.

"Child!" she shouted.

The portal, throughout the fight had been nothing but a stone
wall, came to life again and figures emerged. Demon soldiers under Makraka's command charged with weapons drawn. Delilah did
not move, but she clutched her weapons tight. The general himself
emerged, riding atop a winged dracon.

Makraka surveyed the area and saw what was left of Makaro's
minions around him. He commanded his troops to fan out. They ran
past Delilah up the steps leading to the castle.

Makraka squinted to Delilah. "What are you doing here, woman?"

"What are *you* doing here?"

"None of your concern. Stay out of my way, and we will have no
problems."

"I'm just here for my student."

"I don't give a damn about your child."

Makraka rode past her and up to the castle.

Makaro was in a quandary about the goings on in his domain. His stand faltered as his castle shook. He watched as the rest of his servants grew concerned. What filth had dared to soil his kingdom?

Only his most loyal underlings remained around him, human and demon. He shouted orders in a stammering voice, but it was clear that the mighty Lord of Dracon Peak was cracking.

"My lord."

"What?" he screamed.

"We have activity at the portal."

Makaro's attitude changed in an instant. "W…what? What kind of activity?"

Out of nowhere a winged beast arrived and landed, knocking some subordinates out of the way and others to the ground. Makraka sat on the saddle, the leather reigns in his clawed hands. His stone-like face displayed an expression of disgust. His yellow eyes, the smallest feature on his face, burned to the Lord of Dracon Peak who had fallen on his back. The beast snarled, and Makaro fell to the ground.

Makraka's grip tightened on the leather straps as his winged ride snarled.

Makraka came down, his boots made a loud thump. He looked around but didn't focus on Makaro.

"M…Makraka. So good to see you again. You honor us with your presence. It's always nice to have a…"

Makraka growled at him. "Silence." After a brief inspection at the foreboding castle carved from the mountain, his tone changed. "An impressive little empire you have made for yourself here."

"All for the glory of the Dark One."

"Still the sniveling little shit sack, Makaro?"

"Father thought I was worthy of this kingdom."

Makraka's reply was immediate with the back of his hand. "You besmirch our father's great name. He knew you were a coward, which was why he turned you into a third-rate manager of a mine."

"I have provided the means for your conquests, brother."

"What are you hiding, Makaro?"

Lord Makaro scurried on the ground away from his brother "I… nothing."

"Yes…yes you are," Makraka said as he stepped slowly forward, unsheathing his sword. "Were you hoping you would never be discovered? Shall I give you a reminder of whom you still serve after all these years?"

Makaro held up his trembling hands. His eyes then met Bruk, his loyal bodyguard.

"Bruk. Defend your master."

Everyone's attention was on the bodyguard who stood silent and still for a moment. He drew his sword slowly. Makraka was motionless though curious about his intentions. Bruk stepped forward but pointed the blade at Makaro who cowered, shielding his head.

Makraka touched Bruk's shoulder. "I appreciate your hatred of him, but if anyone is going to kill this worthless pile of dracon shit, it should be family."

The faux lord's jaw dropped as the souls all around him, including those who'd served him for years, all erupted in joy.

It took only a moment for Makraka's blade to bring an end to the reign of Dracon Peak. The general cleaned his blade and noticed the few humans around who were all skeptical about his next move.

Giles stepped forward. "My lord, I speak for everyone here when I say *welcome*. We will all be more than happy to continue our services during your reign…"

Makraka wasn't looking at the human but focused on Bruk. He came up with a test of his loyalty. "Kill this worm."

With no hesitation, Bruk drew his blade. Giles barely had time to look shocked. Makraka nodded.

"A good start." The general said. "Now slaughter all humans in this castle."

Bruk did not waver for an instant. Screams filled the castle.

Delilah arrived, not bothered by the slaughter. The general's minions, a dozen at least in attendance, beamed some hateful glares back at her. One of them smirked, daring her to try something.

Makraka, joined by his entourage, entered the mines and followed the trail back where they had entered. He wanted to see the operation. They arrived at the portal chamber, and the general peered into the nothingness before him.

He stepped through the smoke and witnessed nothing but calm, quiet and dark. No souls were present from the darkness before him. He turned his back but then stopped.

"What is it, my lord?" one of his subordinates asked.

Makraka looked over his shoulder to the void before him. "There's someone alive in there. Go...find and kill them."

TWENTY-FIVE

THE MOURNFUL CRY OF CROWS

ALMOST ALL of the humans were out of the mines, thanks to the secret exit. Dillon groaned through his injuries, insisting that everyone leave before him. Mylo was one of the last, but he hesitated, taking one last check of the mines.

"Boy, come on." Dillon ordered.

"We can't leave without Morgalla. She risked herself to help us, we should do the same for her!"

Dillon walked up to him and grabbed him by the arm. "You go back in there, and you're gonna die. Get out of here, I'll go find her."

They both looked to the tunnel and heard someone coming and fast. They were relieved to see the demon girl come round the corner. She was out of breath, and her body was screaming in pain. She collapsed to her knees, and human companions came to her aid.

"You all right?" Mylo asked.

"I will be. We all need to get out of here, now."

Soon the group had gathered out in the woods. Smoke billowed out of the hole and they coughed, fighting for precious air. They caught their breath and soon a feeling of calm befell them.

"Morgalla, the prism."

Hearing Wulf's reminder snapped Morgalla back to the reality of the situation.

Of course, the prism. Why it's just over….no wait, it's over….

She stood in a clearing of trees, a finger tapping her chin. She turned and saw everyone watching her.

"Did you forget where that damn thing is?" Dillon asked.

Morgalla replied with a blank stare and wide eyes. "Um…no."

She felt their annoyance and patience growing thin and had to remember where she'd buried it and fast. Morgalla remembered the insect hive and sought it out. It didn't take her long to find it.

Bingo. That means the rock is…

She spun around and found the secret spot. Her jaw dropped. The rock had been moved and a massive, empty hole was in its place.

"Oh, no."

"What is it?" Dillon asked.

The demon girl was at a loss for words. She had let them down and didn't know what to do next. Her mouth opened, but she remained silent.

A light breeze caused Morgalla to check her surroundings. Their eyes all focused on the sky and watched the sun as it was shrouded by clouds that rolled in. It was all too fast for it to be natural. The wind picked up in speed, and many in the group found it difficult to remain standing.

Wulfric whispered one word, "Deadra."

Sure enough…his fears were justified as they all turned and saw a figure moving through the trees. One by one the trees came down, cracking and crashing to the forest floor. The witch floated on air, high above the ground, slowly making her way towards them. The look in her eyes was that of a creature possessed with the desire to kill.

Morgalla looked and saw the bag that the witch kept over her shoulder. At the very top, the prism was peeking out. Her eyes widened and hope returned, but they still had to get the gem away from her.

"Sheriff, get your people out of here," Wulfric commanded as he hobbled forward. "She'll kill you. She'll kill us all."

Dillon ignored him. Instead, he shouted a command, "Shoot her!"

The sky filled with deafening booms as they used their weapons to no avail on her. Deadra held up her hands, and the bullets struck an invisible shield in front of her. Her cackles filled the air.

Deadra raised her hands, and the roots of the trees burst from the ground. They wrapped around her foes and dragged them into the earth.

Wulfric spoke a counter-curse, and everyone was freed from her spell. The wizard, using his voice and hands, shot spells at his opponent who deflected them with ease. He was tiring, and with an explosion before him, was knocked to the ground.

The others should have heeded Wulfric's warning to run. Deadra clawed at the air, snarling and hissing as she spoke her incantations. Her spells made some people's bodies fly apart like leaves in the wind. Their screams echoed as they drifted away.

Deadra saw Mylo and grinned, the boy's knife still fresh on her mind. She shot a jinx at him. He was petrified with terror. Dillon pounced, grabbing Mylo. The two of them crashed to the ground, avoiding the spell by inches.

Morgalla ran around the large oaks and pines, dodging the attacks from their foe. She saw black blood dripping to the earth below from her wound. It burned nearby foliage like acid.

Morgalla located some knives and blades from the surrounding dead. She waited for her chance. She jumped from behind a tree and flung a weapon to Deadra. The witch sensed the impending attack before it happened and swatted the blade away. Morgalla was running out of cover as she ducked behind another tree as a shield. Twice more she hurled knives at Deadra, to no avail. The witch was too powerful.

All around them the trees were destroyed and crumbled to the ground. Dillon had pulled Mylo to his feet, commanding the boy to run for his life.

Deadra stepped up her attack, raising her hands to the sky. Dark clouds swirled high above, and flashes of light appeared within. The rumbling built louder and louder until it shook the ground. Surely everyone at the castle and miles away in the town could see and feel it.

The wizard, despite his old, aching bones, got up to his knees and started his counter-curse. Deadra summoned lightning, but her opponent's spell was able to shield the area, deflecting the blast. A strike hit the side of the mountain with such intensity that the inhabitants all fell to the ground.

With a blast large enough to damage the foundation, soon tremors and cracks broke through the stone of Dracon Peak.

Deadra didn't stop her attacks. By then, all of her energy had focused on Wulfric who could only deflect her advances once more, driving the bolt of lightning up and through the castle itself.

"Deadra," he cried. "Do not betray your own people again."

She hissed and spat a mouthful of blood at his feet. The ground sizzled.

"I have failed you as a teacher, Deadra. But do not make your own people suffer."

Morgalla knew this had to end soon. There was only one tree left standing that was close to Deadra. The demon climbed it and ventured out on a limb. The tree shook, its own foundation weak and ready to crumble. Deadra had focused all her attention on the wizard, her hands outstretched and ready to finish Wulfric. His strength had left him.

Morgalla scrambled along the limb as it was collapsing. She leapt. Summoning Hero to her hand, she came down on top of the witch. Deadra noticed her too late, a second after the blade had cleaved through her flesh.

Both women fell to the ground. Deadra screamed and convulsed. Morgalla scrambled away when she saw the still twitching hands on a bed of leaves. Deadra continued to shout incantations in a foreign language, but nothing happened. Morgalla stood, her hand clutched tightly around her sword. The wind increased all around them as she approached her defeated adversary who cast a defiant gaze at the demon girl.

Morgalla was conflicted as she gaped at the helpless creature before her.

Wulfric shouted over the brewing storm, "She's too dangerous. Kill her!"

The demon hesitated but only for a moment. Morgalla's time on this planet had been educational. She realized Delilah was right, and sometimes harsh violence was needed. Morgalla looked into Deadra's bloodshot eyes. She had hoped that maybe there would be some remourse, some hope that there was something more than a monster there. Her senses knew better. Morgalla had, like all demons, the gift of seeing into someone's heart, to see their very soul. Morgalla could see nothing but a black pit where Deadra's soul was, lost long ago to evil magic.

With a lightning strike, Hero answered the call, and Deadra went silent.

In an instant the air was still, the clouds had dissipated, and the sun returned. Crows flew in lazy circles, swirling in the bright blue sky. They let out mournful cries for their mistress who was gone.

Morgalla recovered the Prism of Akubar from Deadra's bag and held the diamond-like gem which gleamed with magic in her palm. She wrapped it in her cloak. She turned to Wulfric. He was on his knees, his body heaving. Dillon staggered onto the scene, an expression of relief on his face. Mylo hurried to join them.

Dillon looked to Mylo. "I told you to run." He said.

Morgalla felt the relief from the souls around her build into a flame of joy. With their enemies defeated and the prism in their possession, there was a ray of hope for their future.

Their joy was short-lived as a tremendous crack echoed through the valley, shaking them all. Dillon and Morgalla both stared up at the mountain above them and looked to each other.

"Uh-oh."

They moved as fast as they could, helping the injured and weak as the troupe ran from the mountain.

Elsewhere at the castle, Delilah, Makraka, and his minions all felt the tremor as well. The ground beneath them started to list to one side.

"It is time we leave," the general ordered.

Delilah took to the sky.

There was no argument as the group of demons scampered, running to anywhere they might feel safe. The mountain shook as it started to rip apart due to Deadra's attacks, taking the castle with it. People in the town of Freedom Ridge looked on as the castle on the horizon crumbled.

Makraka and the rest of the demons made it just in time. They peeked over a ledge of stone as Dracon Peak crumbled, taking with it the magnificent castle of the faux Lord Makaro.

The crash shook the ground for miles. It sent up a cloud of dirt and debris that filled the valley and covered all creatures in dust and filth.

Makraka stood with his soldiers atop the ledge. When the dust had cleared, the new side of what was left of the mountain was exposed to them. On the side of the cliff, nothing was left of the mines. The portal to Hell was bathed in sunlight on the sheer, new precipice.

TWENTY-SIX

A WELCOME SIGHT

FOR MORGALLA and her friends, Freedom Ridge was a pleasant sight. The sun even came out to say hello and bathe the town in brilliant, golden light. A small band of Dillon's deputies, the Izari, and Morgalla, all entered the town. The explosion of the mines had awakened the entire populace, and they came out to see what happened, greeting their liberators.

The mayor made her way through the crowd of people and ran up to the sheriff.

"What's happened?" she asked.

"Makaro's mining operation is done for, ma'am."

Many people seemed shocked at the news.

"What? He'll surely seek revenge."

"I don't think so, Madam Mayor. We got something that will help."

They all gathered in the town square by the massive eagle statue. The sheriff motioned for Morgalla to step forward. She unveiled the gem from her cloak. All eyes looked in wonder at the jewel. Morgalla saw the mouth of the massive bird in the square, it seemed like a good a spot as any. Placing it in the mouth of the bird, The Prism of Freedom Ridge had found its final resting place.

Everyone gasped when they saw that the girl, normally with raspberry hair, had the face of a demon now. Sounds of disapproval erupted from the crowd, and Morgalla felt the tidal wave envelope her heart. She closed her eyes and turned around. Her eyes, now lilac, saw the look of horror on most of the faces before her. One of them pointed and said, "She's one of them."

"Wait," Dillon shouted. "She helped get the gem. She and the Izari were instrumental in saving us all."

The people were not convinced, shouting still. Morgalla couldn't look at them, only staring at the ground.

"She destroyed the mine and also got rid of the witch for us!"

Dillon's words only calmed the mob down a little. Morgalla glanced up and saw the mayor herself, fear apparent in the woman's eyes. She looked away.

A voice called out, "Wait."

As the crowd died down, a figure emerged. It was Dottie.

Morgalla felt a knot in her throat and swallowed hard. She seemed terrified as the old woman approached her. Morgalla fought for the strength to keep eye contact. Dottie, on the other hand, never stopped looking at the young woman.

The demon could feel all the emotions, a whirlwind within the woman's heart. Every feeling was there including anger, fear, and love. But as the sensations swam about, one finally made its way to the surface and won the battle.

Dottie took Morgalla's hand. The demon girl stared up and saw the hurt in Dottie's eyes, but she also felt the love in her heart.

Dottie turned to the crowd. "We will all face the same cold winter and the same dangers. Family is more than just blood, but it's in a person's heart."

Verbal approval whispered through the crowd, but Morgalla knew that most people didn't like the idea of her living there.

"She can't."

Wulfric hobbled forward.

"What do you mean?" Dillon asked.

"The prism was designed to not only shield us from demons but also work against them."

His words hit Morgalla in the stomach. "Wait…that's why my real face was revealed when I touched it?"

"It will never shield you because you are a demon."

Morgalla looked angry, and she stepped up to the elderly man. "You knew this, didn't you? From the very beginning?"

"Don't pretend you didn't search the gem out of your own sense of goodwill. You knew you could use it, too."

Morgalla's lip clenched as her hands flexed into fists.

Wulfric's face was blank. "If you wish to exact revenge against this old man, I won't stop you. I'm not long for this world. My people will be free and safe, and that's what's most important."

Dillon saw the expression on Morgalla's face and was ready to stop her from making a big mistake. He didn't need to. She wanted to yell at him at least, tell him what she really thought of him. In the past, speaking her mind gave her something in return; whether she be standing up for herself, or using her words as a weapon, or just because it felt good. This time, however, she had nothing to gain by calling him a name or stating any fact.

"That's not fair," Dottie said with a dropped jaw. "Surely you gotta be able to do something."

Wulfric shook his head. "I cannot. It is magic far older than I, made eons ago by wizardry that is beyond me."

"Makaro could never have used the gem," Morgalla said. "It would not have shielded him."

Wulf nodded. "That is correct."

Morgalla stepped even closer and everyone grew concerned about what her next action might be. Dillon inched closer. He thought for a moment that he might have to stop her. Wulfric was still and silent. The old man's soul was prepared for death, but he didn't show a bit of fear.

Morgalla's lip quivered for just a moment, and her eyes squinted. After a couple of deep breaths, she turned her back to him. The crowd parted as she strolled away. The old man seemed confused as she stormed off. His old bones creaked as he took a seat on the stone next to the statue. He drew a long sigh.

A man called out, "Three cheers for Sheriff Dillon."

Hip hip, hooray. Hip hip, hooray. Hip, hip hooray.

Dillon did not join in on their celebration. He focused on the old wizard, limping towards him.

"I'm shocked she didn't kill you," the sheriff said.

"So am I."

Morgalla was surrounded by the overflowing joy that the people of Freedom Ridge and their new Izari neighbors were free. They cheered, sang, danced, and embraced. The demon girl's heart ached, and she felt a lump in her throat. Her eyes were red.

"Morgalla, wait."

She turned and saw Mylo running her direction. The expression in his eyes was that of utter disappointment.

"You're not leaving, are you?"

"There's nothing for me here, Mylo."

"It's just not fair."

Morgalla sighed. "Life is seldom fair."

The boy's mouth hung open, but no words came out. Among a sea of happiness throughout the town, he was one of the few people who wasn't celebrating. Morgalla reached into her pocket and found one of the guava seeds from Usteron she had been keeping. She had forgotten they were there. She handed one to the young man. He studied it curiously.

She smiled at him. "They're called guavas, and they're yummy."

He didn't smile at the gift. Morgalla noticed he still had his dull blade at his side. She reached down to her boot and took her knife, handing it to him. It was a demon blade of black steel, the craftsmanship perfect. It seemed just the right size for Mylo.

"Wait, you'll need this more than me." He said.

"Oh, don't worry. I still got mine close by." She replied with a pat on her medallion. "Besides, there's no shortage of weapons where I'm go…"

Morgalla didn't finish her thought, having seen Dottie come walking up. The old woman placed her hand on the Morgalla's shoulder. Morgalla saw the tears in the woman's eyes.

"I…thank you for everything you did for me." Morgalla said.

"It was my pleasure. Please promise me you'll be careful, wherever you go."

"Always."

She spun on her heel and started to walk away, sensing the eyes of four people behind her.

Don't turn around…

She ignored her own good sense. With her throat aching still, she turned and saw Mylo, Dottie, Dillon, and even Sera, all watching her. Pain radiated in their hearts. Even Dillon's wife was conflicted. There were no smiles on their faces, but their eyes told Morgalla what they were feeling. Her own bloodshot ones burned with the tears clawing to be released.

Morgalla winked before turning and walking away. She heard the commotion of the town behind her. All the people in celebration. For the first time in their lives, there was hope that they were truly free of the demon scourge and the Dark One's minions.

She continued up the dirt road, her eyes set on the mountains in the distance. As soon as she stepped through the gates of the town, the voices were silent, and the souls she'd empathically felt were gone. Morgalla stopped and turned around again. Where people had been just an instant ago, now were there none. The buildings had disappeared, replaced by wilderness. No signs a town had ever been there.

She gritted her teeth and clenched her jaw. Just in time, too, for she felt the coming presence of demons in the distance. They were getting closer by the second. She had little time to put on the armor of hate over her heart.

Makraka's orders had been simple. "Search everywhere and kill anything you see." He wasn't convinced the area was secure, so he wanted it sterilized. Soldiers swarmed the surrounding woods and finally came across a road. Following until it ended, they approached a section of wilderness. It didn't seem remarkable in any way, other than the ground being unusually flat. Among the trees and rocks, the soldiers found a single figure, someone they did not expect: a small demon girl.

Her orange skin and hair made her stand out among the trees and rocks. Makraka himself stepped forward and met the young demon woman, her hair mussed, her face and clothes dirty.

"*You,*" he said.

Morgalla knew with great ease he was not happy to see her. His massive form approached, his boots thumping as he walked, his clawed hand on the base of his sword. With demons surrounding her, all looking down, Morgalla remained still.

"Did you see my worthless brother, child?"

Morgalla's eyebrows raised for a moment.

"Yes," Makraka answered his own question. "He and his kingdom are no more. But what I wonder is how you have emerged from this apparently unscathed."

Morgalla's eyes were tired, but she concentrated on how much she hated that she could not stay in this world. The annoyance and anger kept her shielded.

"I haven't exactly come out without a scratch," Morgalla said with a fatigued voice. "There is nothing left here for you, General."

His eyes squinted, and he stepped closer, his hand gripping the sword. Morgalla remained still.

Out of the corner of her eye, she noticed a figure fly out of the sky and land on one of the large rocks nearby.

Makraka frowned and turned his back to her. "Come."

His soldiers obeyed and followed. Soon there were just two women in the forest. For the rest of her life, Morgalla would wonder just why Makraka spared her. Delilah's heart was overjoyed at the sight of her apprentice. She took the child, arms and wings wrapping around her. Morgalla was shocked at her teacher's reaction.

Delilah released her and came to her senses.

Morgalla noticed a strange look in her eye. "Are you…happy to see me?" she asked.

Delilah's lip clenched. "I am…pleased to know you are still alive."

Morgalla smirked at her.

"Come," Delilah said. "Time to go home."

Morgalla remained behind for a moment, taking a glance where Freedom Ridge had been. She waved to the wilderness. Delilah noticed what she was doing, and a hint of confusion showed on her face.

"What are you doing?"

Morgalla replied with a frown, "Nothing. Let's go."

Delilah saw her student's filthy appearance and noted the fresh scars on her soul.

"What the hell happened to you?"

"It's a long story."

"I want to hear it."

As her apprentice walked away, Delilah did a double-take towards the valley. There was nothing there but rocks and trees.

They made their way through the wilderness where the portal to Hell was located…the portal to home.

TWENTY-SEVEN

SOMEONE TO TALK TO

MORGALLA'S WORLD seemed both bigger and smaller than before. She returned to Hell in a foul mood, seeming like a caged animal, ready to strike at the first demon who looked at her the wrong way.

Delilah was on the edge of her seat as Morgalla told about her adventures.

"A witch, hmm? Please tell me you kept a trophy."

"There wasn't time," Morgalla replied with a melancholy tone.

Before they made their way to the town, there was something Delilah had to know. She touched Morgalla's shoulder to stop her.

"Child, your story is one for the ages, and I'm sure you'll entertain many at the next party, but why do I feel you're holding something back?"

Morgalla didn't answer, only watching her mistress with eyes half-open. She knew she couldn't keep anything from her. Any incomplete thoughts would be seen as a lie.

Delilah's eyebrow raised. "You're only telling me part of the story. You fought Makaro and his army? His witch? That's not all of it..."

Morgalla interrupted, "Thank you."

Delilah looked confused. "For what?"

"For…for everything. For everything you've done for me until now. And for coming for me."

"I was ordered to, child."

Morgalla smirked, having caught her teacher in a lie. "You came looking for me because you wanted to." Morgalla's face went serious. She had more to say. "I also know why we left Usteron. The real reason."

"And what might that be?"

"Sure, it wasn't safe for us, but that's because the demon invasion had failed and finally drove them off their world."

Delilah said nothing.

"Demons conquer or kill everything they see. The Usta were completely within their right to kick demons out of their land."

"You mean our kind, right, child?"

"I have little to nothing in common with them."

"They would not have seen it that way, and you know it…regardless of your pacifist attitude." Delilah then gestured to the town. "After you."

Delilah didn't have to tell Morgalla to put on a brave face when they strolled back into town. Her student was so angry with the day's happenings that the ball of fury within her heart was real, tangible.

Some heads turned as the duo passed. Morgalla's torn clothing and dirty appearance had drawn their attention. Most demons just gave a fleeting glance, but soon both women heard a snicker that built into a laugh. They looked and saw Vex, the demon Morgalla had met at the doxer races, leaning on a post. He took a huge bite out of a black apple. Both women stood motionless as the male stepped forward.

"Delilah, does your student even know how to bathe herself?"

Other demons laughed at his words. They were clearly part of his entourage.

"She looks like a hog," one of them said and leaned in to sniff the air. "Smells like one too."

Joyous laughter filled the square as four demons took pleasure at Morgalla's expense. The young demon looked up to the much taller figure whose bellowing laughter carried through the air. Others were joining in. Somehow it wounded her, but Morgalla thought of something else: Much like Deadra, she could see into this monster's heart. He wanted to wound her and possibly more. She could tell the void of where a heart should be, without mercy, compassion, or remourse. There was nothing there to admire.

Delilah glared at them all, her claws wrapped around the grip of her sword, ready to make their leader pay. Her student beat her to the punch as Hero was unsheathed. With lightning speed, the blade cut through the air and quieted the demon who'd made a comment.

Silence. Everyone, including Delilah, were shocked about what had just transpired. Morgalla was even surprised at how easily she'd taken the beast's life, but she knew that little, if anything, was lost. She didn't show any emotion as the demon's body fell and crumbled to dust. She only gripped her blade tight, eyes blazing at the young Vex who'd returned an intense look. Both women were ready to defend an onslaught, but nothing came. Though rage burned within the trio of aggressors, they made no moves.

Delilah broke the silence. "Come."

The two walked away from the scene. Morgalla knew she had possibly added an enemy that day. Delilah swelled with pride, for she realized her apprentice had gained more. All those demons had seen how ruthless Morgalla had cut down the smart-mouthed one and for only making a disrespectful comment. She had shown no fear.

DELILAH RECEIVED a piece of bad news soon after that: Zorach himself had requested an audience.

She was sure the demon lord was enraged over something. She reported to his chamber within his castle. The massive doors unlocked with an echoing metallic sound. It all made Delilah jump.

Get a grip...

As the doors opened, she felt a rush of chilling air envelop her. She saw her breath through her own trembling lips. The lights dimmed. From the chamber, a shadow emerged that flowed around the room, filling every corner and crevasse. A form took shape, and Delilah noted broad shoulders. From them, a horned helmet appeared. Though featureless, she sensed the eyes upon her. A pair of black gauntlets appeared at the creature's sides.

Delilah's heart raced. The beast spoke softly.

"Delilah..."

She bowed her head. "My lord, please forgive me for bringing Morgalla here. I understand my mandate..."

"Silence. I am aware of the conditions on other worlds and the need to bring her here. You have taught her skills that will ensure her survival. For the time being, that is all that is needed."

"She is to explore an alien world."

"I know of the world she is to indulge."

Delilah seemed confused. "My lord?"

"She will be safe in this world. Her skills will see to that."

"I...do not understand."

"Morgalla is essential to my plans. For now, where she is will have to do. The world she will explore is dangerous, but it is a human world. No human can pose a threat. Her skills will protect her."

Delilah bowed. "Yes, my lord. But what shall we do for the time being?"

The beast retreated into its chamber, and soon the light returned to the room. "Keep your eye on Morgalla, nothing more. I have plans for my daughter, but it will take time. The Dark One's demands are great, but we must obey."

"What is in store, my lord?"

"A great cost in life."

The doors shut and Delilah felt the room return to a normal temperature. Her body still shook.

MORGALLA SLEPT soundly for the first time since she could remember. It was more out of exhaustion if anything. She liked her new bed in her new home, and the mattress conformed to her body.

"Morgalla…Morgalla, are you there?"

She woke and rose from the comfortable bed. Much to her surprise, Wulfric was standing in the room.

"Creep factor is at about level twenty right now, pal."

The old man shrugged. "Really the only way I could communicate with you."

"How'd you get in here, anyway?"

"I'm a wizard. Though I think the Dark One might just start to sense my presence, so I gotta make this brief. There are plenty of worlds, Morgalla, and humans are on many of them. You have the gift of invisibility among us, use it."

"Others wanted me to kill." Morgalla said with a sound of regret.

"It's never weak to value life."

"Value life? Like Mylo's? Maybe other people's lives who you affected in all your years?"

The old man shook his head. "Look, I did what I did because I had to. I'm not proud, and I'll pay for it when I face God. I'd like to point out that you just might have to do some things in your life you won't be proud of. I got a guilty conscience, and you're part of that. I wanted to try and put things right."

"That's why you're here?"

"To give advice, yes."

Morgalla crossed her arms, a frown on her face.

"I hope you know the joy of being part of a much larger community, Morgalla. To be part of something much bigger than yourself."

He leaned in to say something more serious as evidenced by his expression. "Demons are dying, Morgalla. Some of them must know it, but their culture is self-destructive and arrogant. The sooner you abandon them, the better off you'll be."

"If that's true, then I have nothing to fear from them, neither does anyone else."

"That's where you're wrong, girl. You know what they say about a wounded animal. I fear that Hell will try to take as many innocent lives down with them as possible."

Morgalla soaked in what he was saying, feeling the significance of his words. "Thank you."

"Oh, and I know you don't have many people to talk to around here, so I left something on your desk that will help."

"I don't have a desk."

"Now you do. You'll see it when you wake up."

"Wake up?"

"This is all a dream, Morgalla. But when you wake, I hope you find your gifts useful."

"Sure. Any other bits of information that you wanted to tell me?"

"Why, yes. I happen to know precisely which world you should look for, one where you will be hidden and free."

Morgalla woke the next morning reeling from the dream, or so she *thought* was a dream. She climbed out of bed and realized she was alone. She also noticed two holes left on her pillow. *Oh, the horns.*

"Aw, damn."

Though annoyed, she was surprised to see an old, small desk. On top of it was a large book. She approached it, running her hands over the dark red leather. There was a note which read:

Just say Dear Diary.

"Dear Diary?"

The front cover opened, and there was a small burst of flame on the page. She looked and watched the words she'd said written in what appeared to be black ink.

"Wow."

There was another burst of flame and the word Wow appeared.

Yeah, that's cute.

THE NEXT few days were uneventful for both Morgalla and Delilah, but their lives didn't stay that way. Soon Morgalla's reputation went from being a cowardly child to as fierce a warrior as anyone else in Hell. She was approached by some, they had seen potential in her skill and daring. She gave the same answer every time: "I'll think about it."

She needed friends, allies. She had Delilah but being part of an army felt safer somehow. Then finally a group of demons approached her with another kind of offer, one about exploring different worlds, knowing the people there, and reporting back to them. They selected her out of her size, her surgical-like skill with a blade. They thought she would be invisible. With Wulfric's words of wisdom still ringing in her head, thoughts boiled over. The demons thought they would use her, but she could also use them.

They mentioned some sort of test that she would have to perform in order to achieve this great position. All Morgalla had to do was show them her human disguise. They smiled.

When Delilah found out about her student's new position, she was livid.

"Where did I go wrong?" she asked Morgalla.

TWENTY-EIGHT

BURY YOUR FEELINGS

DAYS HAD passed, and it seemed Morgalla might slink past anyone's eye. She spent little to no time with other demons. Finally, Delilah had to come looking for her and found her in her room.

Morgalla knew whose soul it was from the other side of the door. Delilah was the only one who ever came visiting, but thankfully Morgalla never opened the door to anyone else.

"And where have you been?" Delilah inquired.

Morgalla held up the file given to her by her superiors. "My job."

Delilah rolled her eyes. Her soul fumed. "And what piece of the crap world are they having you explore?"

Morgalla had the file in her hand and showed it to Delilah. She rolled her eyes, and a laugh echoed in the room.

"What is it?" Morgalla asked. "Something wrong with this world?"

"No, nothing is wrong with it, if you like a planet infested with humans. And I do mean *infested*." Delilah took a moment to massage her temples. "Look, I don't know what your true intentions are with this world…"

"I don't know what you're talking about."

"Please. No one knows you better than I. If you have any sense, you will do what you are told."

Morgalla turned her back. "All mighty Zorach? Making all in his sight kneel before him?"

"You speak so ill of your own father?"

Morgalla spun around. She stared at Delilah whose expression was blank. No deception from her soul.

"You...how long have you known?" Morgalla asked.

"There's a lot I suspect, young one. But there is also much I keep to myself. Years ago, I wondered why Zorach wanted me to watch over a young child."

"You never asked?"

"One does not ask questions here. But it was clear to me that you were of value to Zorach, and that was all I needed to know...at the time."

"And now someone told you?"

Delilah stepped closer and lowered her voice. "He wants his eye on you, child. No longer will my protection be enough."

Morgalla plopped down on her bed. She gripped the sheets, and her jaw clenched.

Delilah said and did nothing at first, but finally, she felt compelled to bestow another lesson. "Fear is a savage peak we all must face, Morgalla, and we all face it many times in our lives. You will conquer it."

Morgalla absorbed the words and was silent only a moment. "Can I be alone, please?"

Morgalla stared at the floor. Delilah left her with much to contemplate.

WEEKS PASSED, and for a time, Morgalla had slipped into a routine. She kept her mouth shut and did everything Delilah told her.

Pretty soon her constant visits to an assigned world started to feel like a mini-vacation every day. Surrounded by humans, she felt as though she could relax and not put on a fake persona even though she never wore her real face.

Dear Diary,

Two minutes after arriving here, I almost got killed by a monstrosity screaming past me at an incredible speed. I didn't know what it was, but it was made of metal, and it had a lot of wheels.

After doing some exploring, I discovered that these devices are called cars and the one that almost killed me is called a semi.

The portal dropped me into a wilderness near a town. I don't think the tunnel could have held more than one person at a time. For a moment, I even thought I might get stuck.

This town is very different from Freedom Ridge. 'Lectricity and tek-nology are rampant everywhere, in every building. The people even carry tek-nology with them wherever they go.

The souls of people are strange, too. They stand right next to each other, yet they seem so distant from one another. I can't quite put my finger on why or how.

In Freedom Ridge, the people were like an iron chain that nobody could break. Maybe it was the constant threat of blizzards or demons that kept them together. Here…the people are very safe. I wonder if they realize that. I doubt they appreciate it.

I really doubt it.

They also don't know about us. Magic, demons, it's all myth. They take pride in their tek-nology and their logic, yet they also cherish fantasy and faith. They are a paradox.

From what I can tell, it seems like a nice place. Nicer than Hell, anyway. Who knows, maybe I'll like exploring it.

ONE EVENING at a gathering at Zorach's castle, everyone in attendance was dressed in the uniform of leather and metal, all black. Symbols of gold were adorned up their arms, some more than others. Delilah wore her uniform with pride. Her heart swelled with joy, walking among her own kind again. She was home.

She looked around and didn't see Morgalla. Some inquired where her apprentice might be.

Child, you had better be here, Delilah thought.

Morgalla had noticed that Zorach's castle was much less opulent than Makaro's. The high red stone was worn from the centuries. Black marble flooring didn't shine, and the walls were blank except for a large vanity mirror that stretched almost as high as the ceiling.

She stared at the uniform in the mirror. The leather was tight and uncomfortable, and the armor didn't make her feel any safer.

"There you are."

She turned and saw Delilah approaching, cloak of black flowing behind her. Morgalla held up her arms and referred to the golden symbols on the backs of her hands and on the plates of armor on her shoulders.

"What are these? A rank?"

"We all must start somewhere. But that's not all. The symbol is a reminder to everyone of your standing in society. But you must exceed that."

"Bury my feelings?"

Delilah paused. Her next words came with serious conviction. "Yes…and more so. You must grow up." Her student gave a deep inhale, and her lips clenched. "You don't like that? Well too bad. It is life, young one, and we all must live it. Do you choose to be a victim or a predator? Because if you are not one, you are the other. Choose carefully."

They both felt the presence of their master and turned to the chamber doors. Delilah spun on her heel and walked away, but she had one more lesson to add before she left.

She looked over her shoulder as her voice carried throughout the great hall. "Oh, and you had better choose the latter because I didn't teach you to be a victim."

Morgalla gave a sarcastic bow to her teacher who disappeared in a huff.

The young demon sighed. She felt her heart, a raging animal within her rib cage. The pounding echoed through her ears, and the twist in her stomach had become an unwelcome companion in recent weeks. Her eyes studied the castle that felt like a tomb. She fought the stinging in them and sought out something happy to latch onto. She couldn't.

Morgalla heard metal latches echo inside the hall. At the opposite end, the massive black doors slowly parted. A rush of cold filled the room, making it as freezing as any winter. Morgalla exhaled and saw her breath linger in front of her.

A shadowy image emerged from the doorway, the black of its cloak appearing alive as it sought to envelop the walls and floor. She watched the helmet of an emotionless beast and the black horns that stretched from either side of its head.

Its soul was like iron, an ancient monster that had seen many centuries and whose black heart revealed nothing. She could, however, feel his eyes upon her.

Morgalla took a strong hold of the golden symbols on the backs of her hands and on her shoulders and tore them off. The metal clanged on the stone floor. To hell with rank, and to hell with status. She inhaled another deep breath and stepped forward to meet her father.

EPILOGUE

IN FREEDOM Ridge, it had seemed like a miracle had happened. The Izari were part of the community and they were all united and safe. They would keep an eye to what was left of Dracon Peak, but for the time being it was silent and still.

Mylo put his skills to good use building furniture and making wooden sculptures on the side. He had gotten a job in a small shop down main street, just down from where the prism shined. One day he was working, putting the finishing touches on an elaborate rocking chair when the bell chimed, alerting him that someone had entered. He looked and saw an elderly woman leaning on a cane. He took his goggles off and the cloth he had over his mouth and nose. He removed his leather gloves and ran his now bare hand through his sawdust covered hair.

Dottie's nose filled with the scent of the different kinds of wood that he had been using, primarily cedar. She looked around the furniture and saw a nice rocking chair that had just been stained a few days prior. They exchanged hello's and a smile, having recognized each other from the day their mutual demon friend had left.

"Your work?" Dottie asked.

"Yeah, feel free to try it out."

Her old bones creaked as she took a seat and tried out the chair, giving it a few rocks back and forth.

"Nice." She said. "I've been needing a new chair for my living room. How have you been holding up?"

"Oh, just fine. There's plenty of wood around and people are always going to need something to sit on, right?"

The woman chuckled. "How are you holding up otherwise?"

Mylo looked confused. "What do you mean?"

She paused a moment. "I miss her, too."

She looked out the window and her lips clenched. Mylo pulled up a stool and sat next to her. "I...I just feel so helpless. I know my friend is in danger and there's nothing I can do."

Dottie put her hand on his shoulder. Mylo stared at the floor a moment, not sure just what to say but no words were needed.

"Do you think she's okay?" He asked.

"Oh, don't you worry about her." She replied with a smile. "I know a fighter when I see one."

ABOUT THE AUTHOR

Born and raised in Southeast Michigan, Jon David was a nerd long before it was ever popular. He hoped to be a comic writer/illustrator when he created Morgalla in college. Since then, between working various jobs, he's honed his craft and turned his misunderstood demon heroine into a four-part epic series.